To my two friends

Dorothy Davies

DEATH BE PARDONER TO ME
The Life of George, Duke of Clarence

Fiction4All

Dedicated to the memory of George Plantagenet, K.G.,
Duke of Clarence,
Lord-Lieutenant of Ireland.
1449-1478
Requiescat In Pace.

It is also dedicated to the memory of David Millard,
medium and friend.

The Duke of Clarence came from what seems to
us to have been a time of courtly knights, chivalrous
adventures and behaviour (on the surface, at least.)
David was a latter-day 'white knight' who often came to
the rescue when mediums were needed for the church I
served, to help during Open Days when he would do
seemingly endless readings without charge. He was there
when called on if he was not booked elsewhere, no
matter what the weather. (He had to get a ferry to reach
us and David was no sailor!)

David had his own demons to fight, his own
treachery to battle and his own suffering to endure; his
was not an easy pathway. He is sadly missed on this
side of life.

David, you are not forgotten and never will be.
Requiescat in Pace.

From Immortality
Olton Pools, Sidgwick and Jackson Ltd.,1917

*There in the midst of all these words shall be
Our names, our ghosts, our immortality.*

Last Confessional

John Drinkwater,
(From Swords and Ploughshares, Sidgewick and
Jackson, 1917)

For all ill words that I have spoken,
For all clear moods that I have broken,
  For all despite and hasty breath
  Forgive me, Love, forgive me, Death.

Death, master of the great assize,
Love, falling now to memories,
  You two alone I need to prove,
  Forgive me, Death, forgive me, Love.

For every tenderness undone,
For pride when holiness was none
  But only easy charity,
  O Death, be pardoner to me.

For stubborn thought that would not make
Measure of love's thought for love's sake,
  But kept a sullen difference,
  Take, Love, this laggard penitence.

For cloudy words too vainly spent
To prosper but in argument
  When truth stood lonely at the gate,
  On your compassion, Death, I wait.

For all the beauty that escaped
This foolish brain, unsung, unshaped,
  For wonder that was slow to move,
  Forgive me, Death, forgive me, Love.

For love that kept a secret cruse,

For life defeated of its dues,
This latest word of all my breath –
Forgive me, Love, forgive me, Death.

Author's note:

Any historian, amateur or professional, studying the life and times of Richard III and Edward IV will be aware of their brother, George, duke of Clarence. He is mentioned in all their books but only one has been written about his life: 'False, Fleeting, Perjur'd Clarence, George Duke of Clarence 1449-78' by Michael Hicks, to which I am indebted for much detailed information. It is a mystery why other authors have not found him worthy of attention. The title is the description given to him by Shakespeare and it is that description which has come down the ages, along with the myth surrounding his execution.

Mary Clive's comment in *'Sunne of York'* (the life of Edward IV) that Clarence was 'essentially insignificant' gave me the extra incentive I needed to write this book, just to prove otherwise. No one who was brother to two Kings, who held great estates and power, who switched sides seemingly on a whim, who allied himself with the great Warwick, then became reconciled with his brother King Edward IV and had his estates and lands restored to him but who was finally executed at King Edward IV's command can be 'essentially insignificant' in the annals of history. Such a man leaves his footprints on the lives of those around him in a most emphatic way. In many ways, George, duke of Clarence, is as maligned as his more famous brother, King Richard III, as he is known for only two things: being a traitor to King Edward IV and allegedly drowning in a vat of malmsey wine. Research shows there was much more to this charismatic Plantagenet than that. It is my hope that I have brought something of the real duke of Clarence to life and, by looking past the historical statements written about him, have perhaps revealed the reasons for his many strange acts. The book has been a challenge to write; one I have welcomed. I consider myself a Clarencian as well as a Ricardian!

I wish to thank the following people for their assistance:

The staff at Tewkesbury Abbey.
Robert Yorke, Archivist at the College of Arms, for his help in supplying articles and the detail from the Rows Rol showing Clarence's arms.
The Richard III Foundation for articles from their extensive library.

I would mention here my dearest friends Mary Holliday and Terry Wakelin, both of whom supported me throughout the writing of this book. I also want to mention AW and GP, for ongoing support and help.

A percentage of the royalties generated by this book are to be paid to Tewkesbury Abbey, site of the tomb of the duke and duchess of Clarence, to aid restoration work and to contribute to the ongoing costs of maintenance.

Dorothy Davies,
Isle of Wight, the year of Our Lord 2008

So incompetent has the generality of historians been for the province they have undertaken, that it is almost a question, whether, if the dead of past ages could revive, they would be able to reconnoitre the events of their own times, as transmitted to us by ignorance and misrepresentation.
Horace Walpole, 1768

FOREWORD

George duke of Clarence was the third living son of Richard, duke of York and Cecily Neville. Their first two sons were Edward, earl of March, later Edward IV, and Edmund, earl of Rutland, murdered on the battlefield at Wakefield, December 1460, during which Richard duke of York was killed. George's younger brother, Richard, became duke of Gloucester and later King Richard III.

The duke of Clarence lived at the time historians refer to as the Wars of the Roses, although it was not known by that name in the 15th century. This was actually internecine warfare between two major 'houses', Lancaster and York.

Henry VI, a Lancastrian, was king of England from 1422 to 1461. He had a son, Edward, Prince of Wales, by his wife Margaret of Anjou.

Edward IV was proclaimed king in 1461, after winning major battles against the Lancastrians, despite the fact that Henry VI still lived.

An uprising drove Edward IV into exile and Henry VI regained the throne for a year.

Edward IV returned to England and reclaimed the throne, sending Henry VI to the Tower, where he later died.

Despite further uprisings, Edward IV held the throne of England until his death in 1483. His son Edward, by his wife Elizabeth Woodville, was officially Edward V, until the allegations of a pre-contract of marriage rendered the marriage illegal and the offspring of that marriage illegitimate, thus disbarring Edward V from becoming King. Instead Parliament offered the throne to Richard of Gloucester, who was Lord Protector under King Edward's will. He became Richard III.

This is a brief outline of the major players of the time. Within this framework, George duke of Clarence played his not insignificant part in English history.

Chapter 1

I dreamed:

Of being king.
Of being the owner of Fotheringhay.
Of having a wonderful marriage.
Of fathering many children.
Of having power.
Of being part of the York family.
Of living to an old age.

Where has Fortune taken my dreams? Here am I, a prisoner in the Tower of London, in luxurious apartments I will admit, but a prisoner for all that. I was brought here by order of King Edward IV, my own brother.

My liege ran out of patience with what he called a wayward, treasonable, unreasonable brother. My liege took a quill and signed his name on the warrant of execution with bold strokes – I know, they showed it to me, his men who came with mixed emotions to tell me of the decision – and in the bold strokes with which he signed his name, I knew there was no going back. No words would move him; no prayers could reach him.

The men came with eyes that said 'poor man, ordered to die by writ signed by his own brother.'

Eyes that said 'well, Clarence, you overstepped the invisible line. Much you should not have said, much you should not have done, but you said it and you did it. What kind of prize fool are you?'

Eyes that said, 'so much for royalty and aristocracy, the end comes to us all at some time and who are you to think you could outwit it, foolish one?'

Then they left me alone with my thoughts, paper, ink, quills and a supply of malmsey wine. They left me to solitude and loneliness. I reflect on my dreams as the wine fails adequately to dull my senses and my thoughts, no matter how much I drink, for of a surety my very blood must be malmsey wine by now and it makes no difference to me. I pour it out as fast as I pour it in and somehow it passes through my body without affecting me. Too many drunken nights, Clarence, I say, catching myself staring at the jewelled mazer as if I had not seen it before, though it has been in my hand virtually the entire time I have been here. Too many drunken nights, days, weeks, months in the past and now. But hell and damnation, how else do I stop the pain in my head? The pressure that is like a blacksmith tightening his hold on a piece of metal and then hammering it endlessly, endlessly, endlessly until I want to shriek aloud to the heavens, in the name of all that is holy, end this and end it now!

No one knows of this. Pride stops me saying 'I have this problem...' for in all honesty, to whom can I turn? I know, deep inside, in the place where all truth is known and none can disguise it, that my physician could do nothing for me, nothing to take the pain from my head, nothing to prolong my life. I know it and accept it.

I could send a note to my brother the king to say he could hold his hand, he could delay the execution, for I will shortly leave this world of my own accord and thus take the taint of ordering my death from his mind and his reign. Why do I not do it? Why do I hesitate to write such a note? Is there still a part of my conscious mind which resents all that has happened? The way the Yorks acted as if I was not a York; as if I was not brother to both March and Gloucester; the arguments, the battles over land, the forbidding of my marriage, the lack of support at my trial; my complaints seem endless.

But what of my actions over the years, what of my treason? Was my brother the king not right in all he said and did against me? My thoughts endlessly charge at one another, knights in a joust, the one trying to knock the other from position. He was right – he was not right. In reality, it does not matter for it is too late. There is no going back. There is no undoing that which has been done, written, said aloud to the Court. My brother the king would not – could not - reverse his decision now. It would show weakness and he would never allow that.

Of my dreams - let me return to my dreams – I say this.

The dream of the crown was taken from me.
Fotheringhay waits. I will not go there again.
My marriage lasted just seven years.
Of my children, just two are left to the world.
He who supported me, the Kingmaker, was killed.
I always felt like an outsider within my own family.
As for old age, I am 28 but will not live to celebrate the occasion of my becoming 29.

So, do I regret anything? Yes, much. Spending so much time in dispute with my brother of Gloucester. Spending so much time away from my brother of March when he was so good to me. Arranging the demise of the unfortunate Ankarette Twynho for no other reason than she was the perfect scapegoat, she with her herbs and her potions and her shining covetous eyes. I needed a scapegoat, needed to blame someone for taking my wife from me. Too much to admit Isobel died of a natural condition, my distorted mind – I freely confess this now – would not accept a rational, sensible human answer. I sought a solution in witchcraft, in sorcery and alchemy. I regret those who died with her. I know now my son died because he was not strong enough to live, not because he had been poisoned. Fool, Clarence; perfect fool.

I could go on but the paper would soon be used and there is no one to call for a further supply. I also have to ask myself if I want to spend the rest of my life, short as it is likely to be, writing of regrets. No, I need not write of them; I can sit here before the fire – this February is bitterly cold, at least here in the Tower – and go back in memory instead.

Let me then ask the question; what do I most yearn for? Answer: a restoration of family life, that is, to be with my lady mother, my brother of March and my brother of Gloucester. My children? I know them not as people, I yearn right now to be with people I know and once loved. Did they in turn once love me? It is too late to ask. It is too late to seek their forgiveness, their understanding, their absolution for that which I have done. It is too late for many things.

It is not too late to be shriven. I pray the priest will come soon. There is much to confess and my knees will ache with cold from the floor and the pressure of my not unsubstantial weight long before I am through. I will not go to my Maker, my God, He who sees all, with the sins I carry right now on my soul.

Twenty eight years. It seems but a blink of an eyelid since I became aware of the castle of Fotheringhay, of my sister Margaret and the many servants who took care of us, of the child born after me who became at times what I perceived to be my bitterest enemy but I know not if that was all in my head.

Dear God, this pain! Will it not let me rest before I am sent to my eternal rest?

What have I achieved in my time? What will history make of me? How will I be perceived by those who are to come after me? How will my children remember me? How will my brothers remember me?

I have no answers. I have only questions – and now doubts, too. If there is a heaven, if there is Purgatory, then my pure Isobel is long since passed through it and is in the glory that is the domain of God. So I ask and will ask of my priest, when he comes - pray that it be soon and I unload this burden of sin! - how long will I spend in Purgatory, how long before I can be

18

reunited with Isobel, how long before I see the glory of heaven? Or is it all a story given to keep us kneeling at the altar rail in the hope that partaking of the Body of Christ will help us be a little more pure in our thinking and in our hearts?

God forgive me for these thoughts! I will add them to my confession. Of a surety there are hours of confession to come. But Almighty God, look down on this sinner and know that he – I – am suffering much pain, much agony of body as well as mind. Knowing it is all to be ended is in itself a hurt, a pain that is hard to bear, that every minute that ticks by is a minute less for me to live.

How foolish are these thoughts! How foolish is it to think in this way! From the moment we take our first breath in this life the days are counting down to our death, whether it be on the battlefield with full honours of a soldier's demise or trying to escape the battlefield and being hacked down, whether it be coughing up blood and expiring through inability to breathe any more or falling from a rearing horse and breaking a spine or as I am, under a double sentence of death, signed by my brother's own bold hand with a fine freshly cut quill and from that which is in my head and even now pressing, pressing, pressing until I could scream aloud with the pressure that is grinding my skull into small pieces. They know not that I drop things, that my hands are unsure, that my balance is disturbed, that I cannot think straight any more, for these things happen when none are here. I make well sure of that. When they come, those who attend me, I do not attempt to stand unless it is with help, I do not attempt to hold things. I have no need of that when they are there to do it for me and I do not need to think when in their presence. I keep quiet for who would wish to willingly attend someone under sentence of death? None. My squires attend me by order of the Constable of the Tower and they go. They come because they must; they go as soon as they can. It is as if I have some contagious disease. If they knew the truth – that if left here I will die without my brother's command – what would they say, how would they show their pity to me? Would they show their pity to me, or would embarrassment at being in the presence of someone who is dying cause them to leave even sooner than they do? Such questions have no answers.

From my viewpoint it is as well they do not know. My speech is affected now and they would not understand me. Even more foolish then is my desire to ask the priest how long I would spend in Purgatory for he would not understand a word I utter. Would it help to have the thoughts of someone who does not know? He would only guess and that would not help me. I will have to find out by going there myself, presenting myself to the Avenging Angel or whoever is in charge of Purgatory and saying 'here I am, traitorous, deceiving, drunken Clarence, do with me as you will.'

As far as the squires are concerned, I pretend I cannot be bothered to speak. I gesture to them and they understand I wish to be bathed, dressed, fed – and wined, for it does dull if not kill the pain. Eventually.

How do I know my speech is affected? I have shouted my anger at my fate and heard the sounds that issued from the mouth which once spoke honeyed words, or so Isobel told me. Like honey, she said, my words of love were like honey. Now they are no more than pips and stones as in the fruit I devour as if there is nothing else to eat. The words stop, the words crash over one another, the words make no sense.

I will write this page and I will burn it, for the ink is smudged with tears. I have no control over my tears now, either. I will write it for it is in part helping me to release that which is within me, a huge stone, a boulder sitting somewhere behind my ribs, behind that which continues to pump the malmsey wine around my body. For how long is another guess, an hour, a day or a week? How long before that which eats my brain stops the process of living? Or will the men come at my brother the king's command and stop the process of living before that happens?

And the final question, the unanswerable one, no matter how much I think on it: which would I prefer?

I do not know: I will not know.

Chapter 2

There was a scent of fresh strewn rushes, a perfume somewhere between cut grass and summer, rose into the air of the birthing room as the embroidered slippers of the ladies, servants and midwife crushed them underfoot. The women seemed endlessly on the move, tending the great fire, heating water and sponging the face of the duchess as the contractions rippled through her body. The midwife hovered, encouraging, checking on progress. Perfumes mingled with the pungent oils massaged into the duchess's wildly distended stomach to help the birth process, the smell of smoke from the burning logs mingled with the herbs sprinkled into bowls of water. The room was full of colour, smells and movement; silks and braids flickered their shining glory under the candles and the flames from the fire as the elaborately jewelled and decorated gowns moved with the women who swayed back and forth and the smoke, the oils and the rushes combined to make a scent like no other. And there was noise, the crackle of logs, the voices, the bubbling water, the groans of the duchess as she tried to assist the birth, the midwife murmuring to the child fighting its way into the over-heated room and an uncertain life. Beyond the door to the chamber came the chant of prayers from the priest and his acolytes, asking for a safe delivery. Further away, but distinct, came the sound of metal on metal as halberds clashed and armed guards took up their positions around the castle.

The angel had most of the senses: she could see, hear and smell but touch and speech were beyond her. She could do nothing but hover, unseen, unnoticed, by the great arras covering the stone walls of the room set aside in Dublin Castle, to watch as the movements of the women stirred the tapestry, sent the shining lance of St George stabbing into the snarling death-ridden dragon.

She admired the dichotomy: on the walls, death, on the bed, life.

With a triumphant shriek from the duchess, the baby emerged to the great joy and excitement of those gathered around her.

"A boy, my lady! Another son for the Yorks!" The midwife cleared the baby's mouth and instantly a loud wail was heard, causing smiles all round.

"A healthy son! God be praised!"

The smell of blood and perspiration added to the miasma in the room but none seemed aware of it although it was as palpable as an Autumn mist and as ethereal. Someone coughed but no one commented on it.

The duchess appeared to melt into the down mattress, all tension fleeing from her body and all anxiety draining from her face. She smiled weakly at the congratulations and fussing comments from her attendants and watched as the child was cleaned and wrapped in swaddling bands. She looked for a moment as if she wanted to reach out and take the baby but instead her gaze followed the child as he was laid in a cradle in the corner, away from the lights, away from the crush of people. She closed her eyes.

'Send a messenger to my Lord husband the duke of York: tell him I am newly delivered of another son for the House of York and that the child is strong and well.' This message was passed through the open door to a page waiting on the other side. The chanting priest and his attendants halted their dirge and for a moment there was silence, apart from the rustle of rushes and the crackling of the logs. In that moment of total peace the angel could, had she wished, have spoken to the newborn, the one to whom she had chosen to devote herself as his guardian angel. She decided to stay silent. The child would have problems enough in this age when infant mortality was a given state and where superstitious people would have condemned him as being from the Devil himself had such an occurrence taken place and any become aware of it. But oh, what mischief was there in her heart and mind that made her wish she could do it!

Instead she watched from her vantage point beside the elaborate and expensive arras and wondered what her duties would be like, guarding and protecting this new arrival. Wondered if he would ever become aware of her or whether she would spend her time in isolation; no word or thought from the one she guarded and protected; no recognition of the work. Not that they sought it, those who were guardian angels, but it was always good when the guarded one recognised they were there, it made it easier to whisper, to guide, to advise, to counsel. Without that recognition, it was more a question of attempting to work in semi-darkness and hoping the guarded one finally realised what was being impressed on them, that it would be better to do it this way, if you don't mind, for that way led to disaster...

This was Dublin, in the fair land of Ireland. He would carry no memory of that, this fine healthy York, but the angel would, in time, whisper in his ear that was his birthplace and he could be proud to be a son of Ireland as well as a son of York. If she said nothing else to him as his guardian angel, she would at least do that.

"A fine boy, my lady!" The midwife burned the placenta, washed her bloody hands in one of the bowls of herb scented water and wiped them on a piece of cloth. "What will you call him?" Ingratiating herself, seeking a bigger reward than that offered for a safe delivery.

The duchess's eyes opened and she looked up at the great wall hangings. "George," she said with a weak smile. "Of a surety St George watched over me as I gave birth. He will slay many dragons, this son of York."

"God grant it be so," muttered one of the ladies, looking into the cradle. "Your son, my lady, is bonny."

"I am glad. Pray God that this one lives!"

The ladies crossed themselves superstitiously as the midwife then burned the bloody rags in the fire.

Does a newborn baby think? Are there active thoughts in the mind, or is it all instinctual survival, the need for food, for water, for strength? The angel had many skills, many gifts to bring to the new one but getting into his mind was not part of the deal, it would seem. She tried, she wished to know, but all she met was blankness. She wondered if she had tried too hard, if she had caused damage but everything said no, it was just that he was too young to have thoughts. It was all down to survival and nothing more. She watched closely as his eyes closed and then opened, closed and opened once more as he attempted, even at that young age, to focus on that around him. Finally the eyes closed and for a while he lost himself in sleep. Soon enough the demands for sustenance would wake him, he would howl with his mighty lungs for someone to feed him, clean him, attend to his many needs, not the least of which would be attention.

The angel sighed over the baby as he lay, not forgotten but temporarily neglected as the weary mother was attended to. Quietly she breathed into his mouth as it opened, breathed in pure light and life, poured in that which she had in abundance, pure unconditional love. Then she stood back as the midwife approached the cradle to look down on the one she had just helped to bring into the world.

"A fine boy," she murmured, so low the angel believed only she heard the words. "A fine boy, destined for greatness and for great shame. Oh yes, there will be dragons but mostly of your own creation, little one." She looked around furtively, afraid of being overheard, of anyone realising she was more than just a midwife. No one was near, they were all too busy with their duties, flustering around the Duchess who doubtless would have preferred to send them all packing and just lie there with her child at her overflowing breast. Protocol was everything, though: when a royal prince arrived, protocol had to be followed to the letter, whether the mother wished it or not. Soon he would be carried away to be baptised, to ensure his place in Heaven. Only then could his exhausted mother look at her new child and the wet nurse be able take up her duties.

The woman reached out a gnarled finger and traced a sign on the baby's forehead. It was the sign against witchcraft and the angel sighed again. It would take more than a sign from a wise woman to protect this one from the life he had to come.

Chapter 3

"George, come on!"

He was crossing the Great Hall, a vast area of flagstones, timbers, huge intimidating tapestries and heavy carved furniture, when his sister raced up to him, her blue satin skirts rippling in the afternoon sunlight, copper coloured curls dancing in her agitation.

"Come on, where to?" he asked politely whilst inwardly anxious to get away.

"Our lord father's arriving soon! You said you wanted to see him ride in! I've been looking for you everywhere! Where have you been hiding?"

She looked flustered and irritated, as well as conveying a sense of excitement. Her eyes betrayed her inner feelings more than her face; at the age of eight Margaret Plantagenet was fast learning to conceal that which she felt. George, just five, had no such control and expressed all his feelings with open candour and engaging naivete.

"I wasn't hiding, I was in my chamber and then a squire said there's a litter…" His voice trailed off as he realised what his sister had just told him; their lord father was due at Fotheringhay very soon and he had asked, if not outright demanded, that she go with him so he could watch from the battlements when the duke arrived. He hoped that by going to that forbidden place with his sister, he would avoid the inevitable censure that came from breaking one of the many rules that governed every part of his life.

"Come on! I think there's still time!" Margaret set off at a run, skirts bunched in her small hands, embroidered slippers flashing shards of light from the gold thread stitched among the flowers. George raced after her, leather boots thumping on the flagstones. He skirted the long table, narrowly missing a carver, snapping his fingers at his favourite wolfhound sprawled indolently in front of the hearth. The dog looked up but didn't move.

The bailey of Fotheringhay held the heat of the late afternoon sun within the great stone walls, the grass browning through lack of moisture. Fortunately no one was around at that moment, a rare event indeed; the castle was normally a hive of activity. George grinned as they ran across the brittle grass and climbed the stone steps leading to the walk at the top of the castle walls. That was the place to be, where he could see everything and, with luck, no one would see him, although he was well aware he was wearing one of his brightest tunics, a vivid glowing red bordered and decorated with gold. Against the stonework he would stand out like a misplaced flower. Perhaps they won't look up, he thought. If I keep my fingers crossed like this, they won't look up and no one will know we are up here. I can do magic, I know I can!

He looked at Margaret's deep blue dress shot with cloth of silver and thought she looked like a displaced cornflower. But magic would cover both of them, of course it would. No one would see them.

The gentle breeze brought the scent of summer, of ripening crops and fruit, of dust and dried grasses to George. The smell was as familiar as the herbs and rushes inside the castle itself. The stone was sun heated and rough under his crossed fingers, the walk warm even through the soles of his boots. It was good being so high up, a small person feeling like a large one for a while.

"I hope no one sees us," Margaret panted, dropping one side of her skirt to push her curls back from her face, which had gone red with exertion. "We're not supposed to be up here."

"No one will miss us and it was your idea, you said come on." George, energetic, fit and strong, had no outward signs of being out of breath despite the fast climb.

"I know, but you asked – George, Susanna might be looking for us." Second thoughts were setting in. Margaret looked and sounded distinctly uncomfortable. It was one thing to be brave when down on the ground, another to maintain it when high above everyone, in a place they were strictly forbidden to go.

George leaned against the stone bulwark. "I think you can see half of England from up here," he commented as he looked across the landscape. Then he turned to his sister to give her the charming smile which melted hearts and persuaded people to overlook many of his escapades. "Susanna can shout, but she won't come up here and find us. She's afraid of heights."

"Silly; that won't stop her waiting on us when we go down again," Margaret fretted, tugging at her sleeves and then began pulling the lace from a small handkerchief in her anxiety. She looked at her brother who was as tall as she was, despite the difference in their ages. "George, let's go down. I don't want to incur her anger."

"Not yet, I want to see if anyone is coming. You promised me we could wait up here until our lord father arrived."

"Yes, but -"

"But what?"

"I didn't think-"

"Well, you go down if you're afraid of a servant, Margaret! I don't care if she shouts at me! I want to see them ride in, I want to see the horses, I want to see the pennants and I want to see their swords and lances! I want to see our lord Father in all his royal glory!"

"Typical boy!" Margaret looked at her brother with a fond expression. He might be demanding but he was the golden George, free with his emotions, his smiles and his kindnesses, when he was in the right mood. If he was balked in his desires, he could be a virtual tyrant; stamping his rage into the flagstoned floor and causing mayhem until his wishes were granted. They invariably were.

He turned to scan the horizon, looking for the telltale signs of a large group of armed men on the move, flash of light from weapons, dust from the hooves, fluttering colours of the pennants. The duke of York was coming home and the world had to know it. The breeze stiffened, ruffling George's fair hair and tugging at his elaborate tunic. He looked down and wondered, briefly, if he was dressed well enough for him to be presented to his father that day, or whether he should rush back and ask Susanna to help him change into something else. It would do, he decided, for his father rarely noticed him anyway. The tunic was new, in fact most of his clothes were new, he had seemed to outgrow everything that summer. People had commented on how he had developed, how he had become so much stronger. The tailor had compared his measurements and told everyone he met in the castle how much Lord George had grown since his last visit.

His nursemaid, Susanna, tutted over his wardrobe, muttering dire imprecations on his head and other parts of his body if he didn't take more care when playing with puppies with sharp teeth and kittens with sharp claws, if he didn't stop leaping on ponies and riding out, regardless of what he was wearing. He would throw himself down beside a pond or river and gaze into the depths, trying to see the fish he knew were there, regardless of whether the bank was muddy, riddled with stones or rank sharp bladed grass, indifferent to the state of his clothes when he rode or ran back into the castle, radiant with the sheer joy of being alive. His lady mother had decreed he was not to leave the castle grounds but often enough, when she was away with the duke on official business, George would coerce escorts into riding out with him. They, like everyone at Fotheringhay, had come under his spell, falling for his charm and his winning ways and in truth there was little he was denied. What were clothes other than things to keep you warm or protect you from kitten and puppy teeth and claws? What if they were damaged? There was always something else put away for him to wear.

"There, Margaret!" He gestured frantically toward the far horizon. "There he comes!"

A distant dust cloud, a glint of arms, a flash of colour. George was all but jumping up and down with excitement when a shout reached them.

"Lord George! Come down immediately! Lady Margaret, come down immediately!"

Susanna's tone brooked no argument. Their strict disciplinarian nurse was standing at the foot of the flight of steps, hands on substantial hips, a scowl twisting her already dark visage. Her cap had been partially dislodged; strands of greying hair were escaping which would not please her when she discovered it. She was as severe with her own appearance as she was with those she had in her charge. She never took no for an answer and George knew it.

Disappointed but unable to argue, despite his brave words, he turned and stamped back down the steps, a sullen look replacing the joyous one. My fault, he thought, my fault, I uncrossed my fingers. I forgot for a moment. Magic fails when you forget. You have to hold on to it. Margaret followed closely behind him, equally subdued.

Susanna waited, one foot tapping the bottom step, until the two children finally reached ground level.

"Come! Now!" She grabbed their hands, hurried them across the courtyard and pulled them back into the castle, through the Great Hall and up the stairs, lecturing as she went. "How many times have you been told about doing things like that? Eh? How many times have you been told to wait until someone is with you before you climb anywhere? Eh? Making me search

31

everywhere for you! Your lady mother has asked that you are made ready to greet your lord father when he returns. I've been in every room in this castle, I do swear I have, looking for you! She would not be pleased to find you have been on the battlements alone!"

"But 'tis the best place..." George began, but was silenced as Susanna pushed him into his chamber.

"Wait on me in there, Lord George, do not move! Lady Margaret, hasten to your chamber, please, be sure to wash your face and hands and go down to the Great Hall where your lady mother awaits you. Be sure there is no dust on your skirts, young lady!"

Margaret hurried away without a backward look. George stood, angry as well as disappointed, waiting for Susanna to return. She bustled into the room, grabbed a damp cloth and began to wipe his face and then his hands. The lecture continued unabated.

"Why must you do such things, Lord George? You know you are not allowed up on the battlements! What would your lady mother say?"

"She would say 'tis the best view of the countryside, she would say of course you could watch for your lord father from there, my son, were she given the chance!" George glared his defiance, anxious to be gone, not wanting to be fussed over any more, wanting to be free of the strictures of his nursemaid. Disappointment made him more reckless than usual. The moment he spoke he regretted it but bravado made him stand up for his desire to be taken seriously.

"Hush your cheek, young man, before I arrange a whipping for you! Now, please go down to the Hall and greet your lady mother. Do not dally on the way, do not touch anything to get dirty, do not speak until spoken to, or I will be very angry!"

"All right, Susanna. I'm sorry."

With one last brush at his clothes, Susanna pushed him out of the door. George sighed as he tried to walk sedately down the stone stairs. It was much more fun to run, to race up and down stairs, to see how fast he could get from one side of the hall to the other, to romp in the stables with the puppies and kittens that arrived as regularly as the morning sun, or so it seemed. The occasions when he had to be quiet, to be the perfect prince, seemed to come too often for his liking. The duke coming home was an event that he had anticipated for some time, planning to be on the battlements, to watch the armed guard escorting him home, to see the fluttering pennants and hear the clatter of hooves, harness and arms as they rode across the drawbridge and into the castle grounds. From that vantage point he would have been able to count the escorts, to see his father in his beautiful clothes, then he could have rushed down the steps and into the stables to smell the richness of tired, sweating horses, to hear the men talk of their adventures in the great wide world which he knew only through books and which he longed to see, to experience, to be part of. The formal meal would be endured much easier with memories to help him through the tedium of each course and the polite chatter of those bidden to eat with the family. It had not occurred to him that someone, Susanna of all people, would find him there and be angry.

He kicked the walls as he went down, needing to dissipate his bitter disappointment. By now the group would be close enough to be seen, had he been able to stay up there on the walk, but he also knew that his mother's word was law, as indeed his father's was and if she had 'asked' for him to be present in the Hall when his father returned, it was as good as a command from the King himself. He would be there. He had no choice. Miserably he continued down the stairs, kicking the wall at every step. It didn't help his feeling of being deprived of something so long planned and anticipated, all it did was scuff his boots and make his toes sore, but somehow he couldn't stop doing it.

It seemed as if all the servants, stewards and ladies were present. The hall was filled with colour and movement as they quietly walked around, speaking softly to one another. The crunching of rushes accompanied every footstep, a sound everyone lived with and ignored as part of castle life but which, in his current state of heightened emotions, sounded unnaturally loud to his ears.

His mother, Lady Cecily, was sitting by the side of the fireplace, a delicate velvet cloak draped around her shoulders, its vivid yet dark blue shade complementing the colour of her eyes. Her silver gown was tight laced; dark blue slippers peeked from beneath the hem. Her hair was caught up under an elaborate head-dress and she was wearing beautiful jewels on her fingers, in her ears and round her neck. She looked almost regal and in truth, George was in awe of her. This beautiful being was his lady mother; someone he saw rarely, someone whose word was law. This was someone who could no doubt see right through his mask of quiet obedience and observe the wild child hiding within, the one which longed to throw off all the restrictions of being a royal prince and just do what he wanted when he wanted, the one who found protocol confining and restricting, the one who wanted to say to the servants 'just call me George, just let me do what I want!' He knew, though, even at his young age, it could not be done. It would not be done. He was Lord George; he was of royal blood. The rest were peasants. They were beneath him. Susanna's constant litany rang in his head: 'you are a prince, Lord George, carrying royal blood from your ancestors. One day you will be presented at Court and you must know how to behave. One day the Yorks will hold supreme power and you must be ready to take on the responsibilities that go with that power, with being a York. Your lord father and your lady mother must be proud of you. You must-"

So many times the word 'must' came into the instructions, the lessons and commandments that were issued from those above him. One day I will be free, he told himself, as he stood quietly, waiting for his mother to notice him, free to live my life the way I want it. Quite how that was to happen and quite what he wanted was not clear in his young mind but he knew that when he grew up, he would be aware of precisely what he wanted from his life and vowed he would get it. If you could not do as you wanted as a royal prince, when could you do what you wanted?

He knew the answer to that: when you were the son of the blacksmith and could come and go without anyone asking where you had been and where you were going, or checking your clothes for smudges and stains, looking for tears and rips and complaining about them when they were inevitably discovered. How many times had he hung out of a window and waved to the boy, envying him his freedom? How many times had the surge of envy gone through him when the boy had waved back and raced off on some magical boy-like errand or escapade that George could never dream of doing? Times which could not be counted.

Even with the heat of the summer's day, a fire roared in the hearth, for the hall was perpetually cold; the thick stone walls allowed no heat to penetrate. George felt the chill and hoped for a chance to sidle closer to the flames, if the dogs would let him.

Margaret was already at the duchess's side, looking cautious and excited in turn. George hesitated, trying to read from his sister's face whether anyone knew of the escapade but she was giving nothing away. He had to wait on his lady mother's words to find out if he was in her disfavour or not. The waiting was an agony of apprehension.

The voices of everyone gathered in the hall were a constant buzz, counter-pointed by the susurration of silks, linens, velvets and wool and rushes as people moved around, creating eddies of cold draughts that found his exposed flesh and chilled it. Oh to be outside in the sunshine! Perhaps they wanted to be outside as well, perhaps that was why they couldn't stand still. Perhaps they wanted the garderobe and didn't dare leave the hall. Many thoughts tumbled through his mind and he suddenly realised he needed the garderobe. In despair he knew he had to wait, that he could not leave the hall, either. He should have said when he was with Susanna, but was too preoccupied with being disappointed at having his plans ruined.

He looked up at the nursemaid standing behind his mother's chair. The solemn faced woman was holding his little brother Richard in her arms. The dark haired, dark eyed little boy stared at everything as if he had never seen it before, as if a sense of wonderment had taken over and he did not know what to make of it all. Hurry up and grow up, George thought suddenly, as he bowed to his mother. I know Margaret will be sent away before long and I need someone to join me in my games! But oh, he is only two, how long do I have to wait until he can come and play with me? How long before his miserable nursemaid allows him to come and play with me? If I have to wait too long, the time will be gone! I will be pushed into being too much the prince to be able to go and play!

His thoughts were interrupted as Lady Cecily held out a hand and drew him to her side. "I am glad to see you, George. Come and stand by me. Your lord father will be here any moment, or so they tell me."

"Yes, Mother."

This was scary, this was a test indeed, to stand by his mother's side and be aware of her scrutiny. Was his hair in order, had Susanna washed the dirt from his face adequately? It had been a very quick scrub, which he had welcomed at the time but now … was it enough? Was there any dust on his sleeves, had he marked his boots by kicking the walls on the way down? What would she find to comment on, what would she say if she knew how rebellious he wanted to be?

"It seems you grow taller each time I see you, George."

"Yes, Mother, this year I have had a new wardrobe." Polite, cautious, almost formal conversation.

"So I saw from the accounts! Well, it is good that you are developing so well. You will be as tall as your older brothers when you are full grown. I am pleased."

A silent sigh of relief escaped George's tight pressed lips. If Mother was pleased with him, then she had not noticed the scuffed boots and there could be no dirt anywhere. No, word was that his lady mother never missed anything, not the tiniest error, so she had probably noticed the things he was worrying about but had chosen not to say anything. Her lord, the great duke, was about to ride into Fotheringhay judging by the sound of hooves and the clattering of arms, harness and men. It was not the right time to make a fuss about anything. He chanced a look at her serene face and saw the twinkling eyes. Maybe on this occasion it would be all right. He dared a smile and noticed that her lips twitched a little as if she would actually smile back at him. It didn't happen; her smiles were reserved for one person only, it seemed, the man at that moment striding through the doorway, hat in hand, dust clinging thickly to the riding cloak he flung to one side. A squire caught it and carried it away.

"My lord, you are safely back with us!" The duchess's smile was radiant as she stood to welcome him. George moved back, then edged forward again, not wanting to be noticed yet wanting to be noticed, indecision causing him to stumble a little on an uneven flagstone.

"It is good to be home again." The duke bowed, took her hand for a moment and then cast a sweeping glance over the group gathered in the hall. "It is good to see everyone here. I thank you."

"Wine is being brought for you, sire. Would you care to wash away the dust of your journey first?"

"I will. Wait here for me."

It was as if a gale had swept through the Great Hall at Fotheringhay. In a single moment the duke had arrived, greeted everyone, passed through, gone to his chamber to wash and to change his clothes and after that moment everyone had scattered, going about their various duties. Wine was poured ready for his return, the butler hovered, supervising the placing of the cheese, meats and fine bread on the table by the fire; minstrels were plucking their lyres and other instruments ready to play if he so wished; the duke's Fool, Hagley, wearing his most outrageous outfit of mismatched colours, hovered in the background, reciting rhymes to himself, newly made up to welcome the duke back. Even the great wolfhounds stirred from the hearth as eddies of the duke's powerful presence reached them. George held his breath. Would that he could grow up to be like his father! Everyone bowed down to him, everyone revered him, his word was law; his wish was the ultimate command. That's what I want to be like, George told himself, watching from under lowered lashes as the people left in the hall murmured and moved around, attending to tasks but also gossiping together. The duchess's ladies talked among themselves as they kept one wary eye on her, ready to fulfil her every wish. I also want to know everything, everything that goes on, George added silently. And I will; you see if I don't!

Voices swirled around him, talk of alliances, of changing loyalties, of court rumours and facts. Some of it registered, some of it was beyond his comprehension but he listened avidly to it all, storing what he could not understand against the day it would all become clear. Experience had taught him that if you waited long enough, you found the answers to everything you needed to find out. Knowledge is power. His tutor had told him that, in an effort to get him to study. Yes, knowledge was power, but not from books. Knowledge of people, that was power. For one so young, he understood a great deal.

There was an agony of waiting for his father to return, in the hope he would at least notice the existence of the smallest Yorks. Richard, fretful at being restrained, was struggling in the nursemaid's arms. At a nod from the duchess he was set down on the floor where he immediately ran to one of the wolfhounds. The dog licked his face and then settled down again in front of the fire. George watched his younger brother climb onto the dog, which didn't move. Once again his thoughts ran in many directions. How he did he do that? Last time, no, the only time I tried it, the dog bit me! The scar on the calf of his left leg ached as if memory had revitalised it. Perhaps I was too big; he's only a little bit of a boy. But he's a York, too, I must remember that. I must look out for him, I am his older brother; I am –

Just then his father returned to the hall, taking his place before the fire, his overwhelming presence seemingly filling the huge cavernous space. The dogs moved out of his way. Richard followed his favourite dog and lay down on the floor by its side, resting his head on the warm body. The duke looked only at his wife as he talked lightly of his journey, of his discussions, of the people he had met. Wine was drunk; bread and meat disappeared almost like magic as he hardly stopped speaking. George watched, his stomach rumbling and protesting. How long before the summons to dinner? If my lord Father eats too much now, dinner will be long delayed for the rest of us! And I am bored! This is not real talk!

As if sensing his thoughts, Lady Cecily gestured to the butler to arrange for the table to be cleared ready for the meal. "Forgive me, my lord," she said carefully, "but we must make preparations for the household to eat."

"Of course!" He glanced at George and Margaret, standing patiently by their mother's side and gave them a quick, approving smile. "You grow well, both of you. Where is Richard?"

"Playing with the dog, sire, as you might expect."

A different smile, a softer one, revealed itself as the duke turned and looked at his youngest son. "Ah, so he is. Well, he grows too, despite everything. Come, my dear, let us go to my study whilst we await dinner. There is much I need to discuss with you."

He walked away without another look at any of his children, as if they did not exist. That, too, George felt was right; who need worry about mere children when there were matters of great importance to discuss?

The men bowed and the ladies curtsied as the duke and duchess walked past them. George watched impatiently. The moment the duchess was out of sight, he raced out of the hall, heading for the stables. There was still time to see the litter, if he was careful not to get dirty. He could only hope it wasn't too late to see the puppies with their eyes still closed. In a sudden flash of adult intuition, he found himself thinking what a shame it was that you had to live with your eyes open and see the world. With eyes closed you could imagine it to be so much nicer than it really was. Sadly, you could not close your ears; people's harsh words would still get through.

Shaking his head to rid himself of the unwelcome thoughts, George hurried across the bailey and entered the stables.

The puppies awaited him.

Chapter 4

I did not go near the battlements for a whole year. I did not dare.

I was wrong when I assumed my lady mother had not noticed the scuffed boots; she had and she mentioned it to Susanna, who was not pleased with me at all. Then someone said he had seen me in the stables – I recall I went to bed in tears that night. It wasn't the first time; it would not be the last, either. I was always getting into trouble and being whipped for it. Sometimes it was almost worth it.

Much as I longed to climb those steps again and look out across the countryside, it was absolutely forbidden by direct command from my lord father. Someone had told him about that – there seemed no end to the people prepared to get me into trouble!

But one year later I was six, bigger than most at that age, strong enough to tackle just about anything and I was deeply upset that Margaret was leaving for Kent. I was off my food, not sleeping well, unable to study and showed no interest in the dogs or the new litters born anywhere in the castle grounds. All this was unheard of for me. So for once my lady mother showed concern and asked what I would like to make me feel better. I didn't have to think about it, the desire had been there for the whole year, the need to be above everyone, to look down on them all. The adult George knows precisely why the desire was there, I doubt that the six year old did but he knew one thing, that was where he wanted to be when his sister rode out so he could watch her go, watch her diminish in size and finally disappear from his life. When he saw her again, she and he would be different people.

Of a wonder, our lady mother agreed, provided I was escorted and held in a harness so that I would not fall into the moat.

Why was the desire there? In part because it had been forbidden, but a greater part was to see people small where I was small, to make me feel large, all powerful, inviolate, unreachable on the high points of the castle walls. Too high for anyone to see my face, to guess what I was thinking. I had to learn to shield my thoughts and my expressions. It was not easy. Up there no one who mattered would see my thinking writ large on my small face.

It had been a year of intense tutoring in all the skills, preparing Margaret for her new life in another home. Of necessity I was dragged in to learn to dance, to play the lute, to speak French and read and speak some Latin with her. I didn't have to learn to sew, for which I was most grateful, but was diverted into practising with weapons; that suited me much better. There were endless instructions in manners, it seems we could hardly move without breaking some convention or other. This all came in addition to our lessons in reading, writing an elegant script and learning to figure. Sometimes I felt as if my head was bursting with all the information it had to contain. I realised I was losing my desire to run everywhere; I walked at a sedate pace and bitterly regretted the strictures placed upon me.

I recall even now the longing I had one day when, hanging out of a window to get air on a particularly hot summer's day, I saw the stable boys mock fighting outside, shrieking with laughter. I saw them; they did not see me. They had freedom; I did not. Never had the contrast been so acutely brought home to me.

As if this was not enough, Margaret talked endlessly of going away, what it would be like, how she would find new people to be with, to care about. She did it deliberately, I knew that; she would be watching my face and the moment I showed distress she would throw her arms around me and tell me there was no one she

43

cared about more than her brother George. She fussed, mother-like, over the small, quiet, determined Richard but not to the extent she did with me. I remember an instance that Autumn when she came into the Great Hall with her hands full of ripe plums. She handed some to me, totally ignoring Richard who was playing with something on the floor. I saw him look but he said nothing. He never did. I often wonder, I as the adult George, that is, how much he felt excluded, how much he wished to be part of the relationship. I almost wanted to say to him; 'sorry, you were born too late and too small and we have no time for you' but it would have been unkind and untrue. It was just the way I felt then.

It would be a kindness not to ask me how I feel now. Some things are better locked in the heart and mind and carried to the grave. On that associated thought, I have asked to be buried with Isobel in the abbey at Tewkesbury. I know my wish has been conveyed to my liege lord and it will be granted. It is small consolation at this time but any consolation is to be welcomed.

Everything changed when Margaret rode away. It was as if she had taken the light and life with her. My lady mother was often attending to business and I found my days revolving around studies, the small, dark, often silent younger brother I hardly knew, Susanna and the squires delegated to care for me. It was dull, tedious and held no promise of the future being any different. Apart from the great religious festivals, the visits of dignitaries and my lord father's coming and going, life remained that way for a further four years. Of a surety there were times I believed it would never change, that I would be trapped in Fotheringhay ennui for the remainder of my life. At that time 'the remainder of my life' seemed like eternity. Now it has shrunk to – days? Hours? Minutes?

The flames leap with such energy, such zest for living, yet how soon they are extinguished, leaving no more than ashes for the servants to clear in the morning. If not removed they clog up the fireplace and then there is no through draught to burn the logs when the fire is revived. Even as we humans have to be removed at times to allow a through draught to cleanse the court, the parliament and the country. It was my reason for ordering executions when I had the power to do so. I accept, reluctantly, it is my brother the king's reason to do the same to me. I stand between him and peace of mind.

The knowledge, the understanding, does not help and I have no peace of mind.

Will I be cruel enough to say it is also a tiny piece of evidence I hold in my drink-befuddled mind that also needs to be burned up and thrown out with the ashes, for fear of it becoming public and bringing down the court and all with it?

Beware the unwary tongue, George, beware. You hope and long for mercy from your brother of March, do not put that into jeopardy by unwise thoughts escaping.

Foolish thought. I cannot speak clearly any more, none would understand me and if I write, my tears smudge the ink so much one would think the paper had been left out in the courtyard among the ravens, that they had trodden on it with their clawed feet and destroyed the words.

Yes, but thoughts have life, have power, have energy and –

No, foolish, drunken man, no. No one can accuse you of releasing this secret to the world and they never will.

Look, now I speak to myself as if I was another person. Madness overtakes the pain or is it the pain which overtakes the senses?

Chapter 5

Suddenly life was stood on its head. Suddenly the order had arrived from the duke that they were to vacate Fotheringhay immediately and ride out for Ludlow. Everything was a flurry of preparations, packing, arguments of what and what not would be taken with them. Men rushed everywhere, attending to horses, tack, armour, weapons, women rushed everywhere with arms full of clothes, bedding, possessions of all kinds. There was no time to think, to question, to wonder, it was all they could do to obey the order and make sure everything was packed that should be packed.

For George the sudden removal was a serious shock. Fotheringhay had been home for many years, suddenly it was not home any more. They were to travel to Ludlow, which he had heard about but never actually thought about. It was just 'over there', another of his lord father's homes, a distant place attended by people who were alien to him, for they were not Fotheringhay people. He hardly slept the night before they rode out, sick with worry and fear, wondering why there was this move, what had threatened their quiet life. But there was also a strange sense of excitement, for they were to ride with an armed escort, they were going alone, their lady mother was to follow later. And, when they got there, his two older brothers, whom he had never met, would be waiting for them. Excitement piled on fear piled on worry piled on wonder. It was a miracle he was not physically sick with it all.

Ludlow was a surprise in many ways.

The riding out with the armed escort, the endless lanes along which they rode in the summer heat, the jangling of harness and the clop of hooves accompanying every move, that had at first been strange, then exhilarating, then boring. But two days of riding brought them to the large imposing fortress home of Ludlow castle. The great outer wall seemed fit to withstand any invading army, no matter how big and well armed and George was able to still his worried thoughts. To him, Fotheringhay had seemed inviolate but it was obvious to anyone that Ludlow was stronger and larger than Fotheringhay and he quietened his churning mind for the first time since they had rode out across the drawbridge. Because of his worry, he had hardly spoken a word during the journey which, at first, was a cause of great concern to his escort. He knew they were accustomed to a George who never stopped talking, who asked a hundred questions about every aspect of a day and there they were, riding to another part of the country, to a place he had never seen, to meet with brothers he had never met and yet he had hardly said a word.

Richard had not spoken, either, but they were used to that. The silent, solemn, deep thinking young boy was normally a shadow to the fair-haired ever-smiling George, whose vivid blue eyes missed nothing and who could normally not stop speaking to draw breath. To ride guard to two young boys who were silent when, under normal circumstances, at least one of them rarely shut up, must have seemed strange. George was constantly asked if he was all right; he responded with a nod or a muttered 'yes' and nothing more. By the end of the first day the escort must have decided he wasn't going to speak to them so they gave up asking. Instead they chattered among themselves as they rode, discussing such mundane topics as the changing landscape, when they would stop for a natural break and what reception they would get at Warwick castle, where they were to rest overnight. George wondered why they had to talk, there was enough noise around them, everything from wildlife to the clatter they were making

47

as they rode, but guessed they needed to pass the time in some way.

Warwick castle, whilst dissimilar on the outside to Fotheringhay, felt like home once they got inside; the familiar sense of being enclosed by impregnable stone walls, the echoing of footsteps where rushes had been kicked aside, the tapestries adorning the walls of the chamber where they slept, he and Richard in small beds side by side. George lay awake for some time, listening to his younger brother breathing softly and muttering occasionally in his sleep, feeling superior in years and experience over the small Plantagenet, feeling protective and supportive at the same time. It was odd; it was an alien feeling and he wasn't sure he overly cared for it. George was the centre of his own universe; it was hard to acknowledge that someone else had a right to be in that universe with him.

Worry rode with him all the next day as, saddle sore, travel weary and tired from broken sleep, he constantly gnawed at the thought, why had they been ordered to leave Fotheringhay? Could this place, Ludlow, be stronger and more secure than his own home, which could surely hold off the largest army?

The answer, as they rode into the outer bailey, was yes.

The hustle and busyness of the place was impressive. The moment they were through the gates their horses were secured by men ready to lead them to the stables, people were gathering on the steps to greet them, their possessions were being manhandled into the castle and George, swaying a little with weariness and stiff muscles, bemused by all the activity and the people, walked toward the entrance and found himself gazing up at the tallest man he had ever seen in his life.

"You have the look of a Plantagenet." The voice seemed to come from somewhere in the clouds and George strained his neck to look up at this incredible person. The sun lit up the golden hair and the smile lit up the already handsome face. A large hand reached for him. "I am Edward, your brother. You are George, I know that and there is Richard, the youngest but never overlooked York. Welcome to Ludlow!"

Richard seemed as overawed as George was by the giant who stood smiling at them but remembered his manners; he bowed and held out a small hand.

"I am pleased to meet you at long last, my Lord."

"Such delightful manners!" Edward turned to the man standing next to him, a man a little shorter, with hair a few shades darker but every bit as handsome as Edward, earl of March himself.

George collected his thoughts, bowed and also held out a hand. "I have heard much about you, my Lord." He turned to the other man and smiled his radiant smile. "I am assuming this is my Lord Edmund, Earl of Rutland." It wasn't a question. He hoped he had moved fast enough and diplomatically enough to cover his mistake in not offering his hand to his golden brother immediately; being outflanked by Richard was not a good move when meeting such impressive people for the first time.

Edmund smiled at both of them. "I am indeed. These young Yorks have been well brought up, Ned. We have brothers to be proud of! Welcome to Ludlow. You must be tired; it was a long journey. Come, we will arrange for squires to take you to your rooms so you can wash away some of the dust of the journey. Then you can both eat."

They walked into the great tower, Edward with George, Edmund with the silent awe-struck Richard. Edward was still talking, asking about Warwick and their stay there, whether the journey had been uneventful whilst almost unobtrusively summoning squires to attend to them. The tapestries here were richer and thicker than those in Fotheringhay, the furniture seemed sturdier somehow, well padded and ornately marked. The one familiar item was the huge fireplace with the seemingly obligatory wolfhounds sprawled in front of it.

On the way to their rooms, one each this time, George noticed the armour and arms decorating the soaring walls, taller and more magnificent than – but he could not really continue comparing the two homes. This was the castle he had heard about from the servants and squires, the great fortified home of the Yorks, the place where his two older brothers had been brought up and taught all they knew about arms, armour and warfare, where his father apparently felt most at home, although he professed to love Fotheringhay.

'I want to explore!' thought George excitedly. 'I want to explore everything – but oh, I am so tired!'

Warm water was brought so he could wash. His clothes had already been hung in his room and he was able to change his travel-stained tunic and hose for fresh ones. He ran a wet hand through his fair hair, bemoaning the fact it was not the same golden colour as Edward's, hoping it looked respectable. The bowl of water was being taken away when he heard a sound and swung round to find Richard standing in the doorway, wearing a linen shift and fresh hose, holding a tunic.

"George, could you help me with this, please?" The voice was so quiet George wondered if he had heard correctly. His first thought was to say 'where is your squire?' but he swallowed the comment and nodded. Richard walked over to him; his eyes full of unshed tears.

"I wish we were back in Fotheringhay," he whispered and then hid his face on his brother's chest. George stood for a moment, dumbfounded. His little brother never showed his feelings, no matter what was going on, whether he was being berated for breaking some rule, misspelling his lessons, being told he could not ride that day or even that a favourite animal had died. Not knowing what else to do, he put his arms around the small slim shoulders and held Richard close.

"We'll be all right." It was said with more confidence than he felt but he had to say and do something. This was unprecedented and was in danger of breaking down all his barriers, which would never do. He had worked hard to build them, to shut out the harsh world that threatened at times to invade his peaceful life. If you denied, vehemently, that people went away, that they were injured and sometimes died, if you denied that animals died or were killed by others, if you denied people entry to your love and your emotions, you could not be hurt. From the moment Margaret had ridden away from Fotheringhay, trailing dust and memories, leaving shadows and emptiness behind her, George had built barriers to keep all emotion out. He had functioned mechanically, going to lessons, visiting his mother and attending services without letting any of the homilies reach his mind. All that was under threat by the shaking bone thin shoulders of a small boy who was homesick and heartsick and reaching out to a bigger - but not so big that he was overwhelming - older brother to take care of him.

"Come on," he said quietly, aware that a page was standing in the doorway, no doubt waiting to take them downstairs to eat. "Let me help you with that."

"I wasn't going to bother you…" Richard began, obediently lifting his arms up so George could slide the tunic down over his head.

"We're family, aren't we?"

"Yes, but…"

"But you never asked me for anything before and you didn't want to ask me now. I'm glad you did." A rush of love swept through George, which he bit back, hard. "I miss Fotheringhay too, you're not alone, but we have to do what our lord father wants. Our lady mother will be here soon, all the Yorks will be together." Apart from Margaret, his mind responded immediately. And his other sisters, too, but he didn't know them and they, unlike Edward and Edmund, were so rarely mentioned that they might as well not exist. His two brothers, on the other hand, were mentioned often, usually with great pride. Now he had met them, he understood why. They were golden people indeed, tall, handsome, no doubt incredibly talented and skilled with both weapons and horses.

"Lord George," the page began. George looked over Richard's head and nodded.

"I know. We will be there soon. Grant us a few moments, we are tired, we have had a very long journey, we were two days on horseback."

The page nodded with a sympathetic look. Richard tugged at his tunic, fastened the belt and looked up at George with a brighter smile than he had given for some time.

"Thank you. I will be back shortly."

The small figure hurried out of the room and George sat down on the edge of the bed. They had ridden for two whole days locked in their own private misery, neither of them sharing their emotions with the other. But if they had spoken of it, the escort would have overheard, would have known that the York brothers were homesick, and would doubtless have thought them weak. Overall it was better they had not spoken then, had kept it to the privacy of the rooms allocated to them in this fortress where they were assured of safety, or so it seemed.

In a sudden moment of overwhelming compassion, George knelt down by his bed and clasped his hands, something he had not done voluntarily since he was a very small boy.

"Dear God, give my brother Dickon courage to face life here at Ludlow," he said earnestly. "He is so

52

young, so much in need of protection. Let none harm him here. In Jesu's name."

He hastily got up, hoping no one had seen him, a hope that was shattered when he saw Richard waiting outside the door for him, together with the page. He walked over to them with one of his dazzling smiles. "Are we ready to go down?"

Richard raised an eyebrow in query but George ignored it. Let his little brother think what he wanted, let him think he had found religion, anything but let him know he, George Plantagenet, had said a prayer for someone who, up to that moment, he had managed to exclude from his emotions. His brother had been there, a part of life every bit as much as his squires, his nursemaid, his physician and anyone else allocated to take care of him, but no more than that. In a single moment of weakness he had allowed that small person to make a chink in the armour in which he lived. It would not do. It had to be rebuilt, repaired, restored to full defensive ability again. Soon.

Chapter 6

I recall my lady mother arriving at Ludlow in great style, ornate carriage, huge escort, packhorses and all. I recall being so pleased to see her, I forgot my manners and rushed forward to greet her, then standing back wracked with pain as she scooped Richard up into her arms before she even looked at me. I put it away, told myself it didn't matter, that we so rarely had a hug from our mother it made no difference that I didn't get one this time. But oh it did, it did. She did reach for me and drew me close to her so I could smell her delicate perfume and the ethereal essence that was she. I was held against her silk gown for a few fleeting seconds and heard it rustle as I moved my legs. I was proud when she told us how pleased she was that we had made the journey alone – if you could call riding with what felt like hundreds of men at arms 'alone' – and I was aware of glowing with importance when she said how well we looked. We had only been apart for a week; it felt like a lifetime. So much had happened, for Ludlow itself had cast its own spell, outside of being in the company of my revered brothers. I was proud and yet the pain persisted. I had reached her first, my legs being longer than Richard's but it was he she reached for. It confirmed what I had always suspected but never had proved to me – I was second best. Sadly for me, I continued to be second best for the remainder of my life.

As if in compensation, that summer was golden. My brothers were attentive, understanding, patient; when not at practice in the tiltyards and on the butts, they showed us the castle grounds and gave us arms with which to practice, taught us the elements of hawking and riding to hounds, which we had not been allowed to do up to that time. Our lord father was invariably closeted in some meeting or other, some notable person with his entourage was ever riding into the bailey and there would be fuss and scurry, greetings and formal meals which we were summoned to attend and abjured to be on our best behaviour. I wondered at times why it was easier to be well-behaved at Ludlow than it was at Fotheringhay and then decided it was because no matter how long we were there, it still felt as if we were temporarily lodging in the castle, that we would be moved on at some point. So it behoved us to be good whilst we were there. We knew not where we would go next. Fotheringhay was home; this was not. At Fotheringhay it was more difficult to remember to be a royal prince, that was the place where we had grown up, the castle which had seen our every stage of progression, from incontinent toddler to young aristocrat did not feel like a stage on which we had to perform our very best acts before the exalted company, dukes, earls and lords of all names and places come to confer with our lord father. The sheer number of visitors made it even more apparent to me how important he was, in what high regard he was held, for these people came to him, he rarely went to them.

Being perfectly behaved was never a problem for Dickon, always the perfect royal prince. It was for me. I still longed to kick over the traces, to run to the stables, grab a horse and go riding through the local countryside. I could do none of it, for along with the many visitors was the constant air of menace, of apprehension, of looming black clouds despite the summer sun. The talk was of uprisings, of problems with the king's army, the king's policies, the king's alliances and the king's wife. Name it and the Yorks appeared to have a problem with it. I have asked myself a hundred thousand times since, even more so since being incarcerated here in this prison - call it as it is, not as it appears to be, royal apartments - why the Yorks had so many problems with what was being done in the country as a whole. If we were not in supreme control, we wanted to be. When we were, we were unhappy with this one or that and unhappy with each other. If ever a family needed to work together it was the Yorks: if ever a family was divided against itself, it was the Yorks.

Was it because we were three? Because we divided two against one in every possible way we could divide two against one? I fought with my brother of Gloucester for land and wealth and had my brother of March to adjudicate between us. My brother of Gloucester fought, in that he spent the whole of Christmastide arguing my case, for me against my brother of March. I know; it was brought to my chamber how eloquently he fought for me when he had fought so eloquently against me. Would that we could have been true brothers of the heart as well as of blood! Would that we were on terms when I could go to my brothers and say 'I fear I am dying and none can save me. I beg and plead for your absolution, my dear brothers, that I do not go to my Maker with my sins against you heavy on my soul.'

Ah, the foolish pride that held me back when this began holds me back even now from admitting to my family that Clarence has a weakness, that the pain which devours him from the head down is eating his very soul away and all he longs for is the merciful hand of Death to end it all.

I divert. I divert for my thoughts are as scattered as the ashes which flee from the hearth when the log disintegrates and dies under the power of that which consumes it. Even as I do.

The summer at Ludlow. Full of the companionship of two golden brothers, tinged with the air of menace and apprehension, of meals cut short when riders arrived with urgency written in every line of their clothes and their actions. Our lord father would leave the table and closet himself with them, emerging with a blackness that boded ill for any who crossed his path.

It all ended that disastrous night which we knew was coming, we knew from the quantity of men in the castle grounds, from the quality of the guests, from the intensity of the discussions and from the worried look our lady mother wore. No one need speak to the young Yorks of that which was troubling the family; it was writ clear for all to see. The summer was going to end in violence and bloodshed and we were mere pawns in the endgame.

In my later life I heard some say Richard duke of York lost his nerve when the army came close to Ludlow. None said it in my own court, for I would have nothing said against any of my family, my father more than anyone. But it was said in other courts, in other gatherings, for did I not have my informants in every place there could be informants, to keep me forever aware of what was happening in every place at every moment? I heard of the talk against my lord father, those who tried to say that the recklessness that drove him at Wakefield to ride out into the battle was in compensation for the night his nerve broke and he left Ludlow under shadow of night.

I say to those persons, Richard, duke of York was nerveless. A more courageous man never walked this earth and I say that knowing of my brother of March's valiant fearless fighting on the battlefields of Towton, Tewkesbury, Barnet and everywhere else that he fought under the banner of York. I say that knowing of my brother of Gloucester's prowess on the battlefield, for did he not lead the vanguard in his very first battle and win the day for his brother of March?

And what of me, I might ask? What of me? What was my prowess on the battlefield? Would I have out-fought all who came at me with battle-axe and sword, with dagger and with lance?

Once. Once I rode to battle and heard the singing of the blood lust in my ears and knew no fear.

Once I knew the thrill of the surging muscles of a destrier beneath me and knew I could conquer all. The siren call of battle is deceptive, enticing and seductive. To see men fall, spouting their blood, to hear their final cries, should this be seductive? Yes, if it was your life or theirs, then your own life takes precedence every time.

Would it continue to have been so?

Chapter 7

It was explained to them in simple terms. The duke's secretary, ink stained fingers winding themselves around each other in his distress, sat in a large carver and looked at the two boys standing before him, wearing faces as blank and guileless as it was possible to be. The room where they normally took their lessons had the look of being hastily searched, books had been pulled from their shelf and left where they fell, quills were scattered across the tables and ink had been spilled.

"Your lord father has had to leave Ludlow." He coughed, reached for a handkerchief, did not find it and coughed again. "Your lord father has taken with him the earls of March and Rutland and Lord Salisbury. He has gone with a retinue of men at arms and will be issuing an array to raise another army with which to fight."

"Why did my brothers have to go, sire?"

George turned and looked at Richard in surprise. Never had he heard him question anyone over a decision made by his father during his entire life.

"The king's army is close, the king's army is greater in number than the men we had here. Ludlow, I am sorry to say, did not prove to be as safe a haven as His Grace thought. When the army comes – as we know it will – if your brothers were to be found here, they would be slain, Lord Richard. I am sure you would not wish that."

"No, sire, I do not. I just wished to know why they had to go. You have answered my question. I am grateful for that."

Ludlow had been an adventure, a summer of arms practice, of family meals, of time spent with brothers they did not know but had come to respect and grow fond of. It had all changed, in what seemed like the blink of a tired eye, but George knew of the hasty meetings, the many men coming and going, the air of

59

menace hanging over everything like an autumn mist without being as thick as an autumn mist.

"What happens to us, sire?"

The question was as inevitable as the next breath the man took but somehow he seemed to want to avoid answering it. He looked everywhere but at the boys, found great interest in the rich arras behind them, the pattern in the Welsh granite flagstones, the disarray of the rushes kicked out of the way by anxious feet. A sense of movement, of haste, of something bordering on panic was filling the castle. George sensed it, drew it into himself unwillingly, knowing he had to accept it. The man's delay in responding said 'this is not good and I do not wish to impart it.'

"Sire," he prompted, whilst Richard began to look even more apprehensive as they waited.

"Your lady mother is to surrender herself to the king's army, taking both of you with her."

It was like a dive into an ice-cold pond and yet George had known something like this would happen. He had been woken in the night by the sound of horses, of muttered curses and hasty farewells whispered into the darkness, words caught by the stone walls and hurled back into his ears as clearly as if spoken to him directly. He knew his father had gone; knew his golden brothers had gone with him but had not known why. The talk around the castle in the preceding days had been confused, contradictory, boldly optimistic when people realised his ears were straining for every word.

"The king will be merciful to a lady." The words were said with a sigh. Was his life then under threat? Would the soldiers kill such an old man, one whose only use was as a scribe? But then again, he would know much, being the secretary. Were there papers which should be destroyed … George caught his thoughts before they went too wildly off the target. If this man was any kind of loyal servant to his lord father, the papers were long turned into black ash and lost in the flames of the great fireplace in the hall.

"May I suggest you change into your travel clothes and take just that which is most important to you, then wait for your lady mother in the hall. She will direct you from then on. I have much to do. Forgive me."

The man hustled away, clearly glad to be done with his unpleasant duty, heaving the two boys standing in the room, uncertain, afraid and yet not wanting to admit that fear to each other.

"Has our lord father run away?" Richard asked in the tiniest of voices, which George only just managed to hear.

"No. You heard what he said, he's gone to raise a bigger army so he can fight back."

"And left us here."

"Not only us, Mother is here."

"We're too small to go and fight, I suppose."

"Much too small. There's nothing we could do in a battle but get in the way of those fighting. Imagine Ned being distracted trying to defend us, instead of killing our father's enemies!"

"I know it but I don't like it!" Proudly Richard stood as tall as he could, as if taking on the mantle of a soldier.

"Come, we have our orders: change and find that we wish to take with us. Come on, Dickon, we have to do as we're told, we don't know when the army will arrive!"

The precisely spoken statement was like a command. Richard reacted by standing even straighter, then turning and hurrying out of the room. George raced after him and together the two boys climbed the stone stairs to their chambers.

George swiftly changed into a coarser tunic and exchanged his fine leather boots for stronger ones. Then it was a question of what to take, if anything. He had to hope there would be someone to pack his clothes for him, he had no idea how to start doing that. He grabbed his rosary, his prayer book and some of his favourite jewels, tucking everything inside his tunic for safe keeping. With one last look at the place he had come to like so much, he went into Richard's room to find out how he was faring.

Richard had changed but was hesitating over his possessions, picking up a chain, putting it down again and picking up a ring instead.

"Hurry!" George urged him. "Take what you most favour and let us be downstairs when our lady mother needs us. This is not the time to incur her wrath!"

Richard nodded, still hesitating. Finally he made up his mind, taking a rich amber rosary, a heavy amber jewel and a ruby ring before hurrying out of his room without a backward glance.

The hall was silent. The fire had been allowed to die down, it was nothing more than a sullen glow of dull red covered in fine ash. The dogs had vanished and, by chance, not a single servant was left in the place to attend to them. They stood, unsure, unhappy, in front of the dying fire, a metaphor for their glorious summer of happiness. They did not speak for to break the silence might mean breaking down the barrier of adultness they were trying to assume.

After what seemed an age the duchess hurried into the hall, carrying a small bag. Several of her ladies came too, brightly coloured birds following their leader.

"We must be ready." The duchess fretted, touching their shoulders, tugging at their tunics, fussing with their hair. "Oh, why did this have to happen?"

"My lady!" One of her ladies distracted her attention for a moment. "The soldiers are here."

The words were unnecessary. Boots resounded on the stone floor, spurs jangled, swords swung from belts. The soldiers, led by their captain, stormed into the hall, viewing the tapestries and rich furniture with undisguised glee.

"Your Grace." The unkempt, bearded dirty captain bowed to the duchess but it was a gesture tinged with contempt. The rank smell of cheap wine, body odour and horses reached their nostrils. George was aware of rising anger that such an uncouth person should address his lady mother in such an arrogant offhand way but also knew there was nothing he could do about it. Not then, not there, but in the future - he promised himself – in the future no man will speak to any woman of my family in such a way and keep his tongue in his head. In that moment he felt much older than his ten years. The captain continued: "Are there no men here?"

"There are no men here. Only myself and my small sons, together with my ladies who have stayed to comfort me in my time of tribulation."

"I am bidden to place any who are in this castle under arrest as traitors to our King and country."

"I throw myself upon the King's mercy and beg him to take pity on a poor woman and her two small children."

"York brats!" someone snarled from the mob surveying the hall. "They should be put to the sword, not allowed to live!"

"Silence!" the captain roared, startling George so much that he stepped back. His mother pulled him forward again to stand beside her. "Speak not of royal princes in that way, or I will deprive you of your ears, dog!" He turned back to the duchess. "Of a surety, madam, you give me many problems. I did not expect to find you here. I shall be forced to send a messenger to His Grace and find out if mercy can be extended to Your Grace and Your Grace's sons. Until then, you are under arrest as wife to a traitor. I must ask that you return to your room and stay there until the answer is brought to us."

"Come." The duchess swung round on her elegant heels and ushered her sons before her toward the stairs. "Come!" She indicated two of her ladies who hurried after them. George shuddered as he saw the soldiers grab some of the others and drag them into nearby rooms, hearing their pitiful screams for mercy, knowing there was nothing he could do or say to prevent them being hurt.

"I shall not forgive easily and I will not forgive this!" The duchess waved an imperious hand at the men already stripping the walls and removing the fine furniture even as she walked away. They ignored her, taking her words as empty threats.

Once in the sanctuary of her room, however, Lady Cecily gave way to her emotions, holding her head in her hands and weeping softly, almost silently. Richard clung to her arm, as if pleading with her to stop her tears. George hung back, almost embarrassed to see his proud mother in such distress. One of the ladies tried to console her.

"My lady, the King will grant the pardon, we will all be safe."

"I know that, Helena, but oh the women here, the men who are dying, the thefts, the-" The tears began to flow again freely and Lady Cecily rocked back and forth in her chair, making a high pitched keening cry. George's emotions snapped and he suddenly threw himself at her, pounding her with his clenched fists.

"Mother, Mother, stop it!"

She opened her eyes and looked at her son in complete astonishment. The tears stopped and she managed a shaky smile.

"Forgive me, my sons, I am sorry. For a moment I managed to forget who I was." She fumbled for a handkerchief and dried her face. The regal demeanour was back. "On this occasion I forgive you for your assault, George!"

64

He stood back, scared, ashamed, scuffing his boots on the floor. "My apologies, Mother."

She reached for him, held him close to her bosom, cradling his head, something she had never done in all his ten years of life.

"My dear son, you brought me back from a moment of sheer madness. There is nothing to forgive." She let him go and held Richard instead. His lips trembled as if he was on the verge of tears. "Helena, if you can, arrange for some coverlets, furs, anything, to be brought to us. If we are to stay here until the king's pardon arrives, we at least need some degree of comfort. And arrange for us to have some food and ale or wine. Olivia," she gestured to her other lady, "I would have warm water with which to wash my face and hands. See if it can be arranged, I beg you."

Then she fell silent and for the first time the clamour of the looting soldiers could be heard clearly throughout the castle, coupled with the screams of women and the groans of men, wounded, dying under the swords and daggers of the king's army.

"Proud they were," the duchess said quietly to her frightened sons. "Proud men, signing up to fight for the king. Listen to them now. Long may they rot in Hell and the traitor Trollope along with them!"

George caught his breath. Trollope, a traitor! Someone who had wined and dined at the castle, been his lord father's confidant, knew all the plans of the Yorks – what had he been paid to turn traitor on the Yorks? More than that, how could he?

"Mother, what will happen to us?" Richard asked at last in a tiny voice croaky with fear.

"Us? Nothing, Richard, nothing at all. The king is a just man and will grant pardon and safe passage to a woman and her sons. We have to wait for the pardon and safe passage. But we are trapped here until it arrives, I am sorry to say. Now, did you both secure your possessions as I requested?"

They both nodded and George realised the wisdom of his mother's command. Anything of value would be taken by the soldiers and everything else probably destroyed even as they seemed intent on destroying the very castle in which they were sitting at that time, judging by the horrendous noises which reached them; the sounds of things being broken, of rage and anger, of pain and sheer unmitigated terror.

The duchess settled herself in her chair, holding George in the curve of one arm and cradling Richard on her lap with the other. For a single fleeting moment, George wondered if the whole dreadful experience was worth it to have this moment of closeness, something he had never experienced before. He wondered if he ever would again.

Chapter 8

We were in the room for two days. We slept on the floor with such coverings as we could persuade the men let us have, while outside the screaming, looting and the groans of the dying went on. We ate whatever our mother's lady could scavenge for us and we drank weak watered wine. We were cold, the Autumn air was chill and there was frost in the morning. We used the covers we slept on to wrap around ourselves in an effort to keep warm. We hardly spoke, for there was little to say. My lady mother prayed endlessly for the safety of our lord father and our brothers and for safe passage for us away from what had turned out to be a living nightmare, not the safe haven our lord father had in mind.

After two endless days of utter boredom combined with paralysing terror, the captain returned to say pardon had been granted, we were to go to Coventry to my aunt's home and we were to leave immediately. We gathered up the coverings, in case we needed them, made sure we had our few meagre possessions safe and walked down the stairs into what seemed like a scene from Hell.

The castle was a wreck. Dead bodies, badly wounded men roughly bandaged, discarded food, empty wine casks, battered broken weapons, drunken men, all jumbled together in a way that tormented and destroyed my dreams and waking thoughts for days.

The captain's men escorted us out past the bodies, past the wounded, past the blank bare walls, past the rooms empty of furniture, all gone. Everything I had admired, everything I had cherished about Ludlow, gone. At that moment I really believed my lord father had abandoned us and we would forever be alone. I recall a great sense of desolation falling over me like fine rain, soaking into my clothes, my heart and my mind.

Coventry was two days' ride away, endless as the days before had been endless, travelling through a grey endless landscape that offered no shelter from the harsh winds and cold that chilled our hearts as much as our bodies. A ride of intense loneliness for we did not speak at all. We huddled over our saddles, clutching our cloaks around us, trying for every tiny scrap of warmth we could gain from the thick wool. The horses plodded rather than walked, as if they too resented the long days of travel. The inn where we stayed overnight was not good but good enough. We hardly spoke for there was nothing to say to lighten our journey or our thoughts.

It was not very good living in my aunt's house. She was gracious, she was kind, but she was extremely strict and we attended services what seemed like all day every day. A tall, thin, elegant but stern looking lady who ruled her home with supreme authority. She would allow no laughter; she would allow no conversation outside of ourselves. No visitors were permitted, no letters came. I knew not where my lord father was or my brothers; we heard nothing. No news was given to us. They might have been dead for all we knew. There was heartache, tremendous heartache at this. Coventry was not home and never would be. It was even more of a temporary resting place than Ludlow had seemed but without the diversions of Ludlow; no brothers, no riding, no hawking no hunting, just rigid devout life. For a time it pushed me even further away from having any kind of faith but I have to recall then I was very young and very disillusioned. For such a nice life - and it had been, despite the menacing clouds - had been abruptly, horribly, brutally brought to an end. I could not remove from my mind the pictures of the dead and dying in the castle and the courtyard at Ludlow, although I shut my ears to the screams of the women, nor could I stop bewailing the loss of my precious few possessions. There was no chance at Coventry to have anything new.

We studied, Dickon and I, and we improved our standards of scholarship but we stagnated in the sheer ennui of services and solitude, of silent meals and lack of companionship outside of each other.

I discovered hidden depths in my small brother I had not suspected. He was pious, which I did not know before then, and took real pleasure in the religious life we led. He went willingly to every service where I lagged behind, seeking excuses not to go, for the chapel was ever cold and I was ever in need of warmth. He did not mind the studying, leaping ahead of me in his knowledge of Latin and French. Whilst I laboured over translation, I realised he wrote as freely in those languages as he did in English. I was often told to look at my brother's work as an example of what I should be doing but what I should be doing and what I did were two very different things then and continued to be for the rest of my life. I was never a scholar to that degree; if something interested me, I would pursue it relentlessly, if it did not, then the words found it hard to penetrate this stubborn mind of mine.

What can I say? In later life, when I fought with my brother of Gloucester over points of law I found my arguments equalled his or he equalled mine. I cannot say which was right of those two statements, so perhaps some of those early lessons did sink in after all, for we were well matched, according to those who heard us, trading argument for argument with neither of us able to outdo the other and it all being left to our brother the king to adjudicate for one or other of us. But that was in the future, the troubled turbulent future when money was important and estates were vital and our wealth depended on that which we held.

I think now of those days at Coventry when we were two small boys trying to be as innocuous as possible so as not to disturb my aunt's household or bring censure down on our heads – my head if anyone's for Dickon was better behaved than I at any given moment of a day or night – and where all that was open to us to pass the endless days was study.

Christmas passed in a haze of services and muted celebrations. The meals were good, but there was no entertainment, for my aunt employed no Fool or minstrels, considering them a waste of good money. Dickon bewailed the fact he had no lute. I longed for a dog to run at my heels as I played or rode with hounds. I longed to ride with hounds, too. Horses were kept for travelling, according to my aunt, not for frivolous things like hunts.

The New Year brought little prospect of joy or release from the prison in which I felt we were incarcerated but sunlight burst through with a visitor who came, cap in hand, to ask my lady mother if my brother and I might be lodged with the Archbishop of Canterbury, there to continue our studies. That in itself was a rare event, a visitor, but it was someone important enough for my venerable aunt to allow him to come in.

My lady mother asked, with astonishment, who had provoked such a request, she was told it was my brother of March who had written to the Archbishop from the stronghold at Calais, where he was safe and well and making many plans, arranging for our liberation. Ever will I be grateful to my brother for this act of kindness at a time when his life was in danger, himself attainted and his estates lost! In the midst of his own tribulations he thought to arrange for our future. When I tried to offer my thanks for this on his return to London in triumph, he dismissed it as nothing. Perhaps it was nothing to him, but it was a great deal to us and we never forgot it, either of us.

In later life I realised that the first consideration for my brother the king was family. Methinks I should have remembered that; in my quest for wealth, position and power I overlooked the small fact of family being important beyond anything else. Had I remembered that, many events might not have subsequently taken place and in truth I might not be incarcerated in the Tower at this time.

But to return to my past ...

We had to leave our lady mother behind, in the care and protection – and custody - of her sister. We had to say formal goodbyes whilst behind the stiff faces I know I was crying and I believe Dickon was too, but we had a new and exciting life to look forward to, for some months at least. It helped, as we rode away, to think on that and not what we were leaving, our lady mother in a place of religion and no laughter, with no news and nothing but heartache. Not even her sons to fuss over and care for. With the ability of children to put out of their mind that which hurts, we looked forward to our next adventure.

And so it proved. The archbishop was a kindly man who provided us with clothing, books, musical instruments, a dog to romp with, a stable of horses to ride and tutors to enlarge upon that which we had learned already. I was, for a time, able to stop thinking about my lord father and my brothers, to stop feeling sick inside with worry at their fate, to concentrate instead on attempting to perfect my court manners and my studies, whilst Richard read and read and read until I thought he would damage his eyes with so much reading. He never seemed to be able to get enough knowledge, ever was he asking questions of the tutors and reaching for another book, or writing another essay or translating another piece of work. I wondered if it was his way of dealing with the worry of our transplanted lives, for we had been uprooted from Fotheringhay, then again from Ludlow, then again from

Coventry and even now knew that this was no more than temporary lodgings.

Our lady mother wrote often, praising us for working so hard – which made me wonder who was passing on the information, was there nothing we could do that was secret? – and assuring us all was well, that we would be able to rejoin the family before many months had passed. I wondered how she knew this, too, for we had no news of our lord father or our brothers. We only knew our brother of March was alive and well at the time he wrote his request for our removal to the Archbishop's home because he had written his request for us to be moved there, but following that time we heard nothing.

There were rumours; of course, England was ever alive with rumours. There was talk of uprisings, of revolt, of unhappiness among the nobles of the land. How much was true and how much was rumour was for any to speculate upon and try and find the kernel of truth, if truth there be in such stories. Who can tell when it is passed from one man's mouth to another's ears and from that man's mouth to another's ears and in the process to become changed beyond all recognition? This we knew to be a fact; rumours could not be truth and truth stood out from rumours. So we lived quietly and studied and waited for the truth to be known and for our brothers and our lord father to come home.

I have to say, if this is to be a honest recollection of my life, and at this advanced stage of my condition that life is ever growing shorter by the moment, that during that period I grew to be more than passing fond of my younger brother. He was quiet, steadfast, intensely loyal, devoted and devout. I found him to be intelligent and sharp-witted, thoughtful and considerate and I envied him his quiet pose and demeanour.

Right now, sitting here before this fire this cold February day, aware of the chill of the great stone walls which have absorbed the joys and sorrows of a thousand years – or so it seems to me – it is hard to recall the feelings I had for my brother in their real form. I recall them as a fact, I recall that I did carry those emotions for him at that time. We lived close together, we studied together, we played together and I grew in love and appreciation of him. I ask myself now why it all went so badly wrong, why I chose to walk away from the family, why I considered him in later life to be my bitter enemy, why and then again I ask why. I have no answers.

I can only what I have already thought whilst dwelling on these memories:

I do not know; I will not know.

Chapter 9

Attainted exiles, despised family, traitors to a man according to the current thinking, but word came of how the people cheered when Edward earl of March rode back into London! Rain, such rain as the world had not seen, had dampened everyone's spirits, along with the crops, the animals and the wildlife. The people of England were in great need of something to lift them out of the depression caused by the incessant ruinous weather. What more could they ask than a golden, handsome giant of a man with a huge smile, tremendous courage and an equal amount of charm arriving like a king about to be crowned?

Could there be anything worse for someone bursting with energy and family loyalty than to hear the news of an adored brother marching on London, setting a siege of the Tower, raising a new enthusiasm in his followers as he then turned and marched north to do battle once more? George fretted and fumed at being confined in the archbishop's house whilst the news of his brother, with the Earls of Warwick and Salisbury, kept on coming, men describing the march on London whilst he was unable to hunt, ride, practice his archery or – what he really wanted – to leap on a horse and go and join his brother on the triumphant ride into the greatest city in England. Like it or not, there were still lessons to be learned, manners to be acquired and court etiquette to be forced into his unwilling mind. Ever impatient, the lessons with lute or the dance were purgatory at times, when his mind was on battle and glory, not on the nuances of lyrics or the turn of a foot and the sweep of an arm so as not to discomfit a partner.

He was safe from the inclement, unseasonable, unreasonable weather at least. The rain beat against the shutters and the window glass, darkening the day so that there was need of cressets and rush lights everywhere.

George strode the halls of the house, boots striking hard against the flagstones, trying to kick his way out of the frustration and anger consuming him. He felt he was being closeted against his will with a brother who spent all his day with his nose in a book and merely raised his eyes to look askance at George as he vented his spleen on the world which would not allow him a place in the battles to come.

"George, you are too young." The words were uttered with all the wisdom of an eight year old who had spent many hours reading Latin, French and other hefty tomes and who took to the practice with arms and the work in the tiltyard as if it was a task rather than a pleasure. In the face of such quiet certitude, George did actually feel too young, rather than what he really was: an eleven year old prince imbued with all the manners and skills required to take his place at court, in essence a young man consumed with restless energy and a need to combat the ennui that the rainy summer and confinement had wrought in him.

"Age doesn't matter, Dickon, it's what's in my heart that matters! My heart says I want to be there with our brother of March, riding where he rides, fighting where he fights, sleeping rough if he does!"

"Ha! What then of your fine doublet and handmade boots, might I ask? Why, you know you are overly possessive of your clothes and your belongings."

"To ride with our brother I would give it all up!" George whispered with such intensity and seriousness that Richard actually shut the book and looked at him.

"You mean it, don't you?"

"I do. Don't you feel the pull of the wide world? Don't you want to be out there, where the people are shouting for you, where the men are saddling up and riding with you or taking up arms and walking the roads behind you to help you to take what is rightfully yours? Don't you think I want to be there when our lord father comes back to England to take his rightful place in court again? Of course I do!"

Stamping his feet, throwing wide his arms, head back, George appeared to grow several inches in every direction. "Don't think I am not grateful for the time we have spent here," he said suddenly, his size reverting to normality again as a more serious expression took over. "The archbishop has been more than generous, I trust our family can recompense him for our board and our clothes. The tuition has been above that which I would have expected and the time here truly a sanctuary after all we have been through. Ludlow is – almost – a distant memory now."

Richard opened the book again. "It's good to know you appreciate it," he said with an edge of sarcasm. "Sometimes I think you see no further than the mirror, provided it is reflecting yourself, of course."

"Ah, you have no interest in clothes, Dickon! I find it so strange that with so many wonderful colours to choose from, you allow the tailor to do what he wants, rather than what you want and so your colours are dark and dour!"

"Clothes are for covering the body and keeping you warm, not to let you dress up like a popinjay, George. Now, please, let me finish this section before the bell rings for noon."

"I despair!" With a theatrical flounce that would have better suited a mummer or a Fool, George walked out of the room, wondering if he would ever educate Dickon in the ways of fashion, to appreciate colour and design, to admire the cut of a tunic or the tilt of a hat. He doubted it very much. Dickon was only interested in books, in acquiring more knowledge and then more knowledge and in taking life so very seriously. For one so young he seemed to act and speak so old, as if someone had given him the head of an elderly learned man, not that of a young boy. There was no point in trying to change him.

"Lord George!" one of the servants called to him from the doorway. "Quick, it has ceased raining, for which thanks be given! Come, the dogs are ready for games!"

George hurried out of the door, grateful that in his life, at least, someone understood there was more than just books to be read and essays to be transcribed in laborious italic handwriting, hard taught by tutors who despaired of ever getting him to write neatly, even as he despaired of encouraging Dickon to take life in a lighter manner.

From July to September the agonising wait went on: longing to be reunited with family, desire to escape the confines of what was fast feeling like a prison and an overwhelming need to know what was going on made for broken nights and endless days. To make matters worse, if it could be made worse, word had come that their sister Margaret had returned home and was with their mother. When the letter arrived, written in Margaret's perfectly formed unhurried script, George all but screamed in anger, startling Richard who was reading his own letter at the time and sending a page scurrying from the room in fear of repercussions.

"Margaret's home!"

"Yes." Richard indicated his letter, written in the same neat script. "It seems the family are moving on and so-"

"That's not the point!" George was on the verge of tearing up the paper in sheer rage. "The point is we are here and she is there and I want to be there!"

Richard sighed and with that simple action he deflated George completely. The anger drained out of him, his face returned to its customary ruddy look from the high colour which had consumed him for a few

77

moments. "God's teeth, Dickon, does nothing touch you?" he muttered, clutching the letter to his chest, regretting the impulse which had almost brought its destruction.

"Don't let anyone hear you blaspheme like that," Richard commented mildly, as if for once understanding his brother's intense rage. "No. I let nothing touch me that I cannot control. If I cannot control it or change it, then it has to be allowed to pass by. Sooner or later we will be reunited with Margaret. Until that time, I bid you calm yourself and do not allow such anger to overtake you. In the grip of such emotion, you are not in control."

"Control, control, it's your favourite word!"

"And it should be yours, too. One day – when all is as it should be – the Yorks will be in power and then you will need to learn to curb your tongue, your rages and your enthusiasms. Never let anyone see what you are thinking or feeling, George. It is not good; it gives away too much to the other person. They can use it as a weapon against you."

George stood, astonished at the wisdom coming from his brother. It made sense and yet it was cold, almost icy in its single-mindedness. He had not appreciated Dickon had such depth of thought. It explained so much, the bland face he adopted when speaking with people, his lack of emotion when given news or letters of family members George knew full well he cared about or his singular lack of interest in puppies or foals. Dogs not fully grown could not be commanded, horses not fully grown could not be broken in and ridden. He was on the verge of saying, 'would it not ease you to laugh, cry or rage occasionally?' when the bell tolled for Terce and the mood, the moment, was broken. It never presented itself again and the question was never asked, although it was rarely far from George's subconscious mind. He was teased with the thought of what Dickon might have answered. Was there anything in the calculating mind of his brother to be eased? If there was, in the name of Heaven, what could it be?

September arrived and with it, word was sent for George and Richard to be prepared to travel into London. At long last the much desired release was in sight which somehow made the last few days of waiting to travel even worse than the days which had led up to that time. Impatient as ever, George had his belongings packed and ready to go a full week before they were finally told their mother was arriving the next day to take them on to their London home.

"At last!" he shouted, throwing a new cap into the air and catching it again before it fell to the flagstones and damaged the fine feathers which decorated it. Richard half smiled at his brother's exuberance.

"May I suggest a ride, George? You need to do something to rid yourself of the energy which seems to be your curse in life."

"Energy? A curse? No, Dickon, a zest for life which you are singularly lacking! Yes, a ride would be good. Come!"

He was out of the door, shouting for their horses to be saddled and brought to the courtyard before Richard had even got to his feet. When he reached the hall George was standing on the steps, stamping his feet with characteristic impatience, surveying the sky as if assessing the weather, watching the coming and going of the Archbishop's many workers, hands busy tugging his cap, adjusting his doublet, checking his lace cuffs, playing with the gold chain and the ruby which hung from it, never still for a moment. He turned round as Richard approached him.

"We can dispense with cloaks, Dickon, it does not look like rain. That means we ride free!"

Richard shrugged. "'Tis as one to me, George, riding with or without. A ride is a ride, is it not?"

"No! Of a surety it is not! Riding with a cloak means something to encumber you, to stop the wind pulling at your body, to wrap around your arms, to stop you doing what you want!"

At that moment George's horse was brought round to the front of the house, a fine dappled gelding that he had become very fond of and hoped very much he could take with him to London.

"This is what I mean!" He threw himself at the horse in an effort to do a showy mount, missed his footing completely and landed head-first in the courtyard on the other side of the animal, putting his teeth through his lip in the process. He got up, smiling ruefully, dabbing at the blood, to see Richard throw back his head and lose himself in a genuine belly laugh for the first time in his life. It almost made the incredibly painful lip worthwhile. He snatched up his cap, dusted it and made his way a little unsteadily back into the house for his nurse to put some salve on the wound. When he came back, Richard was sitting patiently on his horse, waiting for him. There was no sign of the laughter, not even a hint in the dark eyes which looked him up and down. It was as if it hadn't happened but it was a memory George carried with him for the rest of his life.

Lady Cecily finally arrived at the Archbishop's on the 15th September, complete with her retinue of armed escort and ladies. George could hardly contain his joy at seeing her again but did observe the almost formal pleasure shown by Richard. It revealed to him yet again how much their exile, for all that they were still in England, had affected his brother.

A day later they were in London. The crowds were good-natured, there were cheers and waves for them as they rode in, despite the fact hardly anyone knew who they were. It was enough that they were Yorkists entering their great capital city. Colour, palpable sense of excitement and joy, masses of people and the prospect of the family coming back together again, joined together to give George a lift of spirits which had been sorely lacking for many months.

They were to stay at a massive home called Baynards Castle, right on the banks of the Thames itself, all turrets and corridors, massive rooms and elegant hall. It was a delight to George, who wanted the security of the thick walls and massive doors to keep him safe. It was something he always desired, security, safety, constancy in his life. He had so little of it.

He found Margaret had changed, she was older, more sophisticated and smart, more aware of herself than she had been before she went away but she was still Margaret, still the loving sister and he was more than happy to be back with her again.

They might be in temporary lodgings yet again, with the prospect of another imminent move, but it was home for a while. George could hardly contain himself, at times running from one to the other to make sure they were still there, finally throwing himself on a settle, allowing exhaustion from the sustained emotion to take over. In those moments he looked very much the prince he would become, rather than a young boy whose feelings at times ran too close to the surface to be contained. His joy was increased by the fact that the temporary lodgings had been acquired for them by his brother Edward, the golden giant who, despite all the demands of politics and court, visited them every day, making time for his younger siblings. This was even more important when their mother left them to go to Chester to greet the duke, who was at last coming home from Ireland. It would not be long before all of them were back together again.

His brother's visits were like the sun coming out each day. George would be busy at lessons, sharing the table with Richard, scowling over Latin or French or primers of some kind, when he would hear the commotion that meant Ned had arrived. There was always the great booming voice, the laugh, the shrieks of the maids and ladies at his jests before the boots made their distinctive sound on the flagstoned floors. George would throw down his quill and rush down the stairs, stopping short of the golden giant and making a perfect courtly bow to his brother.

This would invariably make Ned laugh and he would scoop up the young boy, hugging him fiercely before putting him back on his feet again.

"Soon you'll be big enough to pick me up, brother of mine!" A daily jest and one that never failed to bring a smile to George's face. He longed to grow quickly, to equal his most handsome and glittering brother. Ever would he admire the beautiful clothes and the heavily jewelled rings Ned wore with such nonchalance, as if being wealthy was his natural state. He was somehow unmarked, despite his hard-won reputation as a fearless soldier. How had he fought and not been wounded? Only by luck, judgement and having a faster arm and eye than those who tried to fight him. One day, George vowed, one day that will be me, fearless soldier, victorious in battle, quick with words and jests to entertain the ladies, wearing gold embroidered clothes and beautiful rings.

Then Edward would look past George and he would know that Richard had made his much more sedate way downstairs and was patiently waiting for his brother to acknowledge his presence, which he did with the same quiet courtly air as Richard had about him. This was something else George noted with great care, treating like with like, never imposing. Richard was not the sort of boy you picked up and hugged, he was old before his time so he was treated with the respect someone of a greater age would merit. Clever, he would muse when lying awake at night in his bed, staring up at the drapes and seeing pictures in the pattern of the cloth created by the flickering tallow candle he was allowed for a while. Treat everyone in the way they expect; flirt with all women, regardless of their looks for each is a female, of a surety; you treat two boys entirely differently because of their different personalities; you give respect to the old, be jovial with the men of your own age and somehow everyone – everyone – adores you and you get the attention and service you demand without demanding it. Oh, such cleverness! Night after night George fell asleep determined to emulate his golden brother, to be that clever in the handling of the people around him. Morning after morning he found it hard to do and wondered if he would ever truly conquer the art of being as clever as his brother Edward, who was almost a king in his eyes.

One day I will grow up enough to understand how he does it, he told himself, walking the grounds of the beautiful home. He wished they could stay there for it suited him well, high walls and espaliered fruit trees, neatly laid out vegetable plots and stately trees for shelter and to house the birds that roosted there. One day I will have a home like this, he told himself, standing under one of the trees, looking at the elegant gardens. One day I will have a home like this and none shall turn me out of it, no matter what prevails in the country. One day I shall not have to pack my possessions and be moved on yet again, to accustom myself to another property, another set of rooms, another bed. One day ... oh, are dreams not made of such statements? But I will, I will!

Chapter 10

Such times were not to come again. Such times were and are branded in my mind forever as even more golden than the time at Ludlow and that was sunshine after rain indeed. Golden days when my brother Ned came to visit us, days of walking in the gardens, of being in London with all that London had to offer. I only had to listen to the cries of the street vendors and those who tried to go about their business but were caught in the snares of those who tried to sell them food and items, or caused a commotion by chasing cutpurses and robbers, listen to the carts and carriages, the horses, the dogs and the animals held for slaughter, to realise this was a thriving city, one that had nowhere to go but upward and onward, to be the greatest place in the country. Where else could such things be found? Of a surety, as a boy I could see no further than the boundaries of London and found outside those boundaries wanting. I almost managed to overcome the loss of the dappled grey gelding in the joy of being there for I was not allowed to bring it to London.

It all changed. I know now nothing is as constant as change but as a young boy I sought permanence, not constant upheaval. My lord father came home, to great accolades and much happiness from all of us. Our lady mother radiated her joy and that infected all of us. Whether it was all our lord father needed to make him try and claim the throne of England by right of his blood line, or whether he planned all along to do that, I cannot say. What I do know is, his efforts failed and after lengthy acrimonious discussions, a compromise was made, one that suited no one, especially my lord father. The moods were black indeed and we were discouraged from going near him, as if we dared anyway. Those words were wasted on us, for we knew from the time we could walk we did not approach the great duke unless he held out a hand to us. The times he did that were able to be counted as often as the sun dropped out of the sky and burned a hole in London. My lady mother's affection for us was displayed as often as snow in August but that had been known to happen, according to some seers, and so it was possible to say it happened. Ah, my brother of Gloucester, I look back down the years to when we were small, when all life seemed to be on a constant tidal flow of good fortune/bad fortune and all we had to cling to was one another. Where are you now that I need you so much? Back in the north, in the land you love so well, where the wind is keen and the people as sharp as the wind that scours their land and their personalities? What is it that draws you to the north, my brother? What is it that holds you in landscape that has ever seemed to me to be desolate, no, more than that, lonely?

Ah, the truth emerges from the drunken part of the brain which is not affected by whatever it is that is causing me so much pain. What eats at me, I ask myself, is it some insect which has burrowed its way in, or maggots hatched from eggs laid in their passing? Or has the drink damaged the interior of my skull and it is fighting its way out? I have fanciful thoughts even as I know, oh how I know, what it is and that it will end my life if my brother the king does not end my life first. God willing, that will happen!

Clarence, stop this endless, senseless rambling. Come, you talk of your life, so talk of your life, foolish drunken man!

I ask now, to whom do I speak? Who is listening to this babble of thoughts, reminiscences, twisted thinking and outright admissions of regret and sadness? Are there spirits around me, angels even, here in this room, ones I cannot see and cannot sense? Are we not taught that the Lord sends His angels to guard us? I wonder who needs most guarding at this time, myself, getting ready to walk into eternity, or those who will be left to –

Ah, the questions. Left to what? Grieve? Regret? Dismiss my passing as no more than a date to be recorded in the endless papers which are kept of such things? The one thing that will not be mentioned is the hell I am going through.

Loneliness. Who needs the hell of devils with pitchforks and endless flames and endless pain when there is, in this life, the hell of loneliness? Who needs to fear Purgatory when here is aching emptiness, here is the ever-present need for a love that will overcome everything? Where was and is the woman who will love me not because I am – I was – a handsome wealthy duke with many estates and many homes, who will hold my head when I weep with pain, who will laugh with me in the sunshine and in the bitter cold winds that sweep across this country of ours and bring the bite of northern lands with it, who will lie with me for no reason other than comfort and who will not turn away when I reach out for that comfort in the middle of a dark endless night?

I never found her.

Damn it to hell, I thought I had, twice I thought I had and both times it failed.

I know now, from sitting here in this cold cheerless chamber, Royal apartments indeed, my brother the king should try being closeted here for days on end if he thinks these are Royal apartments! That the reason it failed – twice – is that I did not give, I only took.

If You are listening, Almighty God, to the prayers of a doomed man, twice doomed, under sentence of death from without and from within, if You are merciful as they say You are, grant me another chance to show I can give as well as take, let me have a chance at love once more. I care not if I have to live a life over again, many times, if the seer I spoke with once was right, if I can carry with me the memory of a true love and learn to give true love in return.

Enough! Wallowing in self-pity will not help my state of mind. Where did I divert? Oh yes, my brother of Gloucester, named for a southern area, who became Lord of the North. Became a man of stature there, revered, they say, treated like a king. Well, it's as close as he will come to being King whilst my brother the king is alive and then there are countless of his brood to take on the mantle when he goes to his eternal rest. Mantle? Crown, the crown of England, that which was promised once to me and which was taken from me when my brother lusted after the hair and the face and the bosom of a buxom widow who was as sharp as a northern wind and knew if she kept my brother the king from her bed she would draw him close to her. The wiles of women; they do it endlessly and men endlessly fall for it. None learn from the mistakes of others, each thinks they have found that One Woman who will love them forever and eternally and endlessly and all the time men buy their affections with jewels, with land, with titles and properties and estates for the hangers-on masquerading as family and all the time they know somehow they will tire of the hair and the face and the bosom and they knew deep inside in the place where truth lives and no lies can ever be told that another's face, hair and bosom will do as well if not better when the first one becomes too familiar to the lips, the arms and the rest of the body.

Ha! Cynical Clarence! Was it not ever thus with me? Did I not desire Isobel and did I not realise in a short time that I married for power and not for love? And that she married because her father wished an alliance and acquired that which he wanted, as always?

And the second time … ah, does the memory fly back now to the second one. Not for me the adventuring outside the marriage, not for me the guilt of adultery, for

87

all that marriage disappointed me, I made vows and I stayed within them. But when 'freedom' came, when my wife faded away before my eyes, became a walking skeleton of a figure that hurt my very eyes to see, when I longed for Death to take her and end her suffering, when she was finally taken to her eternal rest, then did I turn to another for comfort and for consolation and for that which I sought as a man with natural desires, a willing body which would match passion with passion.

I thought I loved her. I thought this time I had found that which was missing from my marriage, I believed – really believed – all was well. But I know now she loved me and I used her. How hard it is to face the truth! How hard it is to stare into an empty mazer - God knows I would wish it were full again – and say in truth, I used her. At night her face vanished from my mind, her scent, her touch, gone like early morning dew from the espaliered trees I loved to tend and which, like everything else, has been taken from me now. If I loved her, she would not have vanished, she would have been held in my mind, I could have relived every strand of her hair, every crinkle of her eyes as she smiled, every dimple in the skin, but I did not. I could not. I know now I am a cold man when it comes to love; I take and do not give. Ever was it thus with me, I know, I heard it in the condemnatory words of my brother the king, 'ever do you take, Clarence!' he stormed at me when we fought over property. Clarence. When he was not favoured of me, it was always Clarence. When we were brothers together, it was George. So much said in a change of name. So much said and not said and that which I should have said will remain silent for even if I wished now to express anything, this foolish brain, so eaten away, would not put the words together.

I leave behind a lasting legacy, of a kind. One no member of the York family knows of. A secret - and ever did I love secrets. She told me with shining eyes and a smile that was so different from the one she gave when in the throes of ecstasy, that a child would be born of our union. I gave her money; I gave her money for the child, for I knew then that the sands of time were running out fast for this once proud great duke but told her nothing of it. My condition was my other secret, one I kept to myself even with her, she who loved me full well.

Is she yet delivered? Is the child well? Does it prosper? Will she talk of me to the child of our love? Who is there to know of this secret and bring me the news I so desire?

None. Nor ever will be. If there is another life after this, then I will know from the security and safety of that world, once I am out of Purgatory and into the Lord's Heaven, if He permits me to enter, that is. Until then, I am left to wonder. And hope.

Chapter 11

The small ship tossed on the turbulent seas, throwing cargo and people around indiscriminately. Its sails were torn, flapping wildly in the violent wind, the waves smashed against the hull as if determined to break through and snatch the heart from the vessel.

None of this was more turbulent than the thoughts being thrown around in George's mind.

Exile. Bereavement. Loss. Upheaval.

John Skelton, their tutor and friend, had come to the two boys in haste, insisting they dress warmly and pack a small bag – where had he heard those words before and did they not mean the same time thing as last time?

"For your safety, Lord George, and that of your brother, too." And so the clothes were chosen in haste, the bag was packed in haste, no squire to help, only John Skelton himself fastening the cloak clasp and ensuring his boots were firmly on his feet. "A battle comes, Lord George, I am ordered to take both yourself and Lord Richard from London."

The words meant little. A battle, where? Why could he not go and fight in the battle? Did it involve Ned or his lord Father? Who were they fighting, the dreadful Lancastrians again? Was there to be no peace from them?

He was hurried down the stairs and out into the courtyard, where his chestnut gelding waited, alongside Richard's darker coloured mare, both animals saddled, harnessed, ready. A sharp bitter wind blew and he tugged his cloak closer around him. He was glad of his thick leather gauntlets, for it would be a cold ride, wherever they were going. Apprehension clutched at his stomach muscles, made sharp bile rise in his throat and he was on the point of gagging with it until it subsided and he was able to look calmly around as if it mattered not to him that he was once again being forced to leave home.

John Skelton turned as if to shout, but at that moment Richard rushed out into the bailey and mounted his horse. As usual he was a silent, brooding child, not a thought given away. If he was frightened or outright terrified, none would know it. George sat squarely in his saddle and watched as the escort mounted up, listening to the jingle of harness and the muffled orders. No one appeared to want to make much noise, as if the enemy was close and did not need to be warned of their departure. What enemy? What problems had beset his family now?

"Could I not have a moment to say goodbye to my lady mother?" George leaned over to speak to the squire who was going with them, it would seem, by the load he carried.

"No, Lord George. Tis best to leave your lady mother to her thoughts and prayers at the moment."

The group set off, buffeted by the bitter wind. Gorge brooded, feeling uprooted, outcast. He had to know what the reason was this time.

He reined the horse back until he was riding alongside John Skelton.

"Why are we going?" he asked bluntly. "Why, not where."

He watched as Skelton went through a variety of expressions, from grief to blankness, as if he wished to blot out the thoughts he carried. Finally he sighed and nodded.

"You have a right to know. Your lord father is dead. He died at Wakefield, in a battle with Lancastrian forces. Your brother Edmund of Rutland was murdered on the battlefield. Your uncle Salisbury is gone too. Your lord father's head and your brother's head are on spikes at Micklegate. Your lord father's head wears a paper crown. Ever does the Lancastrian queen mock the House of York."

Words are often sharper than weapons, sharper than knife thrusts and sword impalement, sharper than lances designed to knock a rider from his horse. George clung to the saddle, shocked to his core. He turned to see the blood had drained completely from Richard's face. He had ridden close enough to hear.

"And so..." Skelton continued, "for your safety, Lord George, Lord Richard, I am commanded to take you to Europe where you can stay until the matter is resolved, one way or the other. Even now the Lancastrians are approaching the city. Your lady mother will write to you when you are safely out of the way. I am sorry to give you this news, heart-sore sorry but someone had to tell you."

The great duke dead, the golden Edmund dead. On a blood soaked field his beautiful brother, so young, so talented, so promising, had been murdered. Somewhere a spike held the head of his lord father, adorned with a paper crown. The proud duke, mocked and scorned and dead. The handsome Edmund, a corpse on a battlefield. Somewhere a woman was gloating over the blood which had been shed and the lives which had been lost whilst in London the duchess was left to mourn her husband and her son. Left to mourn alone for her young sons were not permitted to stay with her. For their own safety. Sometimes, he thought, it would be better to stay and be killed than be separated from her yet again. There were no tears. What tears could be shed in front of an armed escort, of squires, of a tutor, without looking like a weakling, despite the immensity of the news? The tears burned inside, though, hotter than any fire, along with a grim cold determination for revenge. One day, somewhere, somehow, he vowed, there would be revenge taken by the Yorks for this appalling act of killing. He sent prayers flying to

Heaven for his lord father's soul and for Edmund's soul, for the comfort of his mother, for the easement of his brother Richard's mind, for the safety of Edward, who was gone, it would seem, somewhere in the country, perhaps? Mr Skelton had not mentioned him. That meant no one knew where Edward was hiding. It was better that no one knew. Edward was big enough and strong enough to take revenge. It just needed time, George knew that. But oh the need to strike back! The need to hit something, very hard, to take out this anger, this bitterness, this grief, on something rather than hold it inside his young body.

What did Richard feel at this time? He would never know, for this was too big to be discussed. He knew that.

The ride to the coast was endless, silent and intensely cold but his thoughts were colder, infinitely more painful than any he had ever endured in his life up to that time.

After what seemed a lifetime, they arrived at the windswept lonely coast where a small ship rode reluctantly at anchor, fighting the waves as if it wished to be gone. They were hustled aboard; almost immediately the lines were cast and they were out on the turbulent winter waters, the darkness all enveloping, the wind seeking every gap in his clothing, biting at his flesh. A sailor helped him down below deck and out of the wind. The ship rolled, dipping and rising through the waves which sought to destroy it. George saw that some of the crew could not contain their last meal and he did not blame them, the motion was enough to cause sickness in the best of sailors. In a very short time he was being sick himself, much to his disgust and annoyance but the motion of the ship could not be denied, it was affecting the hardiest of them.

In the crowded cluttered cabin he clung to the timber support and watched his brother with eyes that were not really seeing him, they were all but blinded with tears he could not and would not shed. He reminded himself that a royal prince simply did not weep, no matter what the situation. He blinked a few times and really looked at Richard, who was white, his eyes wide and staring. So far Richard had held on, not given way to the sickness which seemed to plague virtually everyone on board, including their squires and guardian, John Skelton, and their attendants. George's sickness was as much through fear and anger as sea-sickness. Again! He raged, again I am taken away from family and home! Again I lose everything! God in heaven, what I have lost this time! You have taken from me my lord father, my brother, my lady mother, my sister and my home, cast me out upon the sea, sending me to another land where I know not who will take me in! God in heaven, hear this prayer, I beseech you! We are two small boys, lost and afraid and fatherless. If nothing else, grant us safe passage to France, for of a surety if the wind does not drop we will all be lost in the waters and there will be no princes left to follow our brother of March to the throne and the House of York will fail in its desire to rule all of England and I must be there when he is crowned King of England and oh God hear this prayer and grant us safe voyage and bless my brother for he suffers so and –

Another bout of sickness took over, breaking off the rambling prayer that was going nowhere but paining his heart. There was little left to discharge, his stomach hurt with the retching which brought nothing but bitter tasting bile to his mouth. Richard looked at him with sympathy but said nothing. His mouth was a bitter compressed line, his emotions, as always, tightly under control.

After what seemed like a lifetime of surging waves, howling winds, snapping rigging and the cries and shouts of men trying to hold the ship on course, they

94

found harbour in France and the wild tossing finally eased into a gentle sway that was almost as bad for someone whose stomach had been badly disturbed by the sickness. John Skelton gathered up his two small charges and took them up into the fresh air and their first sight of the land that was to accommodate them for a while. George found himself longing to stand on solid earth, to look at things which did not sway and move in front of his eyes, which didn't confuse and confound his sense of balance.

The welcome sight of horses and armed guards waiting at the harbour drove away the bad memories of the voyage. From one kind of movement to another, he thought, but this one I can handle. They waited impatiently for the men to help them disembark, then walked with Richard to the horses. He mounted the horse indicated to him, threaded the reins through his fingers, leaned forward on the horse's neck and whispered into its ear, knowing it mattered little which language he spoke but using his hard learned French to tell the animal he was glad to be off the ship and onto something that he understood. The horse tossed its head and snorted, as if in agreement. George laughed aloud and Richard shot him a puzzled look but said nothing. They moved off at a brisk canter and George felt, for the first time since the disastrous news had been brought to Baynards Castle, that things might actually be turning around. The grief, coupled with bewilderment at being snatched from family and home, had created a stone that sat somewhere in his throat but it eased slightly as he looked around at the new landscape, heard different voices and sounds, became aware of different smells and thought, with a rising sense of excitement, that this could be a most diverting experience, if only he could suppress his emotions at the reason they were there.

The duke of Burgundy himself welcomed them, complimenting them both on their French, their clothes and their appearance. George instantly decided half of it was rubbish but the other half pleased him very much. The apartments they were given were sumptuous in the extreme, hung with rich tapestries and silks, with good thick carpets underfoot and fine china ewers and jugs for their washing needs. Servants rushed here and there, doing their bidding. They were treated like royalty, albeit royalty in exile.

There is always a downside to good things, he decided later, learning that a tutor had been appointed to carry on their lessons. But there were good times, riding out across the countryside on fresh energetic horses, meeting and talking with one William Caxton, a merchant from Bruges who had many wonders to show them. A room in which all types of weather could be seen startled and mesmerised them. It was something beyond their experience and was awe-inspiring. All this was carried on with one part of George yearning, almost outright longing, for news from England: what was happening, did the family survive, were the Yorks triumphant, were they soon to return to what was, if briefly, home?

Weeks of lessons, weeks of riding, weeks of adapting to the new life, new experiences, no people to meet and hopefully remember, clouded some of the bad memories and the grief subsided to a point when he could think of his lord father without choking back tears. At night he would lie awake, listening to the nocturnal birds and the sound of the guard tramping the walls, wondering why he felt such a sense of loss. His lord father had been a distant figure but an important one, not someone they knew, but someone they revered. It was, he decided, as if the central part of their life had been taken away, the core around which they had all revolved. When his lord father had been away on one of his many missions, life went on as normal. When he was due to return, life became harassed and everything seemed turned upside down. That presence, that person was no longer there. Edmund had gone, too. It left only Edward, tall, strong, valiant Edward to be the central figure in the family. If he survived the battles which were surely being fought.

Despite all his longings, when the news arrived that their brother Edward had been pronounced king and they could return to England, it was an anti-climax, almost a sadness, to pack up their new belongings, their new clothes, and think about going home. The duke's home had become their home, familiar, secure and once again they were on the move, this time to a country where their brother was king.

Then the full implications of the news sank in.

If his brother was King, he was next in line to the throne. This knowledge made him dizzy with the sheer glory of the thought. At last the Yorks were where they should be, where Susanna and everyone who had taught him had said they would be, rulers of England. Surely now all would be calm and quiet, life would become relatively normal, there would be a period of peace and even living in one place for longer than a few weeks, wouldn't there?

Before they could return to England, George and Richard were feted at Bruges, given a magnificent feast the boys could hardly begin to eat and showered with gifts and compliments. It was an outward sign of the great regard in which the Yorks were held. George told himself over and over, I am a York; I am George Plantagenet, second in line to the throne. And my golden brother is king! Can anything be more wonderful than that? The news finally quietened the cold corner of grief he held for his father and his brother, it almost compensated for the exile they had endured and certainly made him feel as if he could take on the world and win.

When they embarked on the ship to take them back to England, John Skelton, the guardian entrusted with their care, told them both he was highly pleased with their behaviour, their impeccable manners, their courtesy and consideration for their hosts and said he would say the same thing to the King when he got back. George smiled, knowing that everyone who had worked so hard to drum manners and courteous behaviour into him would be well pleased to know their efforts had not been in vain.

Chapter 12

It felt as if we had been away for half my lifetime but it was not really that long. Not from this perspective, anyway. From this perspective, this cold chamber, for it is, despite its hangings and rugs, despite its fire and comforts of wraps and cloaks, is dire. To escape from it would be heaven, but that is an impossibility. Edward, my liege lord, holds that power in his substantial hands and he is not releasing it.

So, I escape into thoughts. I think of the Coronation, of the glory of it, the splendour of it, the extravagance of it.

We had new clothes, glittering clothes; more gold than cloth, more jewelled than stitched. We had new clothes because we were part of our brother's Coronation ceremony.

I knew our lady mother was sad but happy for her son at the same time. I knew it as I knew the day was dawning but it made as little impression on me as the new day did. My mind, my heart was wrapped up in the ceremonials for I was to be steward of England for the occasion. I was a major player in the ceremony. I repeat myself again, I know, but at that time the word hardly left my mind, it was more exciting than every Christmas up to that time, more than the wonders of Burgundy and the magnificence we experienced there.

I recall lying awake, listening to London. How different its sounds were to that of Burgundy! Here were the sounds of the watch, the late rioters spilling from inns and bawdy houses - young as I was I knew their meaning and their use - the occasional fight, the sound of dogs guarding their territory, cats squalling in the darkness as they fought for food or a female cat. I asked myself then why did it sound so different? Dogs and cats sound the same in any country, fights start no matter what nationality the people are, but somehow – in

London it was different. It became the London sound, a city that did not seem to sleep. Now, within these walls, I am shut away from the sounds, the sights, the smells that are the city I love. It is yet another deprivation I suffer.

I recall allowing myself to dream, a small boy imagining himself to be as tall as his golden brother and he himself about to be given the crown of England.

How did it feel to govern the whole country, to hold the lives and incomes of men in your hands, to be able to raise up or throw down anyone you chose, for no other reason than that you wanted to?

How did it feel to be able to take the throne of England, to know that your blood-line gave you an inalienable right to do so?

What was it like to have men and women step back from you in deference to that which you are, not that which you were?

These and a hundred other questions flashed through my ever-active mind; the answers were there for the future, the dreams of the future. For if anything happened to Edward – and with a soldier King, who knew what would happen to him? - I would be king. It would be my Coronation being planned, my ceremonial processing being worked out meticulously and I would award the honour of steward of England to someone, with the appropriate assistance if I deemed them too young to take on the role, just as I had Lord Wenlock to help me.

Such thoughts were good for the dark hours of the night: in the daytime they had to be shut away, firmly boxed and locked, for fear of anyone uncovering disloyal thoughts.

I loved my brother the King but I had ambitions, desires, dreams, plans and vowed one day I would put them all into practice. One day the whole world would be in my hands, just as they were about to be put in his.

Being made a Knight of the Bath was ritualistic in the extreme. I can, if I think on it hard enough, remember the intense excitement of riding to the Tower, dressed in exquisite clothes, passing through narrow smelly streets, the houses leaning toward one another over my head, whispering about me and Richard, saying how handsome we were, what fine knights we would be, what chivalrous adventures awaited us – or was I allowing the excitement of the occasion to go to my head? If I was, would anyone lay blame at the door of the Tower where we stayed?

I was scarcely aware of the Mayor and the others who accompanied us. I was only aware of myself, my horse, my clothes, my importance. There are those who would say I have continued to be that way. They might be right but there is no way for a man to stand outside himself and judge his actions and thoughts. It must always be through the mirror of another's words. I have experienced enough of those.

This chamber is cold. It is not like the one in which we rested that momentous day.

We were feted with an elaborate banquet, fine wine and ale, musicians and songsters singing our praises. Only then did I fully take in the number of people to be made Knights of the Bath. More than twenty, I believe, but I gave up counting as everyone was moving about, talking with this one and that. I thought that was foolish, so I stayed in my place, ate my food, drank my wine and kept a close watch on what Richard was doing so he did not over-indulge. There were hours of ritual and vigil ahead. Watching Richard was foolish, actually, he never over-indulged in anything.

We were ceremonially bathed. Hot water, scented herbs, attendants standing respectfully by, we were immersed in the water and then dried, carefully, dressed in silk and escorted to the chapel. There we were to pray all night and contemplate our future as chivalric knights.

The chapel was lit with many candles whose flickering flames brought the paintings to life, seeming as if any of the figures might step out from the wall and embrace us, welcome us into the community of knights before we got that far. There was much shuffling, murmuring, scrape of sandal or boot, coughs, muttered exclamations as someone found a seat too hard, or caught their shin or leg on something. Then, slowly, it all subsided as each of us found a level of meditation or even dozing as we whiled away the long dark endless night hours. Apart from the occasional creak of wood and a sigh here and there, the chapel was a haven of peace.

We were supposed to kneel all night in silent contemplation. We found seats, of course we did, young as we were, and most of us were very young, we could not endure a night spent kneeling on cold slabs. I doubt that anyone would have criticised us for that.

Did I sleep? Probably. Do I remember? No. It seemed an eternity of darkness, of guttering candles, of occasional snores from those who did, until they came for us in the morning.

Confession, Matins, Mass. Solemn, enduring, thought provoking. Committing ourselves to God and the service of the King and our country.

Then a chance to sleep properly... for a short time, anyway.

Another escort, but this felt different; I was almost a Knight, deserving of the respect that being a knight accorded me. We all rode with an individual escort of men-at-arms, in our eyes we were already elevated to the status of Knight. People gathered to stare, peasant stock, London people, shabby, ragged, half starved by the look of them. We were a display of wealth such as they would never achieve in a lifetime. A small part of me said it was wrong, a bigger part of me said you were who you were. They were not Plantagenet or York or aristocracy. The gulf was wide between us. I knew it then, I know it now.

The great palace at Whitehall stood waiting for us, guards of honour holding back the spectators. Squires took the reins as we dismounted, our cloaks swirling around us. I felt part of the group this time, part of a brotherhood, a member of the elite. It felt good. It felt right.

The throne had been draped in cloth of gold for the occasion. Edward was wearing scarlet and black, picked out with heavy gold thread. He looked every inch a king, magnificent, omnipotent, strange. It was not my brother Edward, the golden giant who swung me round and round when he visited but a solemn monarch who said the words, held out his hand for me to take and kiss, thus creating me a knight, a king who kissed me and bid me be a good knight.

I recall being overawed with the splendour of it all and the responsibility which went with it, standing back and watching as Richard was created a knight too. I wondered, briefly, what it meant to little Dickon, if it was just another part of his life to be taken as seriously as study and practice was, if it had touched his heart and mind. I would not ask, it was not something I would want to discuss, for being elevated to the knighthood was a big step, one to treasure and nurture within the heart, not share with someone who in all probability would not look at it in the same way as he did. Then it would be spoiled.

In any event, the time for such discussions had long since passed. Even being exiled together had not recreated the closeness we had built during our time in Coventry. Somehow the return to London and all that happened afterwards had broken down the bridges we had managed to build. Once again we were two individual people, one with a serious outlook on life and the other with a determination to enjoy life to the full, no matter the cost.

There was not that much time to enjoy simply being a knight. Four months later, amid the same sort of ceremony, the gold, the red, the confession, the Mass, the ride to Whitehall, this time accoutred in a superb outfit of blue and gold, I was given the spurs of a duke and the title of Clarence. I was, truly, heir apparent.

I was twelve years of age. The future looked golden. Richard, created duke of Gloucester, was to go to Middleham, to be in our cousin Warwick's care for tuition whilst I would remain in London. I know not why these arrangements were made and I did not question them. We were obedient servants to our liege lord. We did as we were told. The way looked clear for me to make my mark at court. I was determined to do just that. In style.

Looking back at those times, I cannot believe how innocent I was, how much I believed in the House of York, how much I venerated and trusted my brother the king. I cannot believe how much it all changed as the years went on. Listen, angel, spirit or whoever is with me in this bleak room, yes, my brother the king, bleak room! You call it royal apartments and it is a bleak room, it is a prison! I repeat myself, I know that, I repeat myself, I know that ... small joke for an empty mazer to echo back to me. Listen, whoever is here, that boy was innocent of the treason that took over his mind later, so I call him innocent even if he was worldly-wise in the ways of the court and of people through so much tuition. But tutors cannot give you a pathway to walk, that you choose for your own self. I chose mine. Do I regret it? That is not to be discussed right now, there is too much still to remember, to drag out from the recesses of the mind, to examine, dissect, analyse and then throw back into the darkness from whence it came and where it truly belongs. I am not really conscious of why I am putting myself through this torment, unless it truly is because the alternative, thinking of nothing, is far worse.

Oh, then I was innocent. I believed the world was ours, the world being England and all who lived within in its limits, defined only by the sea. I believed I had a place in that world, one that surrounded me with luxury, riches, fine clothes, wines and companions. After all, did my brother the king not have all that: the finest of clothes, expensive Italian boots – and for his great height, they were expensive indeed! – the finest of jewels, the pick of the women, for did he not have to do any more than smile at them in the way he had and offer them a kingly kiss and they were his? He had the finest of apartments, a riotous court where laughter and song were ever present, courtiers by the hundred and a staff of thousands to take care of his every wish. And did I not desire to have a court like that, a place I could call mine, where I held sway and everything was at my command, not another's? Believe me, I did.

We were not to live with our lady mother after being made honourable knights but were given a home, Richard, Margaret and I, in Greenwich. Apartments were refurbished for us, we were given clothes and money and, even more important in my eyes at that time, clerks who doubled as attorneys to help us manage our money. One such was John Peke, who took a liking to me as a young boy and stayed with me until – well, we need not go into that, spirit, angel, whoever. We know, don't we, when John Peke decided to leave my service? Ah, you wish me to say ... all right, I will say, he left when I turned against the family, in his eyes anyway. His loyalty was first to the king and second to me. But there is much for me to remember before that time arose, much for me to contemplate, many blessed and unblessed hours to think on. Why bother, I ask myself again, but then the answer comes, with what else can occupy your last hours, oh drunken foolish Clarence? Would you rather dwell on that which is to come? In truth, I would not. Hence this walk into my past.

And there I did indeed live in luxury. For a start I had henxmen appointed to be my companions. Noble as they were, they deferred to me, for they were not dukes. I had the feather bed, they the floor, albeit on a mattress. For the first time in an age I had no need of my brother and sister to be with me, although they were there, of a surety they were. Well, for a while, then Dickon was moved to Middleham and we began that separation which cost us our peace of mind as a family. At least, that is how I see it. But then, oh then, together we learned the finer arts, adding to that already taught but now adding archery and jousting. I did not overly care for the tournament, but learned to ride well at the tournai which stood me in good stead when riding to battle in later life. That was the only reason I persevered at my training, so I could ride to battle. I recalled so vividly my desire to throw everything away and ride out alongside my brother the king and that was my incentive for doing well. One day I knew I would ride in battle and I did. But I never entered the tournaments. That was for show, for exhibitionism and, despite my desire for the good life, the rich and the luxurious, that was one show I did not care to enter. Come, Clarence, there is none to hear you but the shades who even now surround you as they await your joining them; be honest with yourself, why did you shun the tournament?

Because I did not dare fail. I did not dare find myself sprawling on the turf with another standing over me with raised sword declaring himself to be the winner. That would not do for the proud duke and ever was I a proud duke, from the moment my brother the king created me thus. Even now, drink sodden, desperately lonely, in horrendous pain and despair, I know myself for what I am, a proud duke. No matter what happens to the body I inhabit, no matter what the world may think of me when I am passed from this side of life to whatever awaits me on the other side, I will remain forever the duke of Clarence and none can take that from me. Call me whatever other names they will, it matters not, for whatever they call me must be attached to my name, George duke of Clarence, once heir to the throne of England and owner of great estates, once a loyal if not devoted husband and once owner of great wealth. I have to leave the wealth here, it cannot go with me into that other world, whatever and wherever I find myself, so now it doesn't matter that others live in my homes and share my possessions among themselves, or that my wealth has gone back to the Treasury for my brother the king to use as he wishes. What matters is the pain that I have and the suffering in my heart and mind and my longing for it to be over and the fear that it will be. How foolish is that?

God grant me release from this pain!

Let me say this to whoever is listening to my thoughts, incoherent, coherent, whatever they might be at this moment: I was twelve years old when I had what was virtually my own small court, henxmen, master of henxmen, clerk, servants, horses, wardrobe of expensive and beautiful clothes, my own harness, my own sword, my own quiver of arrows and bow. I had a favourite hawk and a favourite dog. I did not favour alaunts, I found them ugly and without style, whereas the wolfhound is a dog to be proud of. I had a wolfhound of my own. I had thoughts, dreams and ambitions and those were kept very much to myself. If any learned of them it was if I spoke in my sleep for I made myself a vow that none should know of my dreams and ambitions for fear of laughter and derision.   Ever did the spectre of humiliation haunt me! Ever did I fear too that all I had would be taken from me again, as it had been at Ludlow! Ever did I fear that the home I had established would be destroyed by others and I would again be cast onto the uncertain sea of Fate, wondering at all times where I would be washed ashore and what I would find when that happened.   And, of a surety, did it not happen, just as I feared? I did not realise the need for security at that time, no child puts it into words but every child surely longs for that which is safe, familiar, known and trusted to be around them, to protect and guard them.   This I sought, without fully realising it until now, for the remainder of my time on this earth.

Did this influence my actions in later life?

Chapter 13

The years which followed were good. More than good, they were excellent, they were the shining years of George's life. Living in absolute luxury, adored by courtiers, courted by hangers-on, having the ear of the king when he needed it, enjoying growing up, taking part in what were literally state occasions, such as great funerals, his was the life he had seen others lead and had waited impatiently for life and his king to give to him. Money was no object. He was cared for by the king and although he depended on him for his day to day living, his rich wardrobe, his many servants and squires, his stable and his kitchen, he wanted for nothing. Everyone deferred to him and in so doing, made him feel he was second only to the king himself.

Edward dallied with this woman and that, nothing serious, nothing lasting. Whoever caught his attention ended up in his arms and his bed. Everyone talked of who the latest favourite was, no one laid bets on who would be his queen. After all, he was still a young man with many years ahead of him, there was no rush, no hurry, there were plenty of Princesses and others of noble rank for him to choose from – when he chose to choose.

But, paranoia, that ever present 'condition' for those who lived in the full glory of court, convinced George he needed to know all that was going on, not part of it, not rumours and innuendo. He needed facts, cold hard facts. He began to gather information from this one and that, dropping a coin here, a favour there, a release from a debt, anything to gain the loyalty of a devoted band of informers. His Fool, Durian, was the collector of information, someone who had contacts of his own to add to the growing band. George considered himself well informed, but even they were not enough to save him, the whole court and the country from the shock of what came next.

Edward's secret wedding with a Lancastrian widow.

The announcement of Edward IV's marriage to Elizabeth Wydeville hit the court like a thunderbolt. Its repercussions swept on and on, taking all before them as the implications began to show themselves. It was not so much ripples flowing out from a stone thrown into a lake as a boulder crashing into the water and flooding the surrounding land. Questions were asked in every corner of every hallway, in every room and in every heart but none more than in George's own heart and mind and the mouths of those around him. The widow with the silver hair and the fertile womb had ensured that George was dispossessed of his claim to the throne of England should Edward predecease him which, in the natural order of families, should happen.

No one knew of his immediate reaction. He smiled gracefully, keeping as bland a face as possible, offered his congratulations to his brother the king and then asked permission to leave Court, pleading an urgent meeting with his falconer. Ned, lost in the glory of a new wife and a new challenging situation in court, dismissed him without enquiring further. George swiftly gathered his squires around him, threw an ermine trimmed cloak around his shoulders and left to board a royal barge to carry him to his home at Greenwich. As the barge negotiated the troubled Thames currents, his temper grew, souring his expression and causing him to grip the wooden handrail so hard that his nails all but scoured and dented it. Nothing was said by anyone, his squires read his bleak expression and kept their distance, alert for any command but not offering any words. What could be said?

The moment the barge touched land George leapt onto the path and strode into his home, throwing aside his cloak, kicking at the rushes, ignoring his dog Maint which tried to attract his attention. He sought and gained the solitude of his bedchamber, securing the door so none could enter. Then he threw himself on the bed and lay there, shaking from head to foot as the anger coursed through him, burning through his veins.

How could he! How could his golden brother take away from him everything he had promised! Where then was the promise of the crown of England, where then the title of heir apparent, where then the deference and respect that went with being the next in line? Where would he go, what would he do, now he was no more than the duke of Clarence, with no further claim to kingship? How had that conniving bitch planned and schemed and wormed her way into his brother's affections to the extent he had married her in secret? In secret! And for Ned to announce it in a council meeting as if it was a new law of some kind! 'Oh by the way I married this woman, older than me, a widow, with two children and who comes with a brood of Wydevilles, enough of them to staff the court five times over and still have some to spare.'

"God's teeth, eyes, beard and nails! Christ's wounds! The blessed Virgin's womb! How could he do this to me!"

Then, suddenly, shameful hot tears were coursing down his face as anger gave way to utter dismay and heartbreaking humiliation. His place in court was shattered, his position as brother to the king changed completely. No more the next in line, no more the favoured one, no more could he walk with dignity and royal disdain into meetings and have people step back from him as they stepped back from the king. No more. Oh they might, if they were sensible and sought to curry favour for he would still had the ear of the king to some extent, be deferential to him, but it would not be the same. Of a surety nothing in this life would be the same again.

The tears stopped as abruptly as they had begun. He could hear voices and clank of arms outside the door but ignored them. This was his time and his time alone. He would mourn this once and then no more. As if hearing an echo he relived the moment when Edward announced his marriage with a huge smile as if it was the most wonderful thing that had happened to him. Perhaps it was, perhaps she truly was the woman Ned had sought for so long, among every female who had fluttered her eyelids at him or raised a skirt for him to admire a sleek ankle or devised a way that he would not be able to do anything but admire the cleavage presented to him or, in some instances, all but thrust into his face. George, still virgin at this time, envied his brother the charisma which brought the women into his presence and more often than not into his bed, too. Now it seemed that charisma had won him a woman whose charms were such that he had to marry her, not just bed her.

Be sensible, an inner voice warned him, be sensible, George! At some point Ned would have to marry, make some political alliance that would secure land, security and wealth for the country. Some princess, all limpid eyes and weak smile and – damn it to Hell – possibly an infertile womb, was surely the chosen route for him to go. Even in his more sensible moments, George realised he was trying to make the situation turn in his direction; Ned to marry, to have a Queen, but not produce an heir so that he, the duke of Clarence, would of necessity and of surety be there to accept the invitation of the parliament to take the crown in the event of Ned's demise. Instead … instead he marries a woman who has proved her fertility and who would doubtless breed and give Ned the heir he apparently looked for. Or so it seemed, with such a strange marriage. For who would choose a woman older than himself, one already encumbered with children? Everyone knew of the Wydevilles, everyone knew they laid claim to everything and now they would claim everything.

George rubbed his eyes and stared up at the elaborate hangings surrounding his bed. The pattern seemed to move, to merge into itself, as the last of the moisture drained away. Foolish tears, he scolded himself, foolish emotion but oh, the sense of betrayal!

Am I not all but as tall as Ned, he asked himself? Am I not as handsome, as charming, as diplomatic as he? Why then am I without experience with women? Why then am I here, wondering what it is all about, what the attraction of woman is to him? Why am I not doing anything about it?

He sat up as someone knocked on the door, demanding entrance. Rubbing a hand over his face to remove any trace of tears, George walked across the room and opened the door. His clerk, John Peke, was wearing a look of concern verging on worry but his voice was calm enough.

"Your Grace, I came to see if all was well and if I could provide you with anything."

Tactful in the extreme, thought George, standing back to allow the man to come into the room. He had followed through his earlier thought and Peke's arrival was most opportune.

The door closed, leaving the two men in private. George looked down at his clerk, who was several inches shorter than him, affording him a sense of empowerment and confidence to go ahead with his request. If he could find the right words.

"There is something," he began. A sudden fear shot into his mind, a fear that the 'something' would be misconstrued but, knowing he could trust Peke above all the others in his employ, he carried on. "I would like-"

To his credit, Peke did not interrupt, did not attempt to second-guess his Lord's wishes. He waited with infinite patience as George struggled to find the right way to express himself.

"I want a woman," he said finally. "I-"

"No need to say any more," said Peke gently, with great understanding. "It will be done. Now, is there anything I can get Your Grace in the way of food, ale, wine? Would you like your Fool to come and entertain you?"

"Not right now. I am not in a mood for foolery of any kind. I will come to the hall for bread, cheese and ale if it is brought there for me. I can leave-"

"You can, Your Grace. I will arrange it. If you will return to your bedchamber after Vespers alone, if you dismiss your squires on some pretext or other-"

"You need say no more, Peke." He fumbled for coins and handed over a quantity. "Whatever it costs, take the rest for yourself."

"Your Grace is most generous," Peke murmured without checking how much he had been given. From experience he knew it would be more than enough. The duke of Clarence was always generous. He bowed and backed away before swiftly leaving the room to carry out his tasks.

It was as if a great cloud had lifted from George's mind. Sunshine was radiating into his inner being. By nightfall, if all went well, he would no longer be virgin, but a man capable of taking a woman. God grant she be knowledgeable, he prayed swiftly and then felt guilty at the thought. He could no more ask Peke to provide a knowledgeable woman than he could admit to the overwhelming need which drove him to ask for one. He had tried to make it look as if it were a casual request, one to while away an evening, even as he knew deep inside, where all truth resided, that Peke knew full well he had not dallied with a woman up to that time.

114

Peke would know he was virgin, would know he wanted someone capable of teaching him what to do and when and how and to be kind to a youth of just seventeen years. Even as he thought about the evening to come, his body was reacting and he knew, just knew, he would do well.

Food waited. Now he could face the prospect of fine cheese, pure white bread and strong ale, now he could face the attentions of his wolfhound and perhaps even laugh at the cutting jests of his Fool, whose humour matched his own in every way. Now he could begin to put the marriage and all its consequences into its rightful place in his mind.

First, sustenance for the body. Second, relief for the body and experience that was long, way too long overdue. Third, begin to live the life of a duke who could still demand respect, who still had a role to play in the government of the country, who still could work alongside his brother the king, even if he had made an unsuitable and outrageous marriage. There were worse fates than being deprived of the crown of England. After all, look at Dickon, what chance did he have of ever becoming King? Had he long ago accepted that he was further down the line of succession? Had he accepted that the life of a duke was the right one for him? George briefly wondered what Dickon's thoughts would be when the news hit the Warwick household. He knew how much family loyalty meant to his younger brother, he would doubtless wish Ned well in all he did, no matter who was Queen.

It was only as he walked down the stone stairs to the hall did he remember, as in a blinding flash of light, what he knew of Warwick's plans for King Edward. An alliance had been planned; negotiations were in place for a marriage of political convenience to benefit the Neville family as much as England. Ned had thrown all that into the fire and along with it, very likely, the Earl of

Warwick's friendship. How could such a proud man stand to see his plans wrecked so violently, so casually? Warwick would be bound to react, and react badly, that was a certainty.

It could be that my cousin is in need of an ally at this time, he mused, entering the hall and heading for the table on the raised dais where his food awaited, just as he had ordered. It could be that I might write a letter or two and arrange a visit and –

Maint raced to his master's side and George fondled the dog's ears as he sat down in the carver. A varlet poured ale for him and he tore at the loaf of bread, suddenly sensuously aware of the texture of the dough. He broke off a piece of cheese with the other hand, bit a small piece off and appreciated the sharpness of it on his tongue before enfolding it in the bread. It was as if all his senses had suddenly come alive, as if they had been sleeping and were now awake. The afternoon sunshine streaming through the windows lit the rushes here and there; the dust motes created their own dance of chaotic rhythm. George, you haven't touched the ale yet but you think as one who has drunk deep of the vat already! He scolded himself but smiled as he did so.

His Fool, Durian, approached him, for once wearing sombre clothing. His expressive face was contorted into one of deep suffering and he walked with bowed shoulders, as if carrying the greatest burden on his back.

"Alas, I am in mourning for the death of the plans of your cousin of Warwick!" he intoned in a perfect imitation of the voice of a cleric standing at the side of an open grave.

George laughed out loud and thrust a cup toward him. "Here, have some ale, Durian, and for the sake of my heart, tell me more of this!"

Durian cast off the mournful look and flashed his Lord a smile.

116

"Messengers are at this moment on their way to Warwick. What he will make of the news we can only speculate but I think we can assume, Your Grace, that the Earl will not be best pleased."

"For sure he will not," George commented around a mouthful of cheese. "Is this food always this good?"

"Of a surety it is, sire, why should it be different this day?"

"I wish I knew. Something has changed."

Durian narrowed his eyes and stared at George. "No, the food has not changed. Your Grace has changed in some way. I will ponder on this and return to speak with you later," he said in a quiet voice. The varlet had moved away, but there were others still around the hall, attending to various tasks.

"No, stay a while, share the food, Durian. Give me your wisdom and laughter and we will talk of other things later, when we are able." The last part of the sentence was said so low only Durian heard it. George relied heavily on his Fool's far-seeing, his seemingly natural ability to predict future events as if he was actually looking at them, but he did not allow anyone else to know of his abilities. What no one knew was that Durian was also the head of George's extensive, efficient spy network. It was better for both of them that it should be that way. George had Durian's complete loyalty and Durian had George's complete trust. Few knew of the relationship; George believed Peke knew but said nothing. His lady mother might know; the few occasions she had visited her sharp eyes had seemed to penetrate the very walls as if searching for his secrets but again, nothing had been said. They were both extremely discreet and George ensured that his Fool was well rewarded for all the services he did for him, which also bound Durian to him.

Durian spent an hour entertaining George with wicked impersonations of various members of the Court and how they might have reacted to the news of the marriage, which had George holding his sides which ached from laughter. Underneath all the hilarity the thought kept recurring, tonight I find out for myself what it is all about. Tonight I lay with a woman for the first time. Tonight I prove myself as a man. Tonight cannot come soon enough!

"Come," he said eventually, when the laughter tears had dried and Durian had run out of people to impersonate, "we need to take the air after all that. We will walk in the gardens."

The late summer air was soft; the flowerbeds were in the last stage of their showy splendour. George walked slowly, breathing in the mixed scents of the flowers and the heavily fruiting trees. Wasps buzzed angrily around the windfalls rotting in the grass. 'I need to speak with someone to clear these." He gestured toward the fallen fruit. "I dislike to see it lie so."

"Your Grace has not bothered before," Durian commented. "I still cannot understand what has changed in you, sire, but something has. I would have wagered the news of your brother the king's marriage would have shaken Your Grace to the core."

Only Durian and Peke had the freedom to speak this freely to George and they took advantage of it in moments of privacy, ensuring that at all other times they spoke with due deference.

George turned to look into the candid blue eyes of his trusted Fool. "It did," he admitted. "But then I recalled the plans of my cousin of Warwick and I would bid you find out for me whether he would appreciate my approaching him at this time."

Durian's eyes widened as he took in the implications of the thought. Then he smiled. "Now I see the plan! Of a surety you are wiser than your years, sire!

118

Of course! You have been put to one side and so has the Earl. What a match the two of you will make, if you would but be able to work together!"

"This I need to find out."

"That is not the only reason why you found pleasure in simple food today, sire."

"No, it is not. I confess I have asked Peke to find me a woman for the night."

"Tis more than time you stepped into the world of women, sire! I congratulate you and wish you much – pleasure!"

George flushed bright red with embarrassment which made Durian laugh. "For a young man with such confidence, such arrogance, if I may be permitted to say that, sire, I am surprised that it has taken you this long to decide to request a woman."

"For your ears alone, Durian, and none other, this is nothing more than an act. Beneath this confidence, this arrogance which you see, there is a person who fears nothing more than failing at anything. Hence my decision to wait until I was sure I could take a woman and not fail dismally at it, for fear of never being able to attempt it again."

Durian nodded. "Of a surety you make sense, sire. It is not all physical when it comes to women, there is a good deal of mental effort involved, too. First you must be sure of yourself and second you must be sure of your body. The time has come when those two are together in harmony. I see that now. I see that the time is right and your reaction to the news of your brother the king's taking of a wife has triggered that moment. His many dalliances have not had the same effect." He smiled knowingly. "If food tasted good today, I wonder how it will taste tomorrow to Your Grace?" he murmured.

George grinned. "If the woman is good then it matters little what the food tastes like tomorrow. I know only I will be of equal standing with my brother the king by this time tomorrow in that I will no longer be virgin." His body jerked in anticipation at the thought and he smothered a laugh.

Ned, he thought, whatever you can do, I can do, apart from wear the Crown of England but then, there is much else in this life I can do – and I will! Of a surety I will!

Chapter 14

Of all my memories, that night remains one of the clearest, as if preserved forever in glass and kept, to be turned about and around, to be viewed from every angle and forever cherished.

I had, many times, found relief for myself from the pressing needs of the developing man, visualising without knowledge what a woman's body was beneath shift, bodice, skirt and petticoats. I had only the very vaguest idea of what it would look like and no amount of talk among stable lads, varlets or squires could prepare me for the reality.

She came, the one Peke found for me, shyly and hesitantly, not bold and assertive. That I liked, that I appreciated. I found her comely, with dark brown hair which she unbound and which fell in ripples to her very hips. She had dark eyes which held promise of delights without speaking of them and lips which were red enough to have been rouged or bitten to highlight them.

"Your Grace." Her curtsey was submissive indeed, no arrogance, no surety of purpose there, just the quiet acceptance of the difference in our status. I liked that, too.

"Your name?" I asked her.

"Pentecost, Your Grace, Pentecost Green."

I recall my body being ready long before she ever arrived, I remember being afeared it would all end too quickly before I even got as far as the clothes coming off. I remember swallowing hard as I bolted the door against all interruptions and watched as she slowly removed layer after layer. I did nothing; I could do nothing but watch, entranced. When she was naked it was a revelation. I never imagined anything so sensual, so enchanting or mysterious as the slender body, the full breasts and the hidden magic of the join of thighs. She spoke not a word as she helped me remove my tunic, hose and braies and just smiled as she saw I was ready.

Somehow we tumbled onto the down mattress and somehow she was beneath me and somehow she guided me and in a few seconds I knew the magic of woman. Silk, softness, slippery channel and oh, the sensations!

In all the remainder of my life I never had a night such as that, not even with the one who loved me so and with whom I found comfort and solace. I found it not for this was the first time and nothing can ever be as good or as wonderful as the first time, whether it be the first kill in a hunt, the first kiss, the first time in battle with the blood roaring and the metal clashing and the death song singing in your ears. That was my first time and as such was forever to remain wonderful. She taught me much, that patient loving Pentecost, how to hold back, how to pleasure, how to kiss, how to caress, what parts were sensitive and how to arouse them. Of a surety that girl/woman knew much and yet she was as tight and flawless as a virgin. How much do women know by instinct and how much do they gain by experience? I know not where Peke found her and I know not where she lived or what she thought of our night of passion. I know I have never forgotten Pentecost Green and I carry her memory with me and will do so until the moment comes when the door shuts on this life.

I slept, I think, and woke to find long dark hair entangled around my arms and my fingers clutching a creamy breast. Of necessity I had to let her go, for there was discreet knocking at my bedchamber door and I knew another day had begun. The sun was well risen and it was long overdue that I should be up and about my day's business.

She dressed and left with a curtsey, a smile, a kiss and a bag of gold which she had well earned.

And I was left with memories which have never deserted me.

It is too late now to ask someone to find her, to know if she still remembers that night which meant so much to me but which may not have meant that much to her. It is too late for me to ask for another woman at this time, for thinking of her has provoked a reaction I did not expect, crippled as I am with drink and pain and anxiety and apprehension, if not pure outright fear. Ah, only to the shades which surround me will I admit to fear. To everyone else I must remain the proud duke, allow no one to know that for me there is fear as I walk into the valley of death. The Lord may well be with me but that does not stop the fear.

I faced a new life with new confidence.

I spoke with bitterness of the new Queen's family to those I trusted but to her face I smiled and was polite and escorted her into Reading Abbey along with the earl of Warwick and presented her as Queen. I worked with my brother the king on the preparations for her coronation. I dared not do otherwise; I depended upon his patronage until such time as I had sufficient lands and income of my own. It was important I stayed within his goodwill at all times. Without his patronage, how could a proud duke remain proud and live a life that demanded money? A household does not run itself without finance and I needed both clothes and jewellery to present the right appearance to the world.

I also needed a vast amount of people to take care of me. Not as many, I do believe, as that of the king himself, for his household was virtually an army of servants, labourers of all kinds but of a surety I needed people to clean, cook, wash, tend my needs, take care of my body and my soul. I needed entertaining, confessing, praying over and escorting as I travelled from place to place. I needed my own virtual army to take care of me.

123

I needed people tend my animals, my stable, my livestock. All those people employed to care for one person! I thought how important I was to have so many in my employ and that did not include those who were my informants throughout the land, in every place where I needed to know who thought what and who spoke what, even if I did not use the information at that time. I needed it, I garnered it as a farmer garnered his harvest and stored it for the cold times ahead.

How did I know there would be cold times ahead?

Chapter 15

Winter dragged on, Christmas revels were held and everywhere the Wydevilles were making their presence known, taking on this role and that, seemingly incapable of standing back and allowing the court to absorb them. Rather they seemed to work to absorb the court and the king was kept busy allocating marriages, positions, estates and finances to his queen's family.

The coronation plans proceeded smoothly, with George taking an integral role in the proceedings. At times he even enjoyed the challenge of making so many complex and oft times conflicting arrangements for the event.

Quietly and discreetly Durian came with snippets of information from all around the country, how the people spoke against the Wydevilles, how they feared that their king would be so taken by the enchantress that he would forget he belonged to the people first and his queen second and her family third if at all. They spoke of the anger of Warwick, how the people spoke in jest now of the kingmaker who had not been able to control a king he had made and laughed at his frustration and impotence. Some derided the earl for not producing sons but this George dismissed; no one can order the child they so long for and daughters can make dynasties, after all, married to the right person in the right position at the right time.

At times George wondered what sort of person he wanted for his wife and helpmeet. He observed Ned at close quarters and knew him to be obsessed with his beautiful wife but still unable to remain faithful. A wench passing him by with a smile and a cheeky wink would ensure that he sent a page or a squire to seek her out and bring her to his bedchamber. George had vowed in a solemn pledge in the chapel at court that once married he would honour the vows he made, no matter the provocation, no matter the temptation. He knew his brother Richard would be the same, knew it without even discussing it with him on the rare occasions they saw one another.

As far as he was concerned, meeting up with Richard now was almost like meeting a stranger. Dickon was growing up fast under the tutelage of the many tutors at Middleham and was changing into a young man with an even more serious outlook on life than he had displayed when sharing his formative years with George. Occasionally a flicker of laughter would cross the dark eyes but this was rare and worthy of being noted in some great journal, so few times did it ever happen. George loved to laugh and kept Durian close to him when he could so they could indulge in hilarity to lift the days, which that winter seemed endlessly dark and long. It was almost as if he was waiting for something, anything, to break the monotony of the life he was leading.

"It is like my days and weeks and endless years at Fotheringhay over again," he complained to Durian one day when the rain lashed down and deterred even the boldest person or wolfhound from venturing out into the inclement weather. Durian raised his expressive eyebrows at his master and waited for him to elaborate. George kicked the log in the great hearth and muttered curses against the rain. "I thought at times I would never escape Fotheringhay ennui and here I am, enduring London ennui instead!'

"But surely in greater comfort and with greater control than you had before, sire," Durian pointed out with superb logic.

"True words," agreed George, "but ennui remains the same, does it not?"

"Then I must of necessity find a way to distract Your Grace. May I suggest a game of Tables?"

"No, you may not, Durian! I swear by all that is sacred you will be able to retire to a mansion in the country surrounded by many women and every comfort to last you to the end of your days with the money you have won from me this winter alone! God's teeth, do you have Lucifer helping you with the dice?"

"No, I do not, sire, I just have a degree of luck."

"More than luck," George grumbled. With an effort he got to his feet and shouted for a squire to set his minstrels singing and the musicians to play before wandering off to the garderobe, leaving Durian alone by the fire.

I need a wife George told himself in the few moments he was alone, that in itself being a rare occasion. I need a wife to tend to my needs. A Fool is all very well and I could not manage my affairs without Durian's sharp ears and equally sharp mind but I need a wife, a consort, someone to take on the running of the household, someone to understand my needs, to be there when I want to –

I do not endlessly want to arrange for someone to share my bed, for all that it is exciting to have someone different each time. I want –

There the thoughts stopped as he returned to the fire to huddle close to the log burning fiercely, to listen to the endless rain and the endless sound of a large household going about its daily chores. Each person was carrying out his duties, some quietly, some noisily, all combining to make one chaotic sound that he noticed for the first time. At least the weather that day would prevent petitioners coming to ask his judgement on this matter or that or to adjudicate on some dispute or other, or messengers endlessly ferrying orders or requests from Ned to attend to this or look into this matter or that for him. Sometimes he welcomed the tasks, the responsibility, other times he sought solace for himself and his troubled mind. He did not fully understand why he should need solace, why the life was not enough for him, why he sought more, why he could not lose himself in the hustle and bustle of life, of the business of running a complex estate.

I need silence!

The thought came from nowhere and was acted upon immediately. He got up again and, without a word to Durian, walked out of the hall, snatching up his mantle as he went. He pointedly ignored those who bowed or curtsied as he passed, ignored those who tried to speak with him. He did not want to speak to anyone. He thrust them away from him with his very manner of walking.

The chapel was deserted, as he hoped it would be. There was the distinct aroma of doused candles and incense, dust and crushed rushes, a mixture of smells as familiar as his own bedchamber scents and as comforting in many ways. It was gloomy, the heavy clouds outside diminishing the light quite considerably. The altar was in shadow, the statues appearing like illusory spirits hovering in the corners, awaiting a visitor to speak to. The silence was overwhelming and just what he needed, a balm for a mind full of conflicting emotions.

George dropped to his knees and put his hands together in the classic prayer position, looked at them and then allowed his arms to relax at his sides. His back was straight, his head up, looking at the ornate cross on the altar which, despite the gloom of the afternoon, glinted with knowing light.

He crossed himself swiftly, let his arms relax once more and closed his eyes. "Lord God, Father of all, Jesu Christ, the Begotten One…" A stray tear took him by surprise and he dashed it away. "Lord God, hear my prayer." What prayer, he asked himself? Why am I here, what do I want to ask the Lord God that He can give me? What do I seek and why do I seek it? Why am I not settled in my mind? What can I want to add to what I have?

"Blessed Virgin Mary..." he began again, only to stop as a sob shook his body. He sank down on the flagged floor and allowed the tears to flow freely, even as he wondered where they had come from and why they were being shed at this time.

It was like a dam breaking, one he had not realised was there. Something was tearing itself out of him, a deep dark emotion that he realised even in the depths of his sorrow had been tormenting him for a lifetime.

Slowly the tears and accompanying sobs eased and finally stopped. Shadows grew darker; the statues appeared to move as he looked up at them through tear-blurred eyes. Superstitiously he felt a thrill of fear, crossing himself several times and invoking the name of Jesus Christ before realising how foolish it was. Nothing but the shades of the afternoon, nothing but the shades of his own thoughts were in the chapel, a place hallowed by more prayers than there were people in the whole of England. What fear, what evil could there be in such a place?

Slowly he got to his feet and, with the greatest care, walked toward the altar, where he found the candles and lit them. The guttering flames made the statues appear to dance for a moment before the light became as still as it could be in a place so full of bitter draughts. George stood before the altar, saw the light playing on the intricacies of the cross and allowed himself a small smile that felt odd, as if the muscles had not been used for an eternity when he had laughed just an hour before at some cutting jest Durian had made.

"Blessed Mother," he began again, in a quiet emotion-ridden voice. "Blessed Mother, I do not understand my tears this day in this place, except that here I am truly alone, at least here there are no other human beings."

Then he saw in his mind's eye his father, the great duke, his beautiful brother Edmund, his uncle of Salisbury, saw them smiling at him, saw them raise their hands in blessing and knew he still mourned for them, that their memory was as fresh as the day they rode off to do battle, the day he would not forget.

He knew too that he mourned the loss of favourite animals, people who had died, whose funeral he had attended or had arranged and, most of all, he knew he mourned the loss of that which he believed was to be his one day: the crown of England.

"I know she will produce heirs," he whispered, sending the candle flames dancing with the vibration of his breath. "I know it as surely as I know the sun will rise tomorrow. I know it for has she not proved already that her womb is fertile? And has my brother not proved he has the seed, for of a surety there are bastards of his around this court! Do I not know my dreams lie as dead and as useless as the ash in the hearth of my great fireplace?"

And do I not know that until this moment, I have scarcely shed a tear for any of them? That thought came as a great shock, as if he had committed some sacrilege by not crying for any of them but only for himself, for his own loss and his own disrupted life.

"But am I not doing this now?' he whispered to the silent looming statues. "Am I not mourning my loss of ambition and hope for the crown? Of a surety I am! Am I not begrudging my brother the king his wife and hope of children to come to ensure the continuity of the line of royal blood? Am I not seeking to put my selfish ambitions and dreams before those of the brother I love?"

The statues had no answer for him. He turned back to the cross, glittering in the candlelight. It held a

130

message that took some time to penetrate his mind; when it did, George fell to his knees and began a sincere prayer.

"Prince of glory, I beg thy forgiveness. Whatever dreams thee may have had for thy future, they were taken from thee in an act of great drama and ceremony, even as mine will be. The coronation of Elizabeth as Queen to my brother Edward the King will once and for all end my dreams of kingship. But, Jesu Christ, thee made of disaster a lasting legacy, that all may live on forever in the Kingdom of Heaven. I am a mere mortal man; I cannot make such claims, or even aspire to anything like it. I can, though, live a life that will be remembered through history. I pray it will be a good memory. Help me now to turn this pain in my heart into gladness that my brother is happy with his new wife. I pray that thy angels may keep the dark ones from my mind, for thy sake. Amen."

Shakily he got to his feet, disturbed by the many thoughts which tumbled through his mind. He tugged his mantle close around his neck, feeling the damp chill of the ancient stones eating its way into his flesh. He crossed himself, genuflected to the altar and then blew out the candles. He stood still, waiting for his eyes to adjust to the gloom before tentatively making his way to the door. As he did so, a light appeared to move alongside him, as if he was being accompanied by a being cloaked in white. He wondered why he was not afraid, wondered why the being, whatever it was, had filled his mind with peace and music that was out of this world.

Before he reached the door he turned and said, "Who are you?"

He felt rather than saw an answering smile and the light faded, leaving him in total darkness. He took another three or four steps forward and found his hand touching the latch of the door.

He was not surprised to find Durian standing outside, sheltering under the narrow overhang, a heavy wool cloak over one arm. Nothing was said. Durian draped the cloak around George's shoulders, ignored the surprised face that turned toward him and walked with George back into the hall, where he sent someone for mead and another person for more logs for the fire. He pushed George into his accustomed place close to the flames, nudging a wolfhound out of the way with a booted foot as he did so to allow George space to get closer to the fire. A click of his fingers set the musicians playing a light haunting tune. Durian sat down on a stool, picked up his lyre and began to play an accompanying yet contrasting melody with consummate skill. No words, no explanations, no questions, no condemnation for a sudden departure from that which was normal for George.

George felt himself relax for the first time in many days, if not weeks. The tears, wherever they had come from, had released tensions he had not known were there but which had been tangling up many thoughts and emotions.

With a cup of mead to hand and the fire banked up against the bitter chill, he began to feel much better and actually smiled when his Fool pulled a comic face at him.

"Better," observed Durian. "I know not what transpired there and I would not wish to know, sire, but it was nothing but good if your face is any indication by which to judge."

"It is between the Lord God and myself," George said quietly. "I tell you this, though, Durian, I know not what drove me to the chapel at that time but it was good."

"That is all I need to know, Your Grace. All else is not for my ears. But I have something for yours, later."

Idle talk or information. George would have to wait to find out, wait until all were dismissed from his bedchamber, for he insisted he slept alone, had ordered that those who attended him should sleep outside the door to be there if he called but not to intrude on his privacy. A private person with private thoughts, as he often described himself. Servants of any kind, apart from Durian, were an invasion of that privacy. He detested their attentions, even though he had to accept their assistance in washing, shaving and dressing each morning and undressing every night. The least he could do was ban them from his chamber so that he could sleep alone.

Later that night George lay alone in the middle of the thick feather mattress, covered in heavy robes and furs against the cold. The fire burning in the hearth gave the walls a simulated warmth they could never achieve. Durian had left him, after imparting the latest snippet of information gathered from an indiscreet courtier. It was not of great importance but then, trifles were rarely important of themselves, it was when they became part of the whole picture that they were of use to him. He delighted in the piecing together of people's motives and plans, desires and dreams by collecting and collating their unguarded comments, even their discarded letters. All were good to have, for knowledge was power and power was all-important in a world of ever shifting alliances and politics.

He stared up at the hangings as he thought, catching a glimpse here and there of flashes of light which of a surety could not be real. More signs, he told himself, more indications of other-worldly happenings, perhaps of angel visitations. Had that been an angel who walked to the door of the chapel with him? If so, he was blessed indeed and he gave silent thanks to God for His great mercy. Muttering a prayer for protection during the night, he fell into a dreamless, refreshing sleep.

Chapter 16

Ah but those days are long gone, when angels walked the aisle at my side, when lights flashed in bed hangings, when I felt the love of the Lord God with me. Long, long gone, buried in the mire of battlefields, both real and emotional, beneath what my brother calls treason and I call self-preservation, beneath grief and loss, exile and argument. I mourn their passing for right now, here in this cold, cold chamber, I could and would welcome such an apparition to attend my final days, hours, minutes: I know not how long I have left to stand on this side of the door marked Death. My brother the king does not realise he will be merciful in granting me the absolution of death and does not realise how cruel he is in not giving me an indication of how long it will be before the dark angel walks through that door and into my final moments.

But then again, I ask myself if he does know how cruel are his actions. My brother the king has ever been one for cruelty, although of a surety he would not see it that way. I think now of the time when the men were taken from Tewkesbury Abbey and murdered, even though the law forbids the killing of a priest. He went ahead and killed one anyway. No quarter given with Ned. Never has been, never will be as long as he draws breath. He does what he wants to do and sees what he wants to see and never will he change. The words we threw at one another during my so-called trial linger still, but there is time enough, I trust, to come to that part of this sorry life. Before then there are other years to walk, to remember, to drag back into that portion of my mind which still functions with some degree of accuracy. A part not dulled by malmsey wine and pain, not damaged by fear and loneliness.

The queen's Coronation was a magnificent event, staged as much for the populace as for the queen herself. I recall with pride riding into the hall on a richly caparisoned horse and myself equally richly caparisoned, if I can say such a thing. Gold sparkled everywhere in the rushlights. I was gracious, I led her into the Abbey, I held the bowl for her to wash, I supervised the Coronation feast and I did it all with a fixed grin that anyone should have seen was false and none did, for they were not looking for that emotion from me. They were looking for a feast which they had, for a spectacle, which they had, for ritual which they also had. They were not looking for a duke to radiate hatred and resentment so they did not see it.

I was told my brother the king beamed his way through the day, ensconced in his chambers, awaiting the return of his bride, as if he could not be done with smiling at everyone. When I saw him, I realised the smile said 'look at my bride, my prize, my breeding mare. Look at the hair, the face and the radiance of her. Look at her and envy me, you common people!' and we were indeed common people to him, even those of us with royal blood and as much right to the throne of England as he had. For a king to rule supreme, he must be autocratic, superior, arrogant, supremely right in all things. And in all those things Ned excelled in that he wrapped them in charm, bonhomie of the highest order and a great deal of personal charisma so that those around him did not realise he was autocratic, superior, arrogant and supremely right in all things at the time he declared that this should be done or that should not be done. Even if he was not right, the fact became overlooked because of his charm, his easy manner, his jovial attitude but beneath it all was an iron will, a determination that his will would be done, regardless. It was very much a 'God be with anyone who stood against him' reality in the court at that time.

My problem was – is – I do not take orders easily. I do not bow to the inevitable without a fight. I do not easily grant another ascendance over my body, my life, my soul and my ambition. Hence, problems. They were coming as surely as a cloud comes to spoil a summer outing. I knew it but whether others did is a moot point and they are not here for me to ask, any of them. So I must, of necessity, decide in my own mind whether they foresaw the problems I did or whether they were happy for my brother the king and saw nothing untoward in the way he took on the world and laughed his way through the days, the meetings, the travelling, the celebrations and the birth of his first legitimate child. I have just taken the whole of his reign as I know it and brought it down to a few words which would fit inside my empty mazer and leave room for many other tomes, but it is true. Edward, my brother the king, ever lived his life as he wished it, to see what he wished to see and saw no other viewpoint. He lived in a world where he was supremely right and all else, no matter what they were, had to be wrong. We fought many times over the years, Ned and I, many, many times, in court and out of it, in his court and out of it, ever did we fight over many things but always I came up against that determination that he was and would be ever right and all else, no matter what, would be wrong. It mattered not that the arguments made sense, for he dismissed those, too.

I smiled too, as I said, but inside I did not. Inside I was burning with anger at the presumption of the new queen and her family, of the complacent smiles sent my way. Poor Clarence, so we took your chance at kingly status, did we? Well, isn't that just the way Fate is, lifts some and drops others, we were lifted through our Elizabeth's marriage to Edward and you were dropped because of it. Console yourself with your dukedom, young man, with your estates and such

women as you dally with, for it is all you will have from
henceforth.

Did they really think those things?
I do not know: I will not know.

Chapter 17

There were times, mused George, looking deep into a mazer of malmsey wine, when it seemed as if he was at odds with the world, as if he alone walked a sensible pathway and everyone else appeared to be walking a different, idiotic pathway and they could not see his point of view at all because of the divergence of the roads on which they walked. 'I mean,' he said to his squire, who stood silent as always, knowing better than to voice an opinion which could in future be interpreted as being on the wrong side, 'there was Worcester and that fool woman Lady Roos. I mean, tell me how in the name of Christ I managed to lose that dispute!'

More wine was poured and George drank it as if it was water, not an expensive commodity that was difficult to obtain. He had given a standing order that at all times his cellar was to be filled with fine wines, especially malmsey, no matter the cost. Money was ever a consideration but wine had to come before sensible thought of finances.

His chamber was warm, a huge fire blazed in the hearth with a page detailed to keep it fed, for George liked his comforts and would have it so, especially during the bitter months of winter. For him the fires began in Autumn and lasted clear through to the end of Spring, for castles and large homes were never warm, never comfortable enough for him without a huge log burning.

Durian looked up from the lyre he was strumming and flashed one of his mischievous smiles at George.

"Tis pointless to ask these minions for an opinion, Your Grace, for either they have no opinion or they are too polite to voice it. Either way Your Grace will have no satisfaction from their answers."

George waved the squire away and indicated to the page that he could leave, too. At times he preferred nothing more than the company of Durian, when they could talk freely about everything they had discovered. When the door closed after them, he stirred on his chair, tilting it so that he could balance his heels on the table. The mazer turned around and around in his hands and he gazed into it as if the future was written there for him to see.

"How do they do it, Durian?" he asked, almost inconsequentially, knowing full well the next question would be 'do what?' for his Fool had not and could not follow his thinking. He circumvented the question. "Those wise women, so-called, how do they look into something like a bowl of water or a cup and see the future? I see nothing but darkness and the state of my head in the morrow."

"Ah, you see more than that, sire." Durian poured wine for himself without being bidden, taking a liberty that he was permitted when they were alone. "You see the fact that in the wine you lose yourself for a time. For was not a man more persecuted than you are?"

"Wydevilles."

"Said with all the venom one man needs to show another how he feels about his brother's family!"

"At times I do wonder about you, Durian; just how much do you 'see' that is not there for human eyes?"

"I can't tell you that, sire, for I know not myself how much is 'knowing' and how much is my piecing together all that I overhear and gather from the many sources you and I together have arranged to bring us those pieces for us to put together."

"At times you talk in riddles, Durian!" George grumbled, emptying the mazer and reaching for more. The log collapsed in on itself in the hearth, sending ash and sparks flying into the room.

"No more than you do yourself, sire. Of a surety I have never known a man to speak in such riddles as you do in conversation but by a miracle none perceive that you are talking in rings and they are not following a single thread you start."

George laughed aloud and crashed his boots back onto the floor.

"By God's great name, you're right! And they don't see it, do they? Poor fools!" He frowned. "But I would wish my brother the king would fall into the trap, then I could arrange more land, more money, for the coffers are running a little low these days and I am dependent on him more than I would like."

"Then it behoves me to mention to you a certain subject which I have been pondering, sire."

"Ha! I know your pondering! It usually leads me into pathways I can well do without!"

"Not this time. Of a surety have I pondered long and hard on this and feel it is the right way forward, if everyone concerned allows it to proceed, of course."

"Now you speak in the riddles I mentioned, Durian! If you have something to say, then say it."

"All right." Durian laid the lyre aside and stood up. "Is it not time Your Grace thought of marriage?"

"Well, it has crossed my mind, of course it has, but who-" He thumped his fist on the table and laughed. "This is your pondering, is it not? You have already decided who would be right for me and are seeking a way of putting her name before me. Am I right?"

"As always, sire." Durian acknowledged the statement with a nod and a knowing smile. "And I suggest to you that the eldest daughter of your cousin of Warwick, Isobel, would be the perfect bride for Your Grace."

In all his wondering about a future bride, the daughter of his cousin Warwick had not really crossed his mind. He had looked at the women in court, daughters of knights and earls who pandered to Ned's every wish and wondered if he took any of them to be his bride whether he would be taking one that Ned had cast off. It was difficult to know which of the countless pretty women who frequented the courts and homes where Ned travelled and disported and held meetings had actually favoured his bed, too. He was certain Warwick would not have allowed it, especially after Ned had so casually thrown out the plans for the foreign alliance and with it, all Warwick's dreams of power for the future, by making his own choice of a woman. How good it would be to be part of the Warwick entourage and at such a high level: son-in-law.

But what then of Isobel herself? Would she be prepared to be helpmeet and companion to him?

Impatiently George leapt to his feet and strode across to the polished steel which served as a mirror. I am handsome, he thought, looking at his image. I am handsome, tall, healthy, a knight, a duke, I bring royal blood to any marriage and future child and I have wealth although I would like more. I ride well, I could hold my own at a tournai were I asked, I am sure I could and would do well in battle –

His thoughts broke off there. Would any of this be of interest to a bride? Would she care about his battle prowess, would she not prefer him to be home, not risking life, limb and reputation on a battlefield? Would she care about the joust? Would she not prefer words of love and tenderness and some thoughts of how good a father he would be?

An image of Isobel as he last saw her flashed into his mind, her dark brown hair decorously caught up in an elaborate jewelled head-dress that caught every flash of light from the cresset lamps. He recalled her quietly pretty face and wondered why he should think of her that way, quietly pretty. At first he had believed her sister Anne to be the truly quiet one, a mouse, shying away from people and loud noises and yet rumour had it that Dickon was enamoured of the mouse-like Anne. That had surprised George, he had thought his brother would have wanted someone more assertive, but maybe it would suit him better to have a quiet biddable wife. But he also knew that Warwick had other plans for his youngest daughter, plans that none but he knew of, or so he thought. In an unguarded moment he had expressed them in the hearing of a squire who was in George's pay and the news came to him immediately. Anne was to marry a Frenchman and secure a dynasty there, Warwick being determined to have power, if he could, in that unpredictable land.

But Isobel, bring the thoughts back to Isobel, to the one with the quietly pretty face, the dark brown hair and the curves in the right places. Yes, Isobel would be a worthy bride for the duke of Clarence, she would be an asset at the high table, at banquets and at ceremonials. She would doubtless be an asset in the bedchamber too, if he could teach her well enough. But what would Warwick make of such an alliance and even more than that, what would Ned make of such an alliance?

Curses, he thought angrily, that I need to consult the king before making a marriage!

He swung round on his heel and confronted Durian, who had stood patiently waiting for George to speak to him.

"It's a damned good thought, Durian, I thank you for that. I will consider it and approach-"

"Arrange it with your cousin of Warwick first," Durian said quickly. "Let the arrangements be under way before you speak with the king. Let it seem as if it is all but in hand and you might sway his opinion."

"Why should he care who I marry?"

"Because he wants to use you as a pawn, sire, as he uses everyone. Come now, you know your brother the king well enough to know I speak truth."

"That was the last thought I had before I spoke to you just now, that I need to consult the king before making a marriage and I resent it."

"It is protocol, sire, sad to say. You are subject to the king whether he be brother or not, being high born and part of the ruling family."

"Tell me of things I do not know, Durian, things which will not depress me. I will speak with Warwick as soon as I can. I wish to know if the Lady Isobel would entertain the thought of an alliance with me."

"She would be in difficulties to find anyone better, sire."

"Spoken like a loyal friend, but there are many out there who could offer her a good life, apart from the Yorks, that is."

"Maybe, but who else would bring so much royal blood to a marriage, sire? And blood counts for so much with these great families."

"What is yours, Durian?"

A genuine smile split the expressive face. "Part peasant, part Celt and, I am told, a trace of royal blood from someone in my past who was born on the wrong side of the blanket."

"The Celt explains the fey farseeing, of a surety it does, and I can believe the trace of royal blood for at times you speak and act as an aristocrat and it is not all playacting for my benefit."

"Thank you, sire." Durian obviously meant every word of his thanks.

George hesitated, words trembling on his tongue, wanting to be spoken. He looked around as if to assure himself the room was deserted, no hangers-on trying to eavesdrop on what was likely to be a very private conversation, a rarity for him. Life was so crowded with people who felt they had to be treading on his shadow at all times in case he needed them.

Finally he spoke. "You are one of the very few people I trust, you know that."

"I do. And I am grateful for your patronage, sire."

"It's more than that, isn't it, Durian? More than patronage, more than the gold I toss in your direction. It is not that alone which holds you loyal to me."

"We are speaking the truth here tonight, so yes, it is more than that." A half-smile, almost apologetic, crossed his mouth. George watched the expressions fleeting across the dark eyes, calculating, considering, then finally clearing as Durian made up his mind what to say. When he spoke, it was in a quiet, serious voice George had never heard from his Fool at any time.

"I could find another place tomorrow, with more gold, more comfort and better looking women than here with you, Your Grace, if you will forgive me for saying so, but I could not and would not find a better man to serve. Whatever men say, I know the measure of you, as duke, as brother, as son, as friend and as employer of many. I have seen you at your worst, when the temper has taken you and destroyed your common sense, I have seen you at your best when you flatter and charm those you cannot stand. I have comforted you when you were sick from too much wine and I have laughed with you at the antics of others. I have shared bread and meat with you and drank your wine. I have done everything with you apart from three things: I have not worn your clothes, for you are taller and broader than I, I have not dallied with your women, for that is not the way I am inclined and I have not slept in your bed for if I had done so, I would not be responsible for my actions. I know you as well if not better than I have known any man and I say this: high born or not, you are a fine man, one worthy of respect and honour. And that I give you, in full measure, George duke of Clarence."

Durian turned away, grabbing a mazer as he did so, as if embarrassed by his words, embarrassed by his expression. George did not hesitate; he walked over to Durian, took the cup from his hand and replaced it on the table.

"Look at me," he said softly but with a hint of authority to make him obey. "Look at me, Durian."

Durian tilted his head to look up at his master, tears threatening to spill from half closed eyes.

"There are only four people in my life that I trust: my mother, my brother of Gloucester, Peke and you. Of those four only you hold my innermost secrets, only you know my ambitions and my dreams, only you find out that which I wish to know. Because of this, Durian, you hold my life in your hands. Such is my trust in you. I did not think we would ever confess such thoughts to one another but I am right glad we spoke of it. I am comforted by your words and will sleep better this night for knowing the depth of your feelings. Know they are returned, four fold."

He stood, helpless, as Durian's tears finally overflowed and the small man shook with the force of his sobs. Then he reached out and put his arms around the thin body and held him close, recalling instantly the skeletal feel of his brother Richard when they had newly arrived at Ludlow and all was strange and frightening, remembering how good it felt to be the strong one then and realising how good it felt to be the strong one now. He knew, even as that thought crossed his mind, that at times he was capable of weakness. It was something he had to guard against. Thoughts raced through and around his emotions which were raging through him. Sleep? That would not come easy after these words, no matter what he might say to his Fool. It was very unusual for him to declare his deeper emotions for anyone or anything. His usual way was bluster or charm, scowls or smiles but all of that was designed to cover his real feelings, which were kept locked away behind the equivalent of a breastplate. Feelings were to be denied, ignored, crushed, for the moment you began to display them, people took advantage of you. Show softness and they would walk on you, show loyalty and they would deceive you, show love and they would leave you. Give nothing but pretend you are giving and you hold the upper hand. Durian had just got behind that breastplate, in the same way his brother of Gloucester had. I must be on my guard against tears, George told himself, even as Durian pulled away, slowly, and rubbed a sleeve over his wet face.

"My apologies, Your Grace." Formal again, trying to re-establish their previous positions.

"Forget it, Durian," George smiled at him with genuine fondness. "It's too late for titles. Keep that for when we are in public."

"As we are most of our lives, sire."

"Unfortunately. I have cherished this time we spent alone, my friend."

The casual use of the word almost started tears flowing again but with a supreme effort Durian visibly choked them back. George watched the struggle, then handed his Fool the mazer he had picked up earlier.

"Here, I feel you could do with this right now."

"I could indeed."

The wine disappeared and Durian smiled, a little awkwardly. "I did not expect that to happen."

"Neither did I but perhaps we should have foreseen it, opening our hearts to one another as we did."

"We should prepare ourselves for Compline, sire. The time grows short."

George picked up a cloak and swung it around Durian's shoulders, laughing at how much of it trailed on the ground. Durian joined in the laughter as he struggled to walk with the heavy garment dragging around his legs. "No, of a surety I cannot walk in that, sire! Here, you will need it, you feel the cold much more than I, despite your size."

With the cloak on his own shoulders, George walked toward the door, then hesitated, a hand on the latch. "I thank you, Durian, from my heart. Your words have done much for me this night."

"I thank you in return, sire, for the gift you gave me, your compassion. That means a lot to one such as myself."

"Let none speak ill of you in my presence, or they will know my wrath, on that I give you my oath."

"And that is enough to frighten Lucifer himself, Your Grace!"

Chapter 18

Ah, Durian, such memories! Why are you not with me now, to lift my spirits, to walk the paths of my memories with me! What had I done that God took you from me in that terrible winter, when the tertian fever struck down so many and the physician was powerless in the face of your torment? Do you know how much I wanted to be there, to comfort you in the last days and hours, even as I need comforting now in my last days and hours? Do you know how they denied me access to your room, saying I should keep myself away for fear of contracting the condition myself? Do you know how I did not care at the time if I did or not? My one need was to say farewell and thank you to a dear and trusted friend. Peke held me back; demanded I stay away for the sake of my family and those around me. Peke was right but I damned him for it all the same. Ah, that other devoted man, he put himself in dire danger by standing before your door and barring me from entrance, me, in one of my towering rages, too! A brave man, Peke, brave to the end to defy me thus. You know, Durian, only too well, what I am like when the temper takes me. But he stood firm and I knew he was right. So now I say to those spirits I am sure are gathering around me at this time, find Durian for me, find – no, even now I do not say your true name for you entrusted me with that, my friend, and even in my death days I will not reveal it to the world, not that the world can hear me! But you know how thoughts have energies of their own, do they not? I will not speak your name. Durian you were to me and Durian you will stay until I am with Isobel in the tomb in Tewkesbury which awaits me.

Again I ramble, oh how I ramble in these thoughts! Spirits, angels, whoever is with me at this time and of a surety there are phantoms here, I feel them, I sense them, I beg, I plead with you to find the spirit, soul, the essence of Durian and tell him how I treasured his friendship, his devotion, his loyalty, his humour and his music and how I was prevented from saying farewell by those who sought to keep me healthy.

And tell him how much of a joke that is, for here I am, under sentence of death twice over and it is no more than a toss of the dice which decides what will take me from this life! Ah yes, comes the part of me that wishes against all sensible thought that my brother the king's execution warrant is enacted first: I would not, after all, deprive him of the knowledge, the ongoing memory, that he had his brother killed, murdered in cold blood. How cold that blood is, too, for Ned's anger has long since abated. He does not carry it for too long; he is not one to brood on injustices to the point when it interferes with his hedonistic life. It is my wish to remain a regret, a torment in his darker moments. I know my brother the king, I know his sense of loyalty to family and I also know his pride. It is more than he could face to withdraw the sentence of treason from me and admit to being wrong, to restore my lands and my finances to me, after they were all returned to him to use as he wished, to dispose of as he wished and I doubt not that there were Wydevilles only too ready to accept the gifts of my estates. It is a small revenge on my part for his taking of my life. Petty, almost, but right now it is making me feel better and in that sense there is no argument; I will not tell him.

Did I not own so much and now do I own nothing at all but the clothes I wear against the cold of this prison cell? I refuse to call it anything but, it is a prison cell, I cannot open the door and walk out, find a horse and ride to Greenwich, to Tutbury or anywhere else. I cannot visit my lady mother, go to Isobel's tomb and shed tears for her passing and what we might have had, I cannot find Peke and say my farewells to him and offer him my thanks for all his loyalty and devotion, too.

I do swear these walls are closing in, that the room is smaller than it was some days ago, that inch by inch everything moves closer to me until in the end this will be my tomb. I long to go outside, to breathe clean air, to feel the wind on my face, to become wet through with winter rain and feel cleaned by it. I cannot.

I long to go and speak with those I loved and cared for and give them my thanks. I cannot. Even if I were free to walk outside, my words have gone, fled under the power of that which consumes me moment by moment. That of which I dare not think, let alone speak. I cannot allow it to win. I have to hold it back.

The shutters rattle against that fierce wind that is trying to get in. What will it find if it does? One tormented duke whose balance is gone, whose voice is gone, whose looks are gone. I have a beard, what would Isobel have made of that, I sometimes ask myself? I have a beard for it is easier when the men come to tend to me for them not to trouble with shaving me. I shake at times and the blade can slip. I have no colour any more, or so they tell me, for I have not been outside to gain the benefit of the freshness that is out there for those who do not appreciate it. And I am much heavier than I was, for there has been nothing for me to do but pace the floor and of a surety that becomes tiresome in the end, especially when balance has gone. So I sit and hold a mazer, empty or otherwise, stare into the flames and wish for someone to come and speak with me or for it all to be over, for this is not living, this is not death. This is a dreadful time of waiting and not knowing and, I repeat, for I am sure I have thought this already in these rambling memories, there is a cruelty in the not knowing.

On which thought I have to say my brother the king has not visited me in this prison but my brother of Gloucester has.

He came unannounced, walking into my chamber, my prison, as if it were the great hall of Fotheringhay or the state rooms at Tutbury. He came in rich robes which made me feel shabby, for my jewelled doublets are no longer available for me, nor do I really wish to wear them. I wear drab coloured tunics, dark hose and embroidered slippers, for where is there to go and who is there to impress?

It was as if he knew of my condition, for the first thing he said was "do not speak. Let me talk instead." Squires were dismissed, the door was closed and my brother of Gloucester sat down opposite me across the table, his face solemn and the lines deeper than I ever saw them. Characteristically he immediately began to twist his rings, ever did I see him do this, twist those rings around and around as if they bothered him in some way. I pushed a mazer toward him but he shook his head. I recalled he rarely indulged in wine, only on special occasions. I recalled he was abstemious in most things of the body and wondered if I would have benefited from being thus whilst realising it was too late for such thoughts. He sat for a moment, as if wondering how to begin. When he did, the words came in a rush as if he would be done with them and be gone. I did not blame him for this, it cannot be easy to say goodbye to a brother, loved or otherwise.

"George," he said and I thought, oh heaven be thanked, he did not call me Clarence as our brother the king had done. "I come to tell you this. I am leaving for the North in a day or so, when the packing is done and the provisions are prepared. I am leaving because there is nothing more I can do for you. If I stay I would be at Ned's side pleading for your life and you know as well as I that if you demand of Ned he does the opposite, if you plead too much he does the opposite. I have spoken with our lady mother who has tried to intercede for you but also had to withdraw her petition for the same reason."

I recall nodding emphatically for I knew this only too well of my brother the king. He was this way before he became king and having that supreme power had increased that tendency a thousand-fold. I knew just what Dickon was saying to me in the secrecy of my prison cell, knew it for God's honest truth.

"I cannot bear to be here when you are executed. I cannot bear the thought that our brother has caused this to be written and will cause it to be carried out."

Heartbreak. It was not just those who worked for me and were friends with me who would suffer when I finally walked through the door marked Death, but my family too, my lady mother who had suffered so much already and this caring thoughtful brother. My sisters? I did not know them well enough to be able to predict their emotions. My children would have to live with the knowledge that their father was a traitor, so-called, and make up their own minds whether that was the truth. I watched his face, watched the emotions chasing one another: anger, sorrow, love.

"I have arranged for more malmsey to be brought to you, I feel it is the least I can do at this time, George. I wish you-" He broke off, suddenly overcome. Richard, lost for words, Richard, the supremely controlled person, in danger of losing control. He kicked the chair back and stood, holding on to the table with hands that clenched so tight I feared for the wood itself. "I would undo this if it were in my power to do so," he said so softly I wondered if I heard aright. "I would undo this but I cannot. If I go, if all pressures are removed from our brother, he might reconsider. Let them tell you I left without caring, let them tell you I gave no thought to my brother's execution, that the North called instead. Let them tell you what they will but you have the truth, George. I am going because I

153

think it might help and if it does not, then believe I am going because I cannot bear to be here when it happens. I will remember you in my prayers for the rest of my life."

He strode to the door, that fine built man, hammering on it with a fist that sounded like iron. The door opened and he left without a backward glance, as if he could not stand to look upon me again. I had not realised his stature; I had not appreciated his aristocratic bearing until that moment. It was there in my thought, a fine built man.

The door swung shut on me and my memories, now added to by the concern, nay the love, shown me by my brother of Gloucester. Had the men walked in at that moment with their instructions, I would have welcomed them and gone to my Maker on a cloud of understanding and happiness that it was all done.

Sadly, they did not and I was left, am left, here to think on a life that could have been so different, had my brother the king been different with me.

Where did it go wrong? Was it in his denial of my marriage? Was it in the many fierce disputes we had? Was it – dare I voice the thought – insecurity on his part because of my right to the throne? Did he have any thought that I knew of the existence of the pre-contract and might speak of it and wreck his marriage? Or was it the Wydevilles who suspected this and were pressuring him to dispose of that which would displace them in their entirety?

Chapter 19

By some miracle the sea remained calm for the entire voyage to Calais. Isobel was not a good sailor, she clung to the sides of the bunk and refused to attempt to walk on deck, to take the fresh air and see for herself that the Channel was almost as smooth as the fishpond at Fotheringhay. George gave up trying to coax her out and climbed back onto the deck, where he stood with Peke, Durian and his squires, staring at the slowly approaching shoreline, breathing the sea air and listening to the seagulls screaming overhead. A breeze ruffled his fair hair but did little to ease his mind. I would wish my thoughts were as calm as the water, he told himself, clenching his fists and wishing to hit someone, anyone, to release the anger he had boiling in his heart and mind. It isn't logical to hold such angry thoughts in both heart and mind, he knew that but nothing could quieten his turmoil. Months, endless months of dispute with his brother the king and months, endless months of waiting for the dispensation to arrive which would allow the marriage had taken their toll on his nerves and he found himself snarling and snapping at everyone for no reason.

"I will marry Isobel Neville," he said, day after day, to passing servants, squires, chambermaids, anyone who would listen or at least acknowledge his having spoken. Peke tried to reason with him, to counsel him to look elsewhere for a bride in the face of implacable stubbornness by the king, who simply shouted 'NO!' when approached with the suggestion. The 'NO!' then became an ongoing interminable argument that spilled over into every part of life.

The Earl of Warwick wanted the alliance, probably more than he had wanted anything after Edward had thrown all his plans into the very Channel they sailed on, helping him to go ahead with the marriage in the face of all opposition.

"Can I be held responsible for your feelings toward our cousin of Warwick?" George had shouted back at Edward. "Is this not at the very heart of this decision of yours to prevent my marriage?"

"Ha! What do you know of alliances, of feelings, of politics, Clarence? What would you know, you of how many years is it now, just seventeen, if I reckon it right? What would you know of such things? I know where I want your alliances to be and it is not with the Nevilles!"

Edward had paced his chamber, his boots striking the flagstones with all the anger George recalled his own boots doing in the past, when he too had been infuriated beyond all reason. He recognised the trait and accepted that it told him his brother the king was incapable of discussing the matter logically, if there was logic behind the decision, something he seriously doubted. He snatched up the mazer left for him and drank before responding, thinking swiftly how he could turn this to his advantage, or even if he could turn it to his advantage. In the end he resorted to cold logic, which never worked with Ned if it wasn't his own idea. He knew that but it was his last resort.

"You married whom you wished, Your Grace," he said, deciding to allow formality to come into the room, in the hope it would cast its balm on the fiery atmosphere.

"Yes, I did, because I am king and you are just a duke and subservient to the crown, Clarence! I have plans for you which will be revealed in time, when you are ready, when you are old enough to know your own mind – and mine!" It was at that point George bowed and, without another word, stalked out of his brother's chamber, slamming the great door after him.

He stared out at the fast flowing waters but saw only the set face of his brother, wearing the fierce determined look he knew so well. The only sounds were the creaking of the sails and ropes, the slap of the waves against the keel but George heard angry boot heels striking flagstones and barely suppressed anger in the voice. There was no reasoning with him; there was no arguing with him. But there was defiance and that could be done with the right people and the right plans being laid.

It was a risk, of that there was no doubt. You did not defy your king and expect not to have retribution of some kind. In his quieter, saner moments, he asked himself if the attraction of Isobel was as much in his being denied permission to marry her as the charms she herself embodied. At times he thought he actively disliked his cousin of Warwick and other times thought that he was the finest man who ever lived, outside of his family, that was. The whole thing was a ridiculous mess: it could have been and should have been a happy occasion, with the entire family present, not this travelling across water to hold the ceremony!

He had made little secret of his intention to marry into the Neville family, he had written to people and advised them of the time, date and place, invited some to attend, sent an emissary to gain the necessary dispensation to allow the marriage and in all of this, Ned had said nothing and done nothing. Who knew what was going on in his mind: had he decided to allow the wedding to go ahead without interference, was he just too busy to bother or did he really not care after all? Choose any answer, thought George with extreme irritation, and you could well pick the right one, for who really knew the mind of the king these days, besotted as he was with his queen and bothered as he was with a court full of Wydevilles!

He moved away from his attendants and Durian quietly went with him, following the command of the almost invisible hand signal that meant 'come to me.' He stood alongside George at the rail, looking out at the gently rolling sea. He was apparently lost in his own thoughts, but George knew his Fool well enough to know there was a good deal going on behind the bland 'look at me just watching the sea' face. As if sensing his Lord's thoughts, Durian turned and gave him one of the knowing smiles that he did so well.

"Have we escaped the wrath of our liege lord, do you think, sire?"

"I have to hope that is so. I have to hope that when we return to England there will not be a deputation waiting with strict instructions to convey me to the Tower, there to await my brother the king's further instructions!"

"Would your brother the king be so cruel as to deprive a bridegroom of his time with his newly created wife?"

"Would my brother the king be so cruel as to try and stop the marriage in the first place? Who really knows what goes on behind the smiling face, Durian?"

"Of a surety our liege lord is a man of extremes, sire. It is, seemingly, right for him to take to wife whoever he wishes but if his brother of Clarence should desire to do the same, then it is wrong."

"I made the mistake of hinting at that situation during my audience with my liege lord," mused George, realising as he said it that he had already told Durian of that last meeting. Durian nodded, smiled and looked away.

"I feel, and it is only my feelings, sire, that your brother the king tried to deny the marriage for no reason other than the fact that he could."

"That makes more sense to me than any other scenario I have thought about. He does so love the sense of power that being a king has given him. Dickon is more biddable than I, Dickon will go North if his king tells him to, Dickon will rule the North for him in the future, that I foresee." He turned round suddenly to face Durian. "Why did I say that? Where did that thought come from?"

"The same place my thoughts come from, sire. Do you not realise you are fey, even as I am?"

"It is-"

"Our secret. But of course. I am Fool only on the outside."

"That I have known from the moment you walked into my chamber and asked for a chance to entertain me, Durian."

"Ah, that was a time to be remembered! A time when all was peaceful in the household of the duke of Clarence! A time when you just went along with everything your sainted brother told you without asking questions. Then came the time when you thought, why am I doing this? Why don't I do what I want to do, not what Ned wants me to do! Am I right, sire?"

"You know you are, Durian, you know you are."

"And what you want to do right now is marry the delectable Isobel Neville and it is not because I put the idea in your head; you want to do this because it is right for you at this time."

A great burst of laughter came from the helm; someone was telling the Earl a joke that was obviously unsavoury. George recognised the different tone; his cousin had different laughter for different occasions: it was not often he heard this particular one. It usually followed a heavy drinking bout when the women were dismissed and the men huddled together to swap stories. It was something George found abhorrent but of the necessity to keep his cousin on his side if he was to share a life with him he had to go along with it occasionally. He knew already he had a reputation as something of a prude and had to decide whether to stay with that or do something about changing it.

But then, would Warwick have allowed me to marry his daughter if I had come with the reputation of a rake? It was not something he could ask; it was a question he pondered from time to time. Warwick was difficult to read, a blustering sometimes belligerent man who believed himself king of all he surveyed. His estates were vast, his household seemingly endless, numbering thousands, his power seemed limitless and yet, and yet –

He had failed to keep Edward under his control, had failed in the alliance he wished to make with France, had instead leapt on the chance to draw the duke of Clarence into the family. It was probably wrong to assign thoughts to Warwick he did not have but George wondered, again in his quieter saner moments, whether he was second best: not having achieved his aim of controlling Edward, Warwick was making do with George instead.

Well, I've been second best all this time, what difference does it make to me now?

As if reading his thoughts, Durian spat over the side. "I would wish the Lady Isobel came with a more amenable father, my lord."

The words were muttered in such a low tone George was not entirely sure he had heard aright but knew the sense of the words, for they echoed his own thoughts. He grinned at Durian, his back to the earl, aware no sailor was near enough to either hear or see him at that moment.

"Everything has a price, Isobel is no different in that regard."

"Sometimes…"

"I know, sometimes you have to ask yourself if the price is too high. I know that. I have asked it but she is a beautiful person in her own right, she will be a good wife and helpmeet to me. I can take his power and influence and use it, too."

Durian nodded in acknowledgement of the words. It had been discussed several times between them and ever they came to the same conclusion: the price was not too high for a good wife and powerful patronage. Especially when the king has set his face against you!

The wedding was a glorious occasion, held in an elaborately painted and decorated hall in Calais, one fit for a king. Isobel was radiant in blue silk over cloth of gold, George's new brother-in-law George Neville conducted a beautiful service with words that suited the occasion and the many knights and nobles who attended gave the wedding the prestige and esteem it would have otherwise lacked. Warwick beamed his way through the entire ceremony, loudly proclaiming the good qualities of his new son-in-law to all who would listen. George smiled stiffly; wondering whom among the guests was Ned's spy, of a surety someone would report back to the king. He knew that only too well, for did he not have his own spies in Ned's household, reporting back all that his brother did? Durian took the reports. He was a sponge for information; drawing it in and only giving it back when pressed by George himself to release it.

Isobel clung to George's arm, proudly nodding to everyone who called her duchess, which they did just to flatter and please her. She laughed until tears spilled at Durian's nonsense, he excelled himself with rhymes that both flattered and gently mocked her and her new husband. George alone realised the hours his Fool must have spent working them out, for they were clever, subtle and very funny indeed. I wish I could write them down, he told himself, save them for the future. But then I wish many things...

Not least of which was that the day would end and he could rest. Warwick was busy with back-slapping bonhomie that was getting tiresome, as were comments about breeding heirs when he had yet to bed his new wife.

There was also the manifesto to be announced the following day, setting out their joint plans for the future, with a call to array going out, preparing for their own uprising. This was the underlying reason for the marriage, he had come to accept, the fact Warwick wanted to take over, to supplant Edward with George, to create a new regime in England that would put them firmly in the limelight, give them the power that Edward currently held. Would it work? Doubts tormented his waking moments, alongside his desire for more power; to depose those he thought were not fit to govern. Warwick's persuasive words had found fertile ground in his troubled, unsettled mind. Am I that easy to read? He had asked Durian that question one night when in their cups and for a moment Durian had been silent, considering the question from all angles. Finally he had looked up at George.

"No, my lord, you are not. I think your cousin of Warwick is a perceptive man who sees more than we allow of him at times. Of a surety I know you better than any man alive and yet he sees things I sometimes do not."

That to some degree settled George's mind. He kept a bland neutral face for all business dealings and even some social occasions, not wanting people to know of his innermost thoughts and desires. They were kept for those he trusted beyond all reason, few indeed were those people, far too few. It had perturbed him that his cousin might see past the mask of innocent intent.

After what seemed a lifetime of small talk, congratulations and chitter-chatter, they attended Compline and went to their beds where Isobel proved to be shy, naïve and embarrassed about her body and anything she had to do as a wife. George allowed her to fall asleep without possessing her, there was time

162

enough for that. They had the rest of their lives together to please her father and breed heirs. For himself, the desire was not there, not with so much to think about. Muttering words about how considerate and caring he was, Isobel slipped into sleep, leaving George to look down at her quiet calm face and the mass of hair spread over the pillow. He had requested she leave it loose for this one night and she had obeyed. Tentatively he touched the silken locks, marvelling at the many shades he saw in them, looking at her almost transparent eyelids and her soft lips moving gently as she breathed. Maybe when they were back in England, when they were in their own home and their own bed, he would take her, gently and yet positively. Before then, she was entitled to her rest.

While he stayed awake, despite being bone weary, thinking of the problems that could lie ahead of him.

Then he grinned. I have the earl of Warwick as father-in-law! What could assail the house of Neville and win? None!

With that comforting thought he fell asleep against the warmth and softness of his new wife.

Chapter 20

Oh the softness of my new wife's body against mine in our marital bed! Oh the way her hair wound itself around my face and neck, for I did so like her to wear it loose in bed, even if it did mean a lot of brushing in the morning to untangle it. Then it fell in rich waves and I never tired of seeing the brush slide through it and watch as it fell down her back clear to her waist. She was so pretty, my wife, my poor doomed wife who deserved so much better than I ever gave her. I say this now, I say it in my mind and my heart to those who would hear me, those shades, those angels who are around me during these final minutes, hours, days, whenever it pleases my liege lord to end this useless life of mine. I say I was a good husband but I could have been a better one. I could have considered her more than I did; I should have taken her more into my confidence and not taken her for granted. I could have, I should have, these are the thoughts of someone who regrets so much and who cannot turn back the days, months and years and put things right. Oh Isobel, if you be there in Heaven awaiting me, it will not be long now and I can then offer you my apologies. Of one thing be sure, though, I did not stray. Not once. Not that I was without temptations, enough and more of them! A flash of ankle, a tugging at the neckline of a gown to expose more and persuade me to tarry and look, oh I tarried and I looked but I never touched. This I swear on Isobel's memory, her tomb and her soul. Only when she had departed this life did I turn to another, one who had loved silently and long, one who had waited on my command and my wish, one who served me well. Oh dear girl, I would have you know I loved you more than life itself!

'Tis passing strange, though, that now I hope against all hope that my brother the king will stay his hand long enough to let me wander through the remainder of my life in memory. I wish to relive all that I did and accept it, good or bad, before I walk through that black door and greet whatever is waiting for me on the other side. I visualise a door, heavy with iron, great hinges of black and a latch strong enough to withstand the assault of demons who might wish to prance into this life and wreak havoc. I visualise this and can see the grain of the fine oak from which it is made, wrought by hands that were not of this world, of a surety they were not, for it is too finely made for that.

I cannot visualise that which lies beyond it and therein lies the fear.

The fear which constricts my bowels at times and causes as much pain as that I am experiencing in my head. None will know of my thoughts, it matters not that I admit such a thing to those around me, for of a surety they must have known others in this situation, those waiting to die and being that afraid of what is on the other side they are in danger of voiding themselves. I fear this as much as I fear that which is to come. I do not wish to lose control of myself, it is a shameful thing and one I would not wish to live through. Listen to the drunken ramblings of a drunken man! Live through this! Life is all but over anyway! But still I hold to the pride which I had when in my prime, before the wine took over and the enemy which lives within my skull began to take his revenge on me. I was a proud duke, I have said so before, I know that. I say it again. I was a proud duke. Such a proud person should not be seen to be that afraid he cannot control himself.

Clarence, in the name of Heaven take the thoughts back to Isobel, poor helpless loving Isobel, she of the soft limbs and quiet voice, she of the glistening hair and logical mind which I used at times when confronted with conundrums that my own mind could not resolve. It is best not to think of these other dire truly awful possible happenings. Oh how I wish Durian

165

were still alive, closeted here with me, to make me laugh, to make me forget for a moment that which is to come! Oh foolish man, would you have imprisoned your Fool? Of a surety that would have been most unfair on the person who loved you so well! It is also to be asked whether the king would have permitted my Fool to be with me until the last. I see and understand that cruel streak in my liege lord and believe it would have been denied me anyway, even if Durian had survived. I wish, I wish, I wish I had been there at the last with him, for I would have known by his face whether what awaited him on the other side of the door was good or bad and I would have reassurance of my own passage through that door. So much denied me!

Come, time is running out. Come, walk the path of memory once more, come, relive the times, the occasions, the conspiracy and the impending battle. Oh the sense of anticipation that we were returning to England to try and take control! Did my brother the king know of our plans in their entirety? I would be dismayed to think he knew of it all; parts, yes, for many were in on the plans and many cannot control their words in front of others. Spies, oh we were awash with spies: Wydevilles, Nevilles, Yorks, you name a family and there were spies awaiting every incautious and at times cautious words, for match enough words together and you have a complete sentence, match enough sentences together and you have a book on which to base your future plans. Or so it was in my household. From the time I was old enough to understand that knowledge was power, I sought knowledge and appointed Durian head of my spy network. I believe it was supreme, better by far than that of my brother of Gloucester or my brother the king himself. Proving that would be difficult but certainly I was well informed at all times. Some of it was trivial: liaisons, gossip, chitter-chatter, of course, but at other times real information came on the back of an incautious

166

moment, an unguarded letter, an overheard command or message. Matched together plans were revealed, scandals uncovered, deception unfolded before our eyes. I knew the strength of my spy network and I knew the quality of the information which came to me. Durian was a perfect spymaster, throughout his life not one person ever hinted that they knew of his role in my household, outside of his being my Fool. They never saw the other side of him. As always, people see what they want to see. I sometimes wonder if this was something I was guilty of at times, although in truth I suspected everyone, befriended few and trusted even less.

We sailed for England, duke and duchess together on board the same ship which took us on our outward journey. We were greeted with great deference and many congratulations by the captain and his men, looking for largesse which I freely distributed. Once more the crossing was calm; once more Isobel spent the entire time clinging to the bunk, swearing that she would never set foot on board a ship again.

But I have to say, in total honesty, my thoughts were turbulent enough to have caused the ship to rock violently, to even capsize, were they in a form that could affect this life. I was torn apart by what we were about to do. I was about to take a step that would reflect on my life in every way. Loyalty is everything: loyalty to family, to kin and to king. I was about to break that which was virtually the eleventh commandment: thou shalt not betray thy family, especially when that family includes the king of England.

Even as I anxiously and excitedly anticipated the insurrection, I was besieged with doubts, with troubled conscience, with nerves that threatened to overtake me. As I stood staring out at the endless waves, marvelling at their constancy, I wondered what power Warwick had

167

over me that he could embroil me in his plans for insurrection. I wondered what alchemy he cast that made me go along with the conspiracy, to draw me in so completely that I could look at myself as a proud duke, new husband, new son-in-law to my cousin of Warwick and not say 'I cannot betray my liege lord and brother.'

For some time I stood alone on the deck, as alone as you can be on a ship where sailors are swarming everywhere, over the rigging, over the coils of rope, over the boxes lashed to various strategic points and, if I didn't move smartly enough, over my feet too. I had no desire for my Italian leather boots to be trampled by salt laden crusted sailors' feet so I was constantly stepping out of their way. For all that, I felt and probably was alone, as no one spoke to me for what felt like hours. I recall the endless sound of the snapping of ropes, creak of timbers, cry of seabirds, smell of wet rope, salt and seaweed, of bodies unwashed even more than mine was. I recall it as clearly as I recall the last mazer of wine I finished some minutes ago for that journey was one of intense heartbreak and misery, in direct contrast to the outward one, when all I thought of was the great occasion of my wedding, Isobel's radiant happiness – when off the ship – and being allied to the great house of Neville.

Now I faced the reality of treason. It was not comfortable; it was not easy. I had no way of knowing what my brother the king knew or did not know, how much advance planning he had made or whether the insurrection would result in tragedy. Would Isobel be a widow before she was a true bride?

What I recall most is my sense of injustice, right or wrong, and it will be for others to decide in their own minds if I was right or if I was wrong. What I say now to the arras and the walls, to the insensate flames and the empty mazer is that I, George Plantagenet, was consumed by a great sense of injustice. From the moment I was made duke of Clarence I assumed I would be heir to the throne. Foolish as it sounds, I had overlooked the possibility of heirs that would supersede me in that position. This was my arrogance, my short-sightedness, my internal blindness. I know it; I confess it now. At the time, during that period of conspiracy and planning, with the distinct and very real possibility of assuming real power, not that conferred by my brother the king which was mostly make-weight, lacking real substance, the thoughts were seductive in the extreme. The smell, the touch almost of real power held more promise for me than even my new wife's - at that time - untouched, unexplored body.

In that period of planning and intense discussion I understood that driving force which motivates men to kill, to steal, to deceive and to defy all normal conventional 'laws' of life to achieve the ultimate goal: supreme power. I understood it and I gave way to its seduction. I was drawn in and, once drawn in, there was no turning back. No going to Ned and saying 'forgive me, brother, I almost turned against you.' For my sins, I was turning against him. I could not even begin to imagine my cousin of Warwick's wrath were I to do such a thing; I doubt I would be standing for longer than it would take to swing a fist in my direction. I had committed myself to the insurrection: I would go through with it, regardless of consequences. It would at least send the message to my brother the king that this duke was not to be casually ordered to go here or oversee there or marry this one or not marry this other one, that this duke would do what he wanted as befitted his standing in court and in the land, that this duke would not idly stand by and watch his younger, less experienced brother showered with titles, honours, estates and responsibilities beyond that given and awarded to me. Jealous? But of course! Would you not be, oh you who walk the room with me right now, those shades of darkness waiting to accompany me through the door? 'Tis a goodness that you are insubstantial, I have grown somewhat during this enforced sojourn here in the Tower, here in the prison that my brother calls 'Royal chambers', grown so that there would be little room for more than one person to pace endlessly the flagstones which are all that have been left for me. No coverings here to trap the warmth, no comfort here for feet not long left to walk this earth. Is that by oversight or design? Ah, so many questions and my brother the king not here to answer a one of them.

It was in this frame of mind: resentment, arrogance, jealousy, imagined slights and unsubstantiated insults combining to fire the thoughts, to turn them toward insurrection and ultimately, with luck, power, we disembarked and began the journey to our fate.

Had I known how it would eventually end, would I have turned back at that point?

Chapter 21

In the guest chamber at Warwick Castle, George lay awake, staring up at an unfamiliar pattern on the bed hangings, listening to familiar yet unfamiliar sounds. A castle is a castle, he told himself, stone floors, stone walls, rushes, men and dogs, but somehow Warwick sounded different from any other he had stayed in or lived in. Just how different could it be? No other castle —

"Sire, can I get aught for you?"

A tremulous voice, a hesitant squire, aware of George's lack of sleep, standing bleary-eyed and weary by his bed.

"A mazer of malmsey would settle my stomach, I think. Then get you back to sleep, young man, there is much to do in the morrow."

"Sire."

George was alone again. He didn't need the wine but he did need to sleep and it just might help. If it didn't, he would have to call his physician and ask for a sleeping draught of some kind.

The knot of nerves in his stomach did not need settling as much as untangling, as did his thoughts.

What had his brother the king been thinking of? How could he have allowed himself to be taken prisoner by Warwick? How could he have allowed the others to ride away from him and let Hastings, Rivers, Wydeville and his brother of Gloucester just leave him to walk into his enemy's hands? Was it a trick? Was it one of his devious moves, give in and then fight back? It was so unlike his brother to just give in. But then again, Warwick had commented several times that Edward had not shown any urgency in dealing with their highly successful uprising. It almost gave George confidence that he would indeed be king, that Warwick would find a way of deposing Ned, of using the bastardy claim against him to make him abdicate. The thought often occurred, Edward a bastard, the son of a common archer and one of the highest ladies in the land.

But there the twisted thoughts came back on themselves. Our lady mother would never stoop so low. Our lady mother adored and worshipped her husband and each child was a cherished Plantagenet, a worthy heir to the York name. The bastardy claim was no more than another vicious rumour set in place by those who would damage the Yorks in any way they could. So Edward was born in Rouen, did that make a difference? The fact he did not have a big baptismal ceremony, did that mean the family were ashamed of him? Go ask my lady mother for her comments on this, see how far you get! Ah but it was a useful weapon that I might need one day!

"Sire?" There was the unwanted but oddly welcome malmsey being held out to him by a squire almost falling asleep on his feet.

"Thank you. Be gone to your bed now."

He sat up in the bed and drank the wine, surprised how quickly he drained it, surprised at how little effect it had. I must be careful, he told himself; it would seem I am too used to the drink these days. But oh it is refuge from the raging world that seeks to trample in my footprints, to stamp its authority on my life where I should be stamping my authority on the world around me. Why does nothing go as it is planned?

The uprising did, a small voice inside hinted quietly.

Yes, but of a surety it will not last. I cannot see this acquiescent Ned remaining quietly as a prisoner here. I cannot see my cousin of Warwick ruling England. I can see myself ruling England and the first thing I will do is to deprive the dreaded and dreadful Wydevilles of their titles and their land. And I will give that land to –

It was as if someone had crept up and hit him over the head very violently. One moment he was thinking, the next he was blinking open reluctant eyes to bright sunshine and the smiling face of his Fool.

"Ah, the dreamer awakes!"

"Durian." George struggled up in the bed, pushing his long hair back with a tired hand. The sleep had not refreshed him at all. "What be the hour?"

"Sire, you have missed Terce and Sexto."

"What of-" George fell back against the pillows, trying to drag his sleep-scattered thoughts into coherent order and failing.

He watched from under lowered lids as Durian made what was almost a magic trick of sliding the mazer out of sight. I must have dropped it or it rolled from the bed during the night, he thought. I must break my dependency on the drink, or it will be the death of me. He grinned suddenly at the thought. There would be worse ways to go than losing yourself in drink and not knowing what was happening. Of a surety that would be better than facing the prospect of living one moment, dying the next.

"Durian, do you believe in life after death?" he asked suddenly, wondering why he was asking and whether he would get an honest answer. He need not have feared on that point. Durian, as ever, divined his master's thought processes.

"I do, sire."

"Have you proof?"

"Ha! You want proof? I can tell you I see shades around you at times, I watch them hover over you, ministering to your needs, Your Grace. I can tell you they are there but do you believe me? I would say not, for there is no way I can prove it to you."

"I think I am-"

173

"Overly fond of the malmsey wine. I know that, sire, and I would wish it were not so."

"Is there anything I can do?"

"Stop drinking?"

George burst into laughter and then wished he hadn't, the noise seemed to rebound around his head and burst out of his ears.

"God's teeth, but that hurts!"

"Does Your Grace need any more reason to decline the offer of wine when it is offered?"

"It would seem an insult to one's host to refuse."

"Maybe it would, but Your Grace asked for advice on how to break the fondness for the wine and I merely offered a solution."

"I need-"

George struggled to the edge of the bed and sat holding his face in both hands as if it were about to fall off and break on the flags at his suddenly cold feet.

"Come." Durian helped him to his feet and somehow got him to the garderobe, standing back politely as George relieved himself of what felt like several flagons of fluid. What a waste, he told himself peevishly, watching the arcing stream. What an unbelievable waste.

He turned back to Durian who was holding out his mantle, surely knowing he would feel cold after the warmth of the down mattress. "Sometimes I think you make a better squire than those I employ to take care of me, Durian," he muttered, clutching the edges of the mantle around him as he walked back toward the bed.

"They only work for you, sire, they do not carry affection for you," Durian said quietly and George nodded. It was that which made the difference. Only affection spoke of another person's needs without their having to express it in the form of a request or a command. He sat down and closed his eyes against the light.

"Do you have word of my brother the king? How he fares in captivity?" His eyes blinked open and he stared at Durian, trying to stop the room from going around by concentrating on one thing.

Durian laughed. "You make him sound like a fierce animal entrapped for the first time, sire!" He stopped laughing and looked at George. "In Christ's name, so he is! You saw that and I did not! I must be slipping!" He dismissed the squire who was patiently waiting for orders. "I will attend to His Grace this morning. Be gone and get yourself some food."

The young man bowed and, with a relieved look, smiled at George and hurried away.

Durian brought a bowl of water over and began George's morning shave, talking as he did so.

"I did not see it. I think of him as the Rose of Rouen still, not as the Lion of London which he, of a surety, is these days, standing against the earl as he has, but I ask you, sire, what happened with your brother the king these days before he was captured? It was as if he did not foresee the insurrections before his eyes when all others knew of it and he was told of it and yet-"

"I would like to think it was that he could not and would not believe I would turn against him," George said solemnly. "He might have believed it of our cousin of Warwick but his own brother?"

"Could I ask Your Grace-"

"Why I turned against my own brother?"

Durian smiled as he helped George with his clothes. "No. It is not a question I would ask of you for I doubt you truly know the answer yourself: it is made up of many things, resentment from childhood, being set aside in later life, being ignored in matters of state and responsibility – need I go on?"

"No." George stared at the floor, wondering if it was actually tilting or just looked that way. I need to curb the drinking, he told himself again. It's important.

He looked up, with an effort. "So, what did you want to ask me, Durian?"

"How does it feel to hold the king of England prisoner?"

"Disregarding the fact that the king happens to be my blood relation, quite extraordinary, although at this moment my head does not wish to contain any feelings whatsoever. It contains nothing whatsoever, as it happens, outside of a dull ache."

He stood up, settling his feet into his boots whilst running a hand through his hair, smoothing and ruffling it at the same time.

"Is there word of my lady wife, Durian? How fares she whilst I have been in battle and in breach of my matrimonial duties?"

"The duchess is well, learning her duties, learning the names of all who are in your home, sire. Do not give the Lady Isobel a moment of worrisome thought, but turn your mind to that which is ahead of you, a conference with your cousin of Warwick and decisions to make regarding your brother the king. Of a surety these decisions would be easier were you not blood related to the people concerned!"

The door opened and Peke entered just as Durian spoke. He nodded his agreement. "Your Fool speaks well, Your Grace, it would be easier for you if you were not related to the king, for a start!"

"But I am." George sighed and put both hands to his head. "I am and I know it makes everything much more difficult. Life is difficult. I am not at all certain of our future, I wish I could be."

The door was closed on eavesdroppers. Peke held out a letter he had drafted on George's instruction, creating new positions in his household. George glanced at it, groaned as his eyes failed to focus clearly on Peke's impeccable handwriting, handed it back and gestured to take it away. "I will deal with it later. Right now I cannot see properly."

"Your Grace has a long and tiresome day ahead of him," Peke said formally.

George snorted. "Peke, no one is here but Durian and myself. Speak freely! God's teeth, I cannot stand this ache!"

"I'll ask your physician for a draught for you, sire."

"Shortly, Durian, shortly. For the moment, let me try and concentrate, with your help, on what Peke is trying to say to me."

"Your cousin of Warwick is elated at his capture, sire, but you cannot allow this elation to blind him, or yourself, to the decisions which need to be made. Are you going to make an effort to dislodge your brother from the throne of England and assume that role yourself? Are you about to take on Parliament and the country?"

"What is your understanding of how Warwick sees the situation, Peke?"

The narrow face drew lines of thought from brow to jawline. George waited, prepared to stand as long as it took for the ache to recede and Peke to formulate his thoughts. They were invariably worth waiting for.

"I believe Warwick sees great glory ahead, sire, but I also believe he knows the inherent dangers of what is about to transpire. Your brother the king, of a surety, will not be held for long before he begins to roar his unhappiness and God knows that man can roar when he wishes!"

"I referred to him as a lion earlier, I think." George looked at Durian. "Well, one of us did, anyway."

"So, decisions need to be taken, sire, whether you are ready for them or not."

"You're right, Peke. Maybe I'll feel better with food in my stomach, to settle the acid left over from last night. I knew my cousin could drink but I never knew he could drink that much and still remain coherent!"

"Come, sire, it is time..."

It was time. His return to the world of politics and decision-making was long overdue, while he had slept life had carried on, possibly decisions were made without his knowledge. It would not do. The drinking would have to be cut back somehow. A vow he made again to himself and wondered if he could sustain it.

"Durian, get my physician to make up that draught for me, would you? Peke, I have a thought, before we leave this chamber and others might hear us. Could you possibly arrange for someone to water my wine? I know this is sacrilege and it pains me as much as the ache in my head does to even suggest it but I can act drunk with the best of them if I have to. I just do not want to be drunk."

Peke looked at him closely, then nodded. "I understand. You wish to remain in control. In that I see a hint of your brother of Gloucester, sire, who also wishes to remain in control. I also believe he does the same thing, allows his wine to be watered without others knowing of it so he can appear to be drinking with them but is taking half the amount they are."

"I didn't know that," George muttered as they walked out of the room. "I didn't know that but am glad to hear it. At last I can say I share something with my brother of Gloucester."

Now, he thought, let me share something with my cousin of Warwick, words to ensure that the future of the kingdom is placed firmly in my hands. And to hell with Ned's feelings!

Chapter 22

The one thing you are not doing, oh shades or ghosts or angels or whoever you are, those who are rippling the arras and flickering the flames beyond that which is natural and normal for this time of year and the wood which is burning, is asking me questions. Why are you not asking, Clarence, did you ever give up the desire to take the crown of England? So, as you are not asking it, I will say it for you and give you my honest answer: no. Even as the royal children came, one by one, even as the boy Edward arrived, I held on to my dream.

For a while the dream was within my grasp. I walked down to the Hall at Warwick where Ned paced before the hearth, where he turned as I approached, turned on scuffed heels from the pacing and stamping he had done. I saw the anger within him, well disguised but there, behind the beaming smile, the handclasp, the good wishes uttered for my state of health and I wondered if it were that obvious that I drank too much the night before. Damn his eyes, he looked fit and well and as if nothing had passed his lips but small ale and water!

"We greet thee well," he said, as if he were in his own court and greeting his own courtiers, not prisoner of his brother and cousin, not confined to a castle by armed guards who were only too pleased, it seemed, to ally themselves with the Warwick cause.

I spoke with Ned as if indeed we were meeting in his court, as if we were equals, not king-turned-prisoner and duke-turned-possibly king. I was doing well until Warwick proposed a drink and I had a mazer handed to me before Peke could get the new instructions in place. The wine began the hammering in my head again and I found it hard to concentrate.

Ned admitted he had under-estimated our insurrection, the loyalty our cousin of Warwick could generate, admitted he had been laggardly in fighting back and avowed that had he done so, he would have won through, not been a prisoner. Of a surety he was full of confidence and I wondered what trick he had in mind.

He talked of the battle of Edgecote and my heart began to ache suddenly. I had put away the thought of those who died and now it had come back to assault me. Edgecote was a disastrous battle, 5000 dead. The thought of it, a battle which Warwick and I instigated, fought, won, cost 5000 lives. And the execution of two Woodvilles. I wondered if that too would come back to assault me at some time. Ear Rivers and his son John, beheaded on Warwick's and my orders. I thought nothing of it at the time, caught up in the glory of battle, leaving behind me the sickening fear of dying, the feeling of blood draining from my face, the seeming inability to swing a battle axe or sword, the fear of losing control of my bowels, such was the intensity of the terror which swept over me. And then, in a moment, it had gone and in its place came a screaming joy at slashing and killing, at seeing men go down and be trampled by destriers and feet, at blocking a blow which would have taken my arm or my head from my body and in return taking an arm or almost a head from a body, seeking the weak points in armour, delighting in the gush and rush of blood. It was a time of fear and exhilaration, of kill or be killed for despite my banners and pennants, announcing who I was, there were those who would have taken me down and killed me without a second thought.

Edgecote. A living nightmare. I must have showed it, for Ned asked if all was well, revealing what appeared to be genuine concern. I excused myself on the grounds of too much drink and he sympathised. Of a surety my brother the king had indulged in many a night's drinking session and appeared the following morning looking ten years older than he really was.

My brother the king's detention did not go well. Warwick moved him first to Middleham and then to Pontefract but nothing went as it should. Nothing. We could not rule adequately in his name and we could not rule in our own name, for the country as a whole was not with us. We tried, I tried, the trick of bringing doubt on his birth, knowing even as I did so that it would hurt our lady mother but oh the glittering prize of the crown of England put that beyond my reasoning at the time! It did not work. The time was used for knight to set claim against knight, for uprisings, for problems which needed to be resolved. I did my best; history will show that, I did my best to mediate with problems, writing endless letters to try and resolve things, to be the calming influence. It all seemed hopeless.

I confess now to the flames leaping endlessly and silently in the hearth here in the Tower that the day Hastings, together with my brother of Gloucester and a huge armed escort, came to visit and rode away with my brother the king was a relief.

I recall standing with Warwick, recall the glowering look he wore and forbore to speak with him at that time. His dreams had just vanished with the armed men but then again, so had mine and mine were surely of a more elevated status than his, or were they? Did he seek to control the country through me? These are questions I did not ask at the time and it is now too late to ask of anyone, even if Warwick himself were not long dead on the battlefield, killed trying to flee, cut down by those boiling with the blood lust of battle which takes us all at the time. We see nothing but enemy, we feel nothing but the euphoria that battle brings. It is only when the battle ceases and we stand amid the dead and dying, the wounded and the grievously heartbroken, that the euphoria dies and leaves in its place the emptiness, the uselessness of what we have just done. Achievement? Count it as nothing.

I returned to Isobel, tried to resume as if life had not been disrupted by so many happenings, as if the crown had not been within my grasp and suddenly snatched from it. I made a reconciliation, of a kind, with my brother the king. I was aware of his seething anger, his need for retribution, for revenge, felt it in his demeanour when in my presence, or should that be when I was in his presence; after all he was king. Many of my problems with my brother arose from the fact that although part of me accepted he was king, another part saw him only as my brother of March and resented his authority over me. Foolish? Maybe. Natural? Very possibly. Many of my brother's problems with me, I believe, arose from the fact he could not or would not indict me as a traitor at that time or order some kind of punishment, physical or financial, to give him back his dignity which had been sore troubled by being taken prisoner and confined under guard to the grounds of Warwick's homes.

I discovered later that from the moment of my brother the king's release from our captivity he began to shower my brother of Gloucester with honours, estates and political roles. I was then twenty years old, which means my brother of Gloucester was just seventeen years old and was Constable of England, among other things. Did I resent it? Of a surety I did. But I had cast my lot in with my cousin of Warwick and there I remained, knowing of my brother the king's burning resentment but not realising how it would, eventually, bring about my total downfall and my incarceration here in the Tower. He had his revenge after all.

Should I here raise the spectre of the death of the hapless harmless Henry? Dare I walk that path? Who is to hear me if I do? Ah, memory, do not play me false, it is not yet time to talk of this, is it?

Mayhap it is. For I am speaking of my brother the king's desire for revenge and in that desire, I sense and detect cruelty. Have I not said already that he is cruel, in that he holds me here without my knowing when the end will come or, even worse, how it will come? Let me then speak of the death of King Henry in passing. I knew of some of it but was not part of it, so really, truthfully, memory, this is not part of my life, is it? Only insofar as it concerns the two men I know as my brothers. But did that quiet king die by starvation, natural causes or by execution? The stories are mixed, the information scant, the final judgement known only to God and those directly involved. I give thanks to God I was not.

I know only this: my brother the king was cruel enough to order the execution of a rival king, of a surety he was. My brother of Gloucester was - now, the question – strong enough to ensure the order was carried out or weak enough to ensure the order was carried out? Would he have taken the stance that Edward was the rightful king or would he just obey because of his loyalty to the family, to his brother above all others?

I do not know. I will not know until I go to my just rewards and eventually find that harmless old man and ask him what happened right there in the Tower. Then, only then, will all be revealed.

Or will it?

Chapter 23

It was as if life proceeded on two levels: the top level was the life where George was doing his best to cope with a reduced income as the king took estates away from him and handed them out to others, rewarding this one and that for services and a second, lower level where he was still discussing with Warwick the need for a further uprising, even for civil war, in order to restore their positions in life. Dangerous games: in one way, troubling to the mind, for so much could and probably would go wrong; in another way, exciting for danger added a spice to life that might otherwise be missing. George often thought, as he sat through meetings, discussions, or his own courts, where petitioners came with problems relating to estates he still owned, that there was nothing quite like power to stimulate the senses. Ordering executions had to be the ultimate thrill of all, to take someone's life, to render the family of the dead person homeless if he so chose: small people, he told himself, small people held in the palm of one hand, life and death my gift to dispense as I wish. Who needs to be king when you can do this as duke?

Occasionally a letter would arrive from Lady Cecily, advising, coercing, all but pleading with him to reconcile himself permanently with his brother the king, to end the ongoing breach and restore family harmony once more. It was tempting in some ways, but in other ways was an impossible dream. Too much had gone on between them and he was too much in thrall to Warwick to make any kind of move away from him now. Sometimes he answered the letters, mostly he burned them, along with his thoughts of reconciliation. It was appealing, he admitted that to himself, but it was also such a retrograde step when they had come so far. The heady days when he actually had control of his brother the king, actually had him in captivity, seemed like a very long time in the past but the thrill, the euphoria that such an act had given him, was still a very present memory.

But beneath all this ran a deeper thought, one he rarely allowed space, for it hurt too much when he did. It was a thought that sometimes surfaced during the moments of silence in Mass, a longing that had no name in his vocabulary but which was made up of an intense desire to return to Fotheringhay, to have his brothers with him, to have his lord father and lady mother back in overall control of the castle and of his life, to be able to romp with puppies and dogs, to ride where he wished, to hawk and hunt, to party and shed the responsibilities of being in control of so much property and so many people. I would not wish not to be married, he told himself in a moment of honesty, but I would do without all the responsibilities that go with it, if I could.

Unfortunately it was not to be. There was no going back on anything; family, commitments, steps taken, battles fought, taking a king prisoner – some things were so huge, so problematical, that they could not be talked away by anyone.

He walked out of the chapel with Warwick at his side, sensing the rising excitement in his cousin.

"This time, George, this time we take victory! I promise you, we have enough backing to make the honours ours!"

George silently doubted it, for somewhere deep in his mind he knew with a certainty that nothing was as simple or straightforward as Warwick wanted it to be. At times he felt his cousin was a master tactician, other times he thought he over-simplified everything.

Just as at times I like him, other times I don't, he thought. Can I not make up my mind once and for all about this man? Ever does his character slip and slide away from me. Of a surety he is a complex man but are we not all complex people really? Do we not have many roles to play in our lives? But somehow, in some way, he has more roles to play than others I could think of. I wish –

Before the thought *I trusted him* could be brought into words, Warwick's secretary was there, holding a sheaf of paper and wearing an anxious look. The work had begun, even before they had touched their first food of the day.

"George, we can count on-" Warwick was going over the papers, checking names, anxiously seeking confirmation. I know, thought George, we've been over this countless times. "Sir Robert Welles, for one," Warwick continued.

Why tell me the obvious? George's thoughts ran on. The man wears my livery, takes his orders from me. I trust him more...

Sometimes he had to guard his thoughts. Sometimes they were so strong that they threatened to appear as expressions which anyone could read and that could be dangerous. In any event, he trusted his cousin, didn't he? He did, didn't he? Warwick was not a man to cross at any time, but particularly now, when he was planning an insurrection, when all was so tenuous, when plans were so fluid.

A bitter February wind rattled the shutters and caused a draught to ripple around the room. George pulled his mantle closer around him and sighed, wishing for warmer weather and more congenial company. Christmas, the last time he had felt really relaxed and happy, had been spent with his wife with only occasional visits to court to ensure Ned had not forgotten his existence. He limited those visits, knowing full well that his brother the king still burned with resentment and was looking for a way of taking revenge. Did Ned know that he was spending time with Warwick? Comments had been made, on surface off hand but those who knew the king well would take them as commands, that the two should not be together anywhere at any time. As usual George ignored the commands and continued to meet with Warwick, the better to discuss the insurrection and those who were likely to support them, but not very often. Spies were everywhere, surely some of the meetings would be reported but perhaps not all. Sometimes you had to trust and sometimes you had to take chances. What am I gambling with here, George had asked himself? My future, my life, my livelihood? Would Ned make Isobel a widow so soon or would family loyalties hold his hand? Whatever, it is making life more interesting, more challenging. I need much more than the occasional oyer and terminer! I need more than court chatter and gossip and I need more than the crumbs thrown from my brother's table. Surely I am entitled to more, am I not?

When he asked Durian for his opinion on that question, he got the answer he expected from his loyal devoted servant and friend. "Entitled, sire? It is your birthright."

It was that birthright he was ready to fight for, come what may.

Poor Isobel, ever the faithful wife, busy supervising his home, waiting to become pregnant, to give him the heir he wanted, was not the helpmeet he had hoped for. Somehow she lacked the fire he wanted in a wife. He sought someone to work alongside him, to stand with him against the tides of life that would take a man down if he did not stand strong against them. She supported his insurrection because her father was involved, not because she thought the cause was right and justified. She supported him because he was her husband, not because she believed in his cause. "Women!" he had declared to Peke, throwing a mazer across the room in anger. "Will they see no further than the end of the needle they sew with?"

187

"Your Grace," Peke had begun but gave up when he saw the look George turned on him.

"I tell you, there are times I wish I were without the encumbrance of a wife and home, Peke! I wish I were an adventurer, out roaming the land, taking what I need when I need it. I wish-"

But then he fell silent, for he knew, deep in that part of him which held the truth, that he loved comfort, luxury and security and that would be denied him if he were such an adventurer.

Peke, ever the diplomat, was quietly busy with his papers, pretending the words needed no response. Nothing anyone could say would reach the duke when he was in that frame of mind. George knew it and accepted that no one would try and reason with him.

The memory of that last raging temper haunted him as he listened to Warwick planning to recruit this one and that, to move men here and send out an array there. He had realised that throwing temper fits like that got him nothing more than a violent headache which took hours, sometimes days, to leave him, headaches so bad they made him feel sick and rendered him hardly able to see. It was an object lesson in not losing his temper but sometimes he felt pushed beyond endurance and his only resort was violence, resulting in his throwing things, storming around his chambers and venting his anger on all who came within sight or sound of him. Later he would be found holding his head with both hands, calling for his physician to bring something, anything, to take the pain away. Isobel would sit with him, talking quietly and calmly, seeking to still the tensions racking his body and making the headache worse, putting cold wet cloths on his forehead, smoothing his hair and rubbing his hands. Sometimes he tolerated her ministrations, other times he bid her leave him and lay staring up at the hangings, visualising the pain as a series of groups of men-at-arms stamping their way across his skull, iron shod boots leaving their impression at every step, longing for it to go away.

I promise not to lose my temper again, he said silently, watching Warwick busy with papers and words, wondering all the time if this really was the opportunity they sought, if this really was the time when the tide would turn in their direction.

"Unfortunately my brother the king has the backing of so many," he said carefully, dropping the words into an unusual gap in the non-stop torrent of words from Warwick.

"Your point is, George? My point is that your brother the king all but walked into our hands once. He could well do it again!"

"Yes, we had him in our hands, once, and allowed him to walk away."

Warwick snorted. "He rode away! With Gloucester, Hastings and a virtual army to guard him! What could we do but let him go?"

"Fight back?" George suggested, knowing full well Warwick had no answer for that one. It earned him a look of utter disgust and contempt and he resolved not to say another word on the subject.

As Warwick resumed his litany of who could be called upon and when, George allowed himself to dwell on the thought that he wished for more congenial company. Warwick was intransigent, belligerent, over fond of his own voice and of food and wine, besotted with a sense of power and his own importance. He was not a comfortable companion and George longed for the freedom of his own home, where his staff knew his needs and desires and catered to them without his having to remind them of anything. There the days passed smoothly, no doubt due to Isobel's constant efforts with the staff but that was part of her duties. He lived the life of a wealthy powerful duke. But here, in Warwick's domain, he felt more like a callow youth, unable to make

189

a sensible suggestion, unable to ask for wine when he wanted it, or time on his own when he needed it.

God grant that this time all goes to plan, he prayed fervently and silently, getting carefully to his feet and pleading the need for relief to stop Warwick in mid sentence.

Alone in the chamber set aside for him, George stood at the window, the cold wind biting into his skin, cleansing his thoughts. He knew he was afraid of the coming battles, afraid that he would win and it would cause injury or even death to members of his family and equally afraid he would lose and all would be lost, his wealth, his estates, his way of life. What man was ever caught in such a dilemma? Abruptly he turned and strode out of the room. He would confront Warwick now, still doubtless poring over the papers in his study, and tell him he was leaving for London. Time was getting short; if Ned was to be delayed, it had to be done now.

Suddenly the whole atmosphere, the conspiracy, the planning, was too much for him. He sought relief in action; his pent up restless energy would not permit him to remain acquiescent while Warwick continued his seemingly endless machinations.

It was time to be on the move. Much depended on what he could do. I am needed, he thought suddenly; I am essential to this whole plan. Now let me prove it!

Chapter 24

Ah, the days when I could do that, stride out of a chamber, demand that a horse brought for me, watch the men-at-arms scurry to find their mounts so we could ride out, are so long gone they are a distant and lonely memory.

Baynards Castle is a large imposing place, quite magnificent in every way. It is surprisingly small when you are there with a brother who shows his animosity in every word, every movement, even by his mere presence on the dais at meals. He sat far from me during the services we attended. My prayers were not as devout as they should have been; I seemed to spend the time watching my brother the king and wondering if he knew of my feelings, my plans, my ambitions. If he did, there was little revealed in his muttered words, mostly uttered for the sake of politeness and decorum, not of brotherly friendship or affection. I know my lady mother was distressed but she showed such small sign of it I doubt my brother the king noticed. He was far too busy being autocratic and overbearing to his little treacherous brother. It was almost too much to endure for two days but it was needed. Welles was pardoned and my brother the king was delayed, as planned. Such good plans!

I remember we, my brother the king and I, rode in silence for some distance the next day, then I returned to London and immediately set out again for Warwick. Freedom, that word that means so much to a prisoner, I rode, I went where I wanted! I wrote to my brother the king saying I was going to Warwick and would bring him to join the king's army. I recall the honeyed words with which he responded. I recall feeling tremendously guilty at that, almost wishing it were true.

But, like all good plans, it all fell apart as letters were intercepted, apparently, as proclamations were issued and my brother the king issued his orders, including one to me to disband and join him. Warwick received the same order.

We had been close. Damn it to hell, Fate, whatever, we had been close, had we not? Were we not on the edge of success when it collapsed around us? To be ordered to disband our levies and rejoin the king was the ultimate insult to people who had almost, almost, managed to upset the balance of power and gain it for themselves. Once again that crown almost, but not quite, sat on my head.

This same head which right now is threatening to burst asunder with the pressure inside its bony casing. This same head which houses my thoughts, my dreams, my long lost ambitions and my sadness. Of a surety there are far too many of those!

Warwick suggested we pretend to submit whilst appealing for help. Warwick had many plans and most of them fell apart like cheap linen in the wash house when subjected to scrutiny. My brother the king was not of a mind to issue clemency and was determined on a battle. So we withdrew and made our way to the coast, defeated, heading for exile rather than confront an angry king who had just staved off an insurrection. Edward would not be in the best of humours. We decided to leave whilst we could. It was a sudden, instinctive reaction to the situation and although my cousin of Warwick declared it was not a defeat but a tactical withdrawal, I knew the truth. I could use the words and almost save some of my self-esteem but it was very low at that time. This I confess to these stone walls. None knew of it, for I never spoke of it, not then, not later. Such dreams as I had were fading fast, for despite the support I knew I could generate, geography, demography, Ned's superior position and men's weaknesses combined to ensure that I could not gather together a sufficiently strong and – more importantly – loyal group to do battle.

The biggest problem of all, one that never ever passed my lips, nor stayed in my conscious mind for longer than the flicker of a candle flame for fear of someone detecting it, was that I really did not wish to be there. I really did not wish to be fighting my brother the king. I was heartsick and stomach sick, food roiled and rebelled, turned sour and burned, rendering me incapable at times of being able to eat properly or rest easy in my bed at night. It was not supposed to be that way; a knight had a code of honour to uphold, chivalric standards to maintain, fearsome courage in the face of all opposition, laughing as he downs a goblet of fiery wine before charging into battle. Would that it were so! Would that my body could have followed the dictates of the code of the knight! Would that this poor helpless individual could have thrown off the fears, the terrors of the night, the dichotomy of loyalty one to the other, could have lost the sick apprehension of watching a battle plan fall apart through lack of support or simply through plans that were not good enough when actually in progress.

Who is there to offer a defence for me for that time? I was but twenty-one years of age, married, wealthy beyond most men's dreams, fighting my own brother and his army for the sake of my own ambition, bolstered by my cousin of Warwick who doubtless had great plans for afterwards. I could not put from my mind the thoughts that he was making use of me, that he saw me as some kind of callow youth who could be bid to take part in insurrections for Warwick's own ambitions, not always for mine. Mayhap he saw a better future for his daughter should the insurrection go our way, mayhap he just saw his own power growing in proportion to the hold he would maintain over me. Ever did I sense this worm of distrust and wondered why it was there, what was making me look to his motives more than I should or would otherwise have done. Was Durian right, was I truly fey?

Word was sent to my home: my heavily pregnant wife came to meet us at the port accompanied by her ladies, our servants bringing such supplies as we needed, such horses as were required, such money as we would need to see us through an indeterminate period of our lives.

Then we took ship for Calais.

The spies had been hard at work. Reports went back to London so fast I wonder they did not fly there of their own accord. How else could it have been that our tumultuous storm tossed journey ended with my own brother arranging for us to be denied landing in that port. Who does not know that my wife, no sailor in calm conditions, was so traumatised by the storm and the seas which tossed our craft to and fro that the child she birthed was dead when it arrived in this world? Who does not know – no, they know not for I have not spoken of it to a single living person – that my heart was torn out of me that day. It was torn out of me, wrapped in cloth and dropped over the side of the ship, along with all my hopes, dreams and ambitions. Isobel went into labour on the journey to the coast, the storm aided her not at all, the midwife was capable but overwhelmed by the conditions and my wife's inability to fight the labour pains, or so she said. The blood loss was tremendous, the shrieking screams were agonising to hear when nothing could be done about it. I stalked the deck in fear for her life and, if that were spared, her sanity for she hated the sea and was terrified of the birth, that I knew well for she had confided it in our midnight talks when all the house was still. I thought her strong enough to carry a child, to my everlasting regret this son was still born, no breath, no beat of heart. Or so I was told. And so I believe it to be.

194

Finally we found harbour and sanctuary, for a while. Isobel was in need of a long period of recuperation. I could not be sure to give it to her.

Of a surety we caused many problems in France; we were fugitives, we had need of shelter, of sustenance and clothing and sought it where we could. Of a surety it was a time I would rather forget and, as these are my memories, oh shades and ghosts and those who haunt me at this sad desolate lonely time, be aware I will dismiss the thoughts that so trouble me.

I lie even to myself. Not all my hopes, dreams and ambitions were buried at sea along with my poor dead child who never saw my face or drew breath on this earth. My dreams truly died when Warwick arranged a marriage between the Prince of Wales and his younger daughter, Anne.

Allying his family to the Lancastrian regime. I could not believe he would do that, I did not believe he had arranged this without speaking with me about it. Was I not family, was this not my wife's sister?

Never was a youth more unpleasant in his outlook and his manner; never was a marriage more doomed to be made in hell than to ally that – person – with the shy, mouse-like innocent Anne who was no more than fourteen years at that time and naïve beyond belief. I surveyed the marriage in my thoughts and I knew then, with absolute certainty, that Warwick's plans were way beyond those of manipulating a mere duke, even if he was brother to the king of England.

I knew too that once again I was second best. If I thought losing my child was a sword thrust to my heart, then this was surely the stroke which severed my head from my body. It went straight back to my younger days, brought back all the hurts, the 'never quite good enough' feelings I endured then and fought against all my later life. It went straight back to them and revived them as surely as a necromancer breathes life into a dead animal and makes it dance once more.

I would fain have turned my face back to my brother at that time and begged forgiveness, taken what retribution he inflicted and endured it without a sound. I would fain have deserted my cousin of Warwick and left him to his own nefarious plans and schemes.

Why did I not do it then?

Chapter 25

England. No more grating of French voices, no more often unidentifiable food on the plate and no more enforced accommodation with unwilling hosts. At last, home again with good ale, good English food and his wardrobe restored so once again he could dress in a manner befitting his rank and he could relax once more. Or so he told Durian, as they discussed his exile and all that had gone on whilst he had been abroad. A successful Lancastrian uprising, his brother the king in exile – just for once let Ned suffer the hardships of being in that unwelcoming country, he thought with great glee – a king oddly unprepared for the return of the Warwick faction and the victory was theirs. There was a lingering sadness that his brother of Gloucester had chosen to go into exile with Ned but ever was his brother's loyalty to his king more than any other. Had he heard of the marriage of the woman he said he loved so much? If he had, what effect had it on a heart so controlled it was a wonderment it continued to beat of its own accord? Perhaps that was one of the reasons for leaving England, to leave some memories and unwelcome thoughts behind. George knew full well that it never worked that way, no matter where you were, sadness and bitterness accompanied you if it was there in the first instance.

Durian had been busy, along with the other senior members of George's staff. They had maintained the homes still in his name, sought to restore his reputation and worked for his return. Durian had gathered a mountain of information, all of which would need to be sifted and assimilated to bring George up to date with the happenings at court and in every other major city.

"I need to talk to Your Grace about the words I picked up from a member of the clergy."

George's interest was piqued immediately. It was not often that Durian spoke with such seriousness about an item of information; it had to be of great interest. But he also realised that Durian wanted them to be alone when they discussed it, which made it even more frustratingly interesting.

"As you wish, Durian," he said as casually as he could. Durian smiled his all too knowing smile and carried on with the information he had gained during George's enforced exile.

Later that day, with a mazer of malmsey wine in one hand, the other resting on the head of one of his devoted wolfhounds, George surveyed the papers on his table and decided to ignore them for the time being. Isobel had something she wanted to talk about, some gathering of the Nevilles and her need for another gown to be made for her to attend, one that was unlike anything she had in her collection already. George could not deny her anything, he was already prepared to tell her to go ahead but knew she found pleasure in the telling, the minute detail of what it would be like and what lace would be attached here and there. He was patient with what he referred to as 'house matters', knowing it was part of the daily round of living, even though at times he wanted to dismiss it all and stride out to the stables, grab the reins of his chestnut stallion and take off for a headlong gallop across the countryside, letting the movement of his favourite animal and the rush of the wind take all his worries from him. Warwick had told him not to go anywhere without a full armed guard, for there was still insurrection in the air, still many unresolved problems, without the ones they were about to generate in their ongoing efforts to take over the country for themselves. Someone somewhere might have instructions to quietly dispose of the troublesome duke of Clarence. George doubted that his brother the king would go quite that far but whether others in his court would feel the same was another matter. The lessons of the chance remark which had caused the murder of Thomas Becket were not lost on the duke.

My heart's not in the battle any more, he admitted finally, not really. But there was no going back. There never is a way to go back, to unpick the threads of the acts you had committed and their consequences. What you had to do was live with the consequences, whether good or bad. Although his heart was not in it, the desire to be king was still there, simmering beneath the cultivated smile of indifference and quiet acceptance that he showed to the world. Warwick believed him pliable and biddable, Isobel found him a willing and acquiescent husband, the staff could not believe he was not storming around in his ferocious and fearsome rages and his lady mother congratulated him in her letters on a change of attitude. What she had heard, what she had surmised, he didn't know and didn't dare ask. What would she say if she knew he was prepared to use the bastardy rumour to further his cause, despite the fact he did not believe it for a second? No doubt he would go down in her estimation but that would be nothing new. I am proud to be duke of Clarence but King George would sound so much better to my ears and my heart. But let none know of this ongoing desire of mine, let them think I am content with my lot. It is easier for me to manipulate them if they know little of my real thoughts.

What of the thoughts of King Henry right now, restored to the throne of England yet again? What are his feelings now? Would he have preferred the quieter life he had before politics once again invaded and created their own confusion and problems?

Isobel entered his room, surrounded by a flurry of ladies in bright colours, bringing with them various perfumes and high giggling voices. They displeased him but it was Isobel's choice to surround herself with those

199

ladies, not his. Of a surety he would dismiss them all and find people who were sensible and quiet in their demeanour but he knew that his wife took pleasure in their company. For the most part he tried to ignore them.

"How good it is to be back!" Isobel sighed with happiness, sitting down next to George and fanning herself ostentatiously with a beautiful jewelled fan. "Why do you keep your rooms so hot, George?"

"I cannot bear to be cold," he replied, glancing at the women who were smiling and simpering as if trying to attract his attention. It was something he deplored. Did they not understand he had taken a vow of devotion when he married? His brother of Gloucester apparently had a bastard child somewhere but then, he was unmarried and entitled to populate the court with children should he so wish. That was a burning pain somewhere deep in George's mind too, following the tragic death of their first born, Isobel had not become pregnant again and George longed for children of his own, heirs to the name and the estates he had fought for and won against all the odds. Won from his brother of Gloucester, won by his servitude to his brother the king and now by his own uprising. He needed heirs to ensure the land and the money remained in his family, not returned to the Treasury to be dispersed amongst those who did not merit having such a reward.

Isobel chattered on about a great gathering of Nevilles and the gown she just had to have made, not to mention the Christmas revels. George grunted his assent, nodded in the right places, told her to choose whatever was right for her, to ensure the seamstress was a good one and then ostentatiously reached for the paperwork. Isobel took the hint and rose; her ladies fluttering around her as she walked to the door. George would see her again at dinner but that was always a formal occasion when marital talk was not so free flowing.

When the room was quiet again, he put the papers back on the desk, picked up his mazer and gloomily swirled the wine around before drinking it. It isn't what I expected, he told himself. I wanted – what did I want? A companion that matched me in intellect and wit, knowledge and interests, someone of bold mind and inner strength. Oh she is a decorative wife, she has her own charms and there is no end to the delight I take in her body, but she is not of the mind that I am. It is as if we speak different languages, as if she is here in England speaking French and I am only speaking English.

Exile had not been good for the marriage. It had imposed strains that were difficult to overcome and her long period of convalescence following the death of the child had made it much harder. He had tried to be a good husband, to abstain from the demands he would otherwise have made of her, tried to comfort her over the loss which had torn him apart as much as it had Isobel but somehow had not been able to share his grief with her and so she thought he had not been as affected by it as she had. A small misunderstanding that somehow had not resolved itself.

He sighed and leaned back in his chair, propping his heels on the edge of the desk. I am so tired, he thought, so very tired and this pain in my head is worrisome, to say the very least. Maybe I am drinking too much again, despite all my good intentions.

Durian came in, closing the door after him. "I did not think you would wish to wait until after Compline for the news, sire," he said with barely concealed excitement.

George swung his feet back down to the floor and sat up straight, the pain temporarily forgotten. "You're right, Durian, as usual. Do tell!"

"It's one Stillington, sire, a man of some consequence in the church hierarchy and known in court circles. Bishop, I do believe, Bath and Wells? It is said, and I have to insist I cannot prove it yet, that he is aware of a pre-contract of marriage between one Lady Eleanor Butler and your brother the king. That would mean..."

"How much is he aware, Durian?" asked George, his pulse racing as he considered the implications of such a piece of news. A possibility that the marriage to the Wydeville mare was likely to be illegal. Which meant...

"I have to find out more, sire. I have to find out much more but I could not wait to give you this part of the information. I do not know if he was witness to the contract or assisted at the ceremony or – I do not know yet. But I will find out. You know I will."

"Is my sainted brother really living in illegal partnership with Elizabeth Wydeville, Durian? If so..."

"Your Grace follows my thinking precisely." Durian spoke with the quiet assurance of one who is certain of his own thoughts. "I would not mention this to anyone, anywhere, at any time, sire, until we are sure and until we can use it in the right context."

"That means controlling my thoughts completely. I can do that if I curb the drinking and I have been meaning to do that, as you well know."

"It would be wise, sire. All things in moderation, as your brother of Gloucester knows and practices."

"Damn it, Durian, Dickon knows too much about control and not enough about letting go occasionally! He doesn't enjoy life."

"Do you?"

The question was asked with bluntness without a courtesy title attached to it. George was shocked into silence for a few moments while he considered his response. Lie, and be known to be lying or be truthful and admit that which nagged constantly at his heart and mind. Either way it was not something he wanted to confront at this time but the question hung between them like smoke caused by a down draught in the great hall. It could not be ignored.

He sighed deeply and pushed a hand through his hair. He caught himself doing it, realised it was a trait his brother of Gloucester had and dropped his hand immediately. Some time had gone by and still he had not responded to the question. Durian stood, straight and rigid as a guard on duty outside the door, staring at George, willing him to reply.

"There has never been anything other than the truth between us." George spoke at last, breaking what was fast becoming a difficult and embarrassing silence. "There seems no need to disseminate the truth now, Durian. No, I do not enjoy life."

"As I thought."

"What is there to be done about it? I do not have the prize I sought, there is still a rift between myself and my brothers, my income is not as much as I would like and-"

"Your marriage is not as fruitful as you hoped."

Truth. Cold, blunt, unpalatable truth. George all but stepped back from the statement which carried a feeling he did not wish to confront, either. But there was no escaping the truth. He had always told Durian that truth was everything, he could disseminate facts and falsities with the best of them in court if it meant keeping others happy but face to face with the one person who knew him best, there was no hiding the truth.

"You're right."

"That, sire, is in your hands, or your flesh sword, if I may put it like that."

"No, it is in the hands, if not the body, of my lady wife who is not always willing and I will not take her against her will. When she comes to me, she comes with tenderness and willingness and it is in that a child will be conceived, not taken by force if it is not her wish."

"Others would not agree with you, sire."

"My brother of Gloucester would, of that I am sure. How I know this I cannot say, it is just a feeling."

"A rightful one. I would agree with you about your brother of Gloucester. I was thinking of your other brother."

"Edward? He has no need of force, he can and has charmed so many women I wonder there is one left in the land who has not succumbed to his inducements by now, apart from my sister-in-law and my wife!"

"There is your lady mother and your mother-in-law," observed Durian with a wry smile. "You're right, sire, there are so many women who have fallen for the king's charms. It is said he earns much money for his coffers by merely kissing a woman and then asking for her hard earned coins!"

George smiled at the thought and then the smile vanished. "Apart from that, Durian, I am content enough with my life."

"That is the first lie you have uttered in my presence when we have been alone, sire. I would hope that it will be the last!"

Rebuked, George stared at his Fool, at the knowing eyes and the even more knowing smile.

"I give in. I surrender. Is there anything you do not know about me?"

"No, sire, nothing at all. Any more than there is anything you do not know about me."

"I am content with this life, on the surface. Beneath the surface there are emotions which few know of and even fewer understand." He stopped, pressing one hand to the side of his head. Durian looked concerned and asked a silent question with raised eyebrows. "Nothing. A pain that comes and goes. I will ask for a draught later, to help dull it if it does not subside by itself."

"How long have you had this pain?"

"Oh, I don't know, it has come and gone for some time, a year? Maybe more. I do not recall now when it began. It is there, like a bad headache, then it goes and I am not troubled by it for some time."

"Today it troubles you?"

"Indeed it does. But it will go. Worry not, Durian, I am here for some time yet, or so the astrologer tells me."

"Ah, the faith you have in these people, sire, is a wonderment to me."

"They speak true of many things. I am told there is a child to come to me before the next year is out."

"That is something many could predict!"

George laughed. "Of a surety they could, but that was not their sole prediction. They spoke of my brothers' exile and of the king resuming his throne long before it happened."

"I cannot believe in such things myself, sire, forgive me for that. I believe in that which I can see, touch and smell for myself."

George raised an eyebrow. "What of your feyness, Durian, your farseeing?"

"Ah yes, but that is my own intuition. I rely not on the movement of stars and zodiacal calculations and the like."

"The Lord God works in mysterious ways and sometimes His will is not always shown clearly but through the workings of others."

Durian shrugged. "I prefer my own simple faith, sire. I say my prayers, He answers as best He can and together we do what we can for you."

George laughed again. "I can see there is no dissuading you from your position, so I will not try.

Now, shall we go to dine? I am sure I heard a summons to eat."

"Now I know you are all right, Your Grace. Food is ever something you enjoy. Let us see what the kitchen has prepared for us this night."

As he walked down the stairs to the hall, George turned a thought around in his mind. If Durian knew he was unhappy with this life, did his cousin know? If so, would that colour the way he perceived George and his part in the life of the Nevilles? It was something to watch out for, everything could be changed with a wrong word, a wrong expression.

I really do need to stop drinking, he told himself as he walked toward the dais and saw Isobel, pretty, smiling, welcoming, waiting for him. I could not bear to lose everything through a wrong move on my part, even if that which I have is not entirely that which I would wish to have. There are others far worse off than I; my brother of Gloucester has no wife at all. Briefly George wondered if his brother would find anyone to marry, now that the woman he loved had been forcibly married to someone else. Damn Warwick, he thought fiercely. In many ways he has been responsible for a lot of unhappiness. If God is righteous, surely He will rectify this situation, one way or another. I just wish I could see how it could be done.

There was a full mazer of malmsey wine waiting for him at his place on the dais. He raised it to his lips, sipped it and put it down again. Isobel looked puzzled, as if the wine did not please him but he smiled reassuringly at her and she resumed her conversation with the lady sitting beside her, one invited to the table that evening.

It will be hard to pretend I am drinking, he thought and harder to tell people I am not drinking so much. If it means losing the pain in my head, it is worth doing. If it means keeping a strict curb on my tongue, my expression and my thoughts, I will definitely do it. Of a surety there are greater problems to be faced than the fact of not drinking! He gazed at the mazer again, longing for the oblivion that the wine would bring him. It may be worth doing, he thought bitterly, but it is going to be hard. God's teeth, it is!

Chapter 26

At what point was the decision made to leave my cousin of Warwick and rejoin my brother the king? I am not certain. I know only this, disillusionment makes a mockery of dreams, failure makes a mockery of plans and ambitions and I am never one – oh listen to yourself, Clarence – I was never one for such debilitating thoughts. Ever did I seek to prove myself to be worthy of respect and attention and so, in the extremity of disillusionment, I went to my cousin and told him, quietly and carefully, I no longer wished to be part of his plans.

Of course he blustered and blundered and shouted and raged and drank heavily, as was his wont, but he could not argue with the fact most of my lands and estates, including my much loved home at Tutbury, had been taken from me and I was left with far less than I had before the whole sorry affair began. He had no family being pressured: for my part, my two brothers were in exile, my sisters were having difficulties because their husbands were not with them, my lady mother was pressuring me in the way only she could over various matters and in all the circumstances it seemed right and favourable to seek reconciliation with my family to restore my honour and my income. Both were important, for different reasons. Without honour a knight cannot survive. Without income a knight is an unwelcome burden on others. I would not be a beggar in my own land. I made my peace with Ned, my brother and my king – it mattered little at that point that another king occupied the throne of England and wore a crown, to me the crown and the throne belonged only to my brother – and I did the honourable thing and told Warwick myself that I was returning to the Yorks.

Of a surety he had suffered too; loss of land, loss of face, loss of ambition and I knew his bluster and ravings were as much a manifestation of his disappointment as it was anger that I was turning my back on him and taking with me any chance of his being able to control the king. Not that he would have had that chance; my brother was not a person you controlled. Every woman he bedded sought to control him in one way or another but few if any achieved it. I would dare, in the sanctity of this prison cell, state to the arras and the still burning but insensate fire that Elizabeth Wydeville – in view of what I learned of the pre-marriage contract I will not call her Queen – tried to control her wayward husband but despite all her wiles and her ways and her cunning and her resorting to witchcraft, of a surety she did, she had little influence on Edward of March. I believe, because it suits me to believe, that she had some influence in my trial and my sentence, but that is possibly my own black thoughts, for the dispute between my brother and myself at that time was bitter enough without a woman interfering. Especially a woman like her.

I did wonder if my cousin of Warwick would speak with me again after that conversation, he did but it was stilted and very difficult. He wrote to me occasionally but that too was not the Warwick I knew and had fought alongside. I wonder now, looking back down the years – few though they are – whether my withdrawal from him hastened his disastrous decision to commence hostilities against Burgundy.

Not that it matters, what happened was inevitable, in a way. The Readeption parliament was not as strong or as good as it should have been. My brother the king saw a chance to make a triumphant return to his country and what was rightfully his crown, in his eyes and, I freely admit, in mine, too, but then my family loyalty was at its peak and I would of a surety think that way, would I not?

It was easily done. Commissioned to array troops, I put them to my own cause and that of my brother of March, not that of the King who ordered it. When my brother the king landed on English soil again and began his march toward London, he drew in more and more men. I urged Warwick not to fight until he could concentrate his forces and then set out with my own force, ostensibly to fight my own family. I remember I rode with a mind as blank as the face I turned to the world, for it was hard to feel anything. My wife was waiting for me at our home, having whispered to me before I set out that she thought she was with child again. I took that with me, held close to my chest and my heart and told no one, for fear of it being a false alarm. I wished so much that it would not be false, that it was a true pregnancy, that a child of my own might be born at long last. I rode with my army toward two people who were family, my cousin and my brother. The first one thought I was coming to aid him, the other knew I would fight for him.

I saw my brother the king riding toward my group, my brother of Gloucester just a little further back. In that moment I decided on something outrageously extravagant to make him take real notice of me and my intentions. I dismounted and fell to my knees in the dust before him, bare headed and contrite. There was a long silent moment and then Ned came and helped me up, we hugged, we spoke, Richard came and we embraced and we spoke. Before everyone, Gloucester, March and Clarence stood together, embraced, shook hands, spoke words of conciliation. In that moment I knew where I wanted to be, back with the Yorks.

I can say no more on this for it is still a moment of deep emotion for me. I know not how my brothers really felt but we stood and we smiled and we spoke kind words to one another. What my brother the king really thought was concealed behind a smiling face and his usual bonhomie. My brother of Gloucester seemed genuinely pleased to see me, his smile was warm, his hand-clasp firm and strong.

I sought to bring reconciliation to all, appealing to my brother the king to be benevolent toward Warwick and he agreed but Warwick refused to talk so all the work I had done to negotiate new terms was as nothing in the eyes of the man who felt spurned by me. Oh, he never said so, but it was there in his look, in his manner, in his words and in his actions.

So we marched on together, the Yorks as one. Spies reported to us what Warwick had in mind, to trap us between London and his own forces.

He made a large mistake. In the past Warwick had under-estimated Edward's power with the populace and he did so at this time, that and Ned's ability as a soldier and tactician. This was Warwick's downfall. The plans were made, discussed, put into action. London was reached, breached; we turned and went straight back, launching our attack on his army before first light.

I hear; I see, I smell and I sense the roar of battle even as I think these thoughts. I hear metal on metal, metal on flesh, the defiant, the dying, the wounded and the terrified. I see the flash of metal on metal, I see the metal on flesh, I see the blood gouting, I see the defiant standing firm and I see the dying falling, tumbling charging men and horses to the ground. I see the terrified making a bad job of standing up to the onslaught. I smell the blood, the faeces from the gutted horses and men, the sickness that battle provokes in some men. I sense the blood lust that takes over as man attacks man, no matter who they are. I am aware in my heart of my own fear and bravado, I know well that my body was hard put not to betray me, for no matter how many times a man fights in battle, the fear remains the same –this time might be my last.

211

And in this turmoil and chaos and confusion, amid this noise of crashing clashing armed men, my cousin of Warwick was felled.

I could not believe it. The man who had dominated my life, changed my loyalties, led me into exile and back into what should have been glory, was no more than just another corpse on the battlefield. Barnet: a simple word but one that would bring its own pang to my heart and mind for a long time after the event. I felt such shock I doubted I would be aware of anything for some time.

When it was over, and it seemed to be over in such a short time, my brothers were together, tall in their blood-splashed suits of armour astride their destriers, faces agleam with the satisfaction of victory. My brother the king was free with his praise for those who fought so valiantly, myself included. If my shock at the loss of Warwick showed at all, he ignored it, as did my brother of Gloucester. The loyal knights who fought with us also said nothing so mayhap my ability to wear the blank face of one who gives nothing away was in place, despite the inner turmoil. Apart from my own feelings, I had a terrible task ahead of me; I had to return to my home and tell my lady wife that her father was dead.

We rode for London, ahead of a victorious army, into a city that welcomed us. The gates were flung open, the people cheered and shouted for the Yorks. If any Lancastrians were there, they hid, or pretended to be Yorkists.

I bid goodbye to my brothers and went home, fearing giving Isobel the news of her father, whom she loved and feared in equal proportions.

I planned to say nothing when I arrived, but tell her in the privacy of our chamber. It didn't work like that, she must have seen something in my face, for she ran to her room calling her ladies, shrieking her agony.

They wondered what was wrong with her, but I detained one, whispered the bad news and sent her after the others so they knew what they were dealing with.

Later, after a meal, she told me the pregnancy was indeed a false alarm. I felt a sense of relief, for her violent reaction to the news of her father's death would have damaged the child or her in some way. It was then she asked me how he had died. I told her he died a soldier's death, cut down on the battlefield. It was the truth, she did not need to know he was fleeing at the time.

The mourning went on for some time. The whole family had lived under Warwick's strictures, a powerful man with a strong will was no more. If Isobel held me to blame for any part of this, in going back to the Yorks, she never uttered a word of it in my presence. Nor did it make any difference to the way she acted with me, she was still the loving and devoted wife. I heard stories of his death, that he was fleeing the battlefield when the men captured him, that he tried to fight back single handed, that he was a bold and brave soldier, that he was a coward who fled, what is the truth? Would any of us know the truth on the battlefield if it were writ large on a pennant before us? Blood lust and fear fight for control of the mind, battle fever and sheer bowel clamping terror compete with one another for the control of the senses. Who knows what any of us would do confronted with a line of men determined to take your life? I say nothing against my cousin of Warwick, I knew him for a brave and loyal man, even if his loyalty was to himself and the Nevilles. Are we not all guilty of that, taking consideration for that which is ours and all else secondary? Is there a man among you who would know of a surety what he would do in that position? So we allowed the story to stand, that he died as a soldier and it seemed to me to be an epitaph worthy of my cousin of Warwick, Richard Neville. I wish you peace, my cousin. I wish that it had been otherwise with us.

Should I think of Tewkesbury, so soon after Barnet? A mere three weeks passed and it seemed that we were hardly out of our armour before we were back in it again, marching out to yet another battlefield. Margaret of Anjou was not giving up so easily. I will not think of Tewkesbury now, the death, the destruction, the killing that seemed endless. There was the death of my sister-in-law's husband, the young Prince of Wales, cut down on the battlefield, but who is to say that was not a good thing? I say this to the arras and the walls of this prison, was that not a good thing? I will say to the shades around me, those who might hear and take the word back to those who live still, I had no hand in his killing. I saw him struck down but it was not I who struck the blows. I was not near enough to do the deed. Would I have liked to? I cannot answer that. Had I thought it through, mayhap I would have, to have left the way clear for my brother of Gloucester to have the only woman he had ever loved, it would seem. But who has time for rational thought in the middle of a battle, when it is kill or be killed? I had my own life to protect and my own wife to consider; I did not wish her to be a widow so soon after the death of her revered father. There was an additional worry: the callous way my brother the king had men dragged from sanctuary and executed. I could not condone this in my mind: church was sanctuary and should not have been violated. My belief, but obviously not his. I thought then, battle had hardened my brother's mind and heart and he would not be as giving in the future as he had been in the past. I wondered if our lady mother knew of this change in her eldest son and if it would make any difference to her if she did.

After that battle, life seemed to quieten for a while.

214

My brother the king had a boy-child at last. I recall Durian bringing me the news, carefully, as only he could. Whilst the offspring were mere girls I could hold on, no matter how fragile that hold, to the faint hope that I could one day be king. With the coming of the boy-child, a healthy one, apparently, not one that would deliver himself into the hands of Death at an early age, my last faint hope flickered and all but died.

We were required to swear fealty to the boy-child Edward, one who would one day be Edward V, life being fair and equitable and he living to a good age. I went with the crowd of knights, dukes, earls and other nobles to make my oath. I went with sawdust in my mouth and lead in my heart. I forced a smile for all gathered there. I went with the knowledge that there might be a pre-contract which would make this boy-child a bastard but knowing full well that the chances of proving such a thing and demanding that the crown be given to me in the event of Ned's demise was slender indeed. Who would stand for me if such an occurrence happened? Who would be strong enough to defy convention, to put the heir apparent to one side and ask me to take the crown of England? What would parliament make of such a claim? Would Bishop Stillington stand up and declare it to be a fact, taking my side, ensuring that the people clamoured for me and not for Edward V? I asked myself, in the solitude of the night hours, when my lady wife slept softly beside me and the squire at the doorway snored gently and rhythmically, all these nonsensical questions.

What if Ned were taken with some tertian fever from which he did not recover?

What if the Wydevilles proclaimed Edward V as king and I were to ride to London with my armed guards and Stillington and there announce to Parliament that the marriage of Elizabeth Wydeville and my brother Edward

Plantagenet was illegal and void and that I alone was entitled to the crown of England?

What would my brother of Gloucester do if this were to happen, would he kneel before me and swear fealty? How far did his loyalty to the House of York and the crown of England really reach? Could he do that; would he do that?

Would I be content to let him continue to rule the North in the way he had become accustomed, virtually a king in his own land? Would I be content in my mind to leave him with such power? What if he rose up and brought an army against me in the south?

What if Ned lived to an old age and Stillington died? No amount of written evidence would stand in my case, for they would say it could be a forgery and indeed it could. I would need the man himself.

So many thoughts, so very many thoughts. So many imponderables, so many variations on a theme. I was awake for hours, considering them all. They each held an element I did not wish to dwell on, starting with the death of my brother the king.

I recall when I finally did slide into the arms of sleep, my dreams were racked with strange visions of a Coronation at which everything was going wrong and Ned appeared as a spectre, denouncing my right to be king. I woke in a cold sweat, to find Isobel already at her morning rituals of being prepared for the day. I woke feeling as if I had consumed half a hogshead of malmsey wine when in truth I had drunk nothing but light ale the whole day before.

For a long time I tormented myself with my thoughts, asking the questions, asking the Fates, give me a sign, a hint, an indication, should I share my knowledge with my brother of Gloucester or go to my brother the king himself and say 'this I know, brother, your marriage is not as it should be' and always I held back. I could not see a way to approach and confide in

216

Dickon who, in any event, appeared to be spending a lot of time away from court, beginning to make his presence felt as a leader, a commander of men, a person of authority. He seemed to have more power than I, something that rankled and stopped me considering approaching him for fear of saying the wrong thing and causing another breach in the family.

I could not see a way to approach my brother the king who would have immediately taken steps to ensure that the situation never arose and my claim would have been as dead as my ambitions. He was doubtless hoping against all hope that the pre-contract would never be exposed to public knowledge. It was possible that he had forgotten about it, as he had the ability to live for the day and to see only that which he wished to see. I found him full of kingly arrogance: his predecessor had been quietly and effectively dismissed - to the grave - and the kingdom was his to do with as he wished. He seemed to wish to populate the court with his offspring, give his son every honour and lie a sybaritic lifestyle. Could I, in truth, go to him and say he was living a lie and escape with my life? It was debatable, to say the least.

Despite all the doubts, I kept a tiny spark of hope alive, as in a fire all but extinguished but which could be revived with kindling and twigs, brought back into full conflagration once more with a little encouragement.

I lived my life with a mind full of questions, usually starting with 'what if-' and the answers nowhere to be found, except mayhap somewhere in the future, when the fates decreed that lives would turn and events would dictate and situations would change.

One question I should confront right here, shades of night, of Death, whoever you are. I see the shadows move and I move not, I see flickers and I know the flames have not reached that part of the room. I know you are here, ghosts, spirits, emanations, whatever you are. I know time is running out for me and there are years I wish to think on, come to understand and accept, before you and I become one. Hold back the hand of my brother the king for a while yet, I beseech you.

The question is this: why did I take that frightened mouse, Anne Neville, and hide her from my brother of Gloucester? What was really in my twisted troubled mind at that time? Was I so afraid of his finding happiness where I had not? Was it a desire to strike back for some imagined slight I had long since forgotten? Did I not say earlier I was glad of the death of the Prince of Wales as it freed her for my brother of Gloucester who loved her so? I know I did and yet in my confusion and jealousy I decided he would not have her. So I hid her in a cookshop, disguised as a pastry maid and watched as Gloucester searched London for her with a face of stone and a determination that no person or thing would stand in his way. It did not take long for him to find her, to escort her to St Martins for sanctuary, to claim her for his own.

I know now I am deeply ashamed of my selfish, greedy attitude but who is to hear me confess this, apart from those invisible beings with me now? Would the world believe it of me were I able to speak it coherently anyway? Have they not all made up their minds that Clarence is ever greedy, acquisitive, selfish and demanding? These things were said of me many times; I am sad and heartsick to say they were true then. They are not true now but now it is too late, dear God, it is too late!

I confront the question, you shades who move a little closer to me as I speak to you, mind to mind. I confront the question but is there an answer?

Chapter 27

The Warwick lands, estates, power and might devolved upon his family, in particular his widow. George took 'charge' of the widowed Anne and wanted to send her away to be with her sister, ostensibly to take care of her. He heard the rumours, the stories that it had been suggested in many quarters that he had taken control of the young widow so that the world would not be so aware of her claim to any part of the estate, should a bill of attainder be brought against the Earl's name. All this was brought to him via his network of spies and he consistently marvelled that people were unaware their words and actions were being reported back to those who would benefit from the information. It was through his spy system he learned that Richard had sought and gained the king's permission to marry Anne, that possible heiress to great fortune. Was Richard of Gloucester, wealthy beyond reckoning, powerful beyond dreams, virtual ruler of the North, scourge of the Scots, still seeking money and estates? Or was it for love?

George quietly took counsel with his trusted advisers, aware he was bending the laws rather than breaking them, so far anyway. The Countess was still alive, she was still Anne's legal guardian but with his pre-emptive strike, as it were, he had managed to gain the upper hand. The task now was to maintain it. The news that Middleham had been given to Richard infuriated him, not that he had any real interest in the place; he had visited often and quite liked it but that was not the issue. It came with a huge estate and other homes were associated with it, making Richard of Gloucester one of the most influential people in the North.

I see my farseeing prophesy coming true before my very mind, he told himself, pacing the floor of his study, fuming. What is my role, what is my place in this new regime my brother the king is creating? Everything seems to be going to Richard! God's eyes and teeth, am I not the older brother here, am I not entitled to some consideration? I fought alongside Warwick, surely that gives me a right to the estates? But then, Ned will want money for his coffers for he is spending as if the coin of the realm will cease and he wants his pleasures while he has the gold to pay for it. Or the silver, or anything that will create something he can spend.

George's patient staff watched as he paced, aware no doubt of his inner turmoil and unable to do anything about it until he spoke to them of his thoughts.

I am consulted by a king, he thought as he paced. I am consulted on state matters. I am given responsibilities. I am Chamberlain of England, I am Lieutenant of Ireland, I am entitled to Isobel's share of the estates. I am a very important person. Why then do I feel as if I am being offered titbits from the king's table, that all this is being done not so much to honour Clarence as keeping Clarence quiet and on the king's side? Is he so afraid I will turn traitor on him again? Have I not proved my worth and loyalty in battle?

He stopped suddenly, swung round on one heel and pointed a finger at his chancellor. "Facts, figures," he said abruptly. "What am I worth right now and what is my brother of Gloucester worth? I want a comparison of the two and I want it as soon as you can arrange it."

He saw Peke's eyes light up and a knowing smile cross Durian's face. He knew that both men knew him well enough that he needed no other explanation. He had a plan and he would see it through.

The nightly conferences with Durian had become such an integral part of George's life he wondered how he would cope if his Fool were not there. Squires were dismissed, no servants were allowed in the room, the two men were closeted together as George prepared for bed.

It was a time of quiet discussion before he went to Isobel and listened to the litany of problems, resolved and otherwise, of the household, much of which he completely ignored as it was Isobel's duty to resolve it, not his. Durian alone knew of the deep-seated resentment George held against his brother of Gloucester, of his perpetual feeling that no matter how much was given to him in the way of estates, positions of power or titles, he was and always would be second best in Ned's eyes and affection. It was there in the way Ned spoke of his younger brother, in the proud way the name Gloucester was said, as if he, Clarence, for all his skills and abilities, did not measure up. It wasn't possible for him to make overtures of brotherly friendship toward his brother for he was, on the outside, a cold controlled person as he had been throughout his life. So few were the occasions when the control broke that George could count them on one hand and have fingers left doing nothing but record his own times of loss of control. Ha! He thought, I would need an abacus to record the amount of times I had lost control!

As if reading his mind, one night Durian commented very quietly, "your brother of Gloucester is not your enemy, sire."

"No, he isn't, but I feel as if he is."

"It is because you have been pitched against one another too long. You have no way of knowing how he felt when you were exiled, sire, and you have no way of knowing how he felt when he was exiled. I would just put forward the premise that he had a better time of it than you did, having no wife to worry about and a brother who was still king, in many respects, to share your exile, whereas you had-"

"My cousin of Warwick, my wife and a household of hangers on."

"You are determined he shall not have a share of the inheritance, I take it?"

221

"I am. I will find a way to stop him. He has virtually the whole of the North of England to call his own and, unless they stop him, he will walk into Scotland too and no doubt be crowned king!"

They both collapsed with laughter at the thought of Richard being crowned King of Scotland and that, to some degree, restored George's good humour, although it was tinged with two worries: the persistent pain in his head and Durian's persistent cough which he insisted was responding to the physician's treatments. George did not think so, he did not believe it to be getting any better. He wished to avoid embarrassing his friend by insisting he take good care of himself as he was needed; one such night of emotion between them had been more than enough, but it was there in his gentle tone when speaking to his friend in these private moments and Durian knew it, responding with his own affection.

It was during this particular conversation that Durian said something profound which stayed with George for a very long time. "Beware of your brothers, sire. Your brother of Gloucester has but one devotion, to king and country. No one else matters, no one else is worthy of his consideration, unless it be the pretty little Anne Neville. I would say to you, walk cautiously with your brother for he will fight you for all that he considers rightfully his.

"Your brother the king shows a face of great humour to the world but beneath it lies a cruelty that is not seen or appreciated by the many who are around him. Feel not that he has forgiven everything, remember that his wounds were deep and his memory is long. One day he may wish to exact his revenge."

It was a thought to take into the darkness of the long nights, when Isobel tossed restlessly by his side, coughing from time to time, as if the illness she had contracted whilst in France had not quite left her. There was a promise of a new pregnancy and this time it seemed to be right, her blood flow had not shown itself now for three months and George had every hope that this would be his much longed-for child, son or daughter, it did not matter. He longed only to hold a child, his own child.

At times like this he envied Ned his easy-going manner and ability to sire children seemingly at will. While he envied him, he kept Durian's words in his mind for Durian had never failed him with wisdom and sharp observation. It was all too easy to believe, in the closed world of the court where money and titles were everything and he had both, that Ned had forgiven him his trespasses. But would I have forgiven and forgotten, he asked himself and came up with the answer: no. Forgive, yes, forget, no. Given the chance of revenge, would I not take it? Of course I would. So Durian's words are right and to be remembered at all times. Walk carefully with my brothers, for either of them could cause problems for me in the future, for different reasons.

Yes, but I hold a secret and I hold the dice of Fortune in my one hand too. I was son-in-law to the Kingmaker and as such I can use my knowledge to influence events. I will keep Anne Neville from my brother of Gloucester as long as I can. I will argue with him that the estates are mine. I will ensure the greatest part comes to me. Of a surety I will not get it all, Ned does so favour his loyal and devoted brother above all others! I will have a child I will need to favour, to ensure they have what s rightfully theirs, as offspring of the daughter of the Kingmaker and a prince of the royal blood.

That comforting thought eased him into sleep that night.

Not all of life goes according to our plans. Isobel's cough became worse and the coughing brought on convulsions which caused the loss of the child. For a while Anne, lodging with them while the inheritance problem was resolved, was companion and nurse to her sister, listening to her endless weeping that she would never produce the much wanted heir. George became impatient with the dispute, demanding that it be settled and soon, as it was interfering with his running of the many estates and the manifold tasks he had through the honours heaped on him by his brother the king. But the dispute went on and on and became steadily more bitter as it did so. Both brothers were well versed in law, both well versed in the matters of estates and land, their arguments were so precisely matched that Ned found it hard to adjudicate on the matter.

When George learned of Richard's plan to take Anne away from his home with the intention of arranging their marriage, he swiftly hid her away in a cookshop nearby, with orders that no one was to allow anyone near her. Unfortunately that too did not go as planned; the owners of the cookshop were over-awed by having nobility in their presence and word soon got out that she was there. Richard 'rescued' her and arranged sanctuary for her in St Martins In The Field. George was fuming that his plans had been so easily and swiftly disrupted and this embittered him even more.

I will find a way to get back at him! Thoughts raged through him as he spent yet more time simply pacing, sometimes in the elaborate gardens he loved to maintain or in his rooms, away from all eyes but Durian's, endlessly pacing but unable to walk away from the pain in his head and his heart. Durian was visibly fading before his eyes. Isobel was not of good health but George knew, in his totally honest moments, that he was more afraid of losing Durian than losing his wife. He could find another wealthy heiress to marry, he could not find another Fool with the skills, the abilities and the devotion Durian brought to his life. Once, in a moment of frustrated emotion, he shouted at Durian, 'I order you not to die!'

Durian just smiled sadly at him. "That, sire, is in God's hands and, great as you are, you are not God."

Chapter 28

How endless and tedious were the arguments over land! How angry I was when Richard married the mouse-like Anne! Oh, those who said he was after her estates were only half right, you only had to see the way he looked at her and she at him, you only had to watch them in each other's company to know it was a love bond as much as a financial acquisition for my brother of Gloucester. When he marched into my home and demanded that I hand her over, his face showed true emotion for the first time in many years, to the point when I hardly recognised him as the cold controlled person who had shared so much of my life. When I said she was not there, he stormed out, not walked, stormed. He was almost not touching the flagstones, so great was his anger. He had what seemed like half of London searching for her so she was soon found. Then, to see them together was to see the other side of him, the loving consort, solicitous in the extreme. Their marriage was a true love-bond and I said so to any who dared raise a voice otherwise. There were two forbidden subjects in my household: my brother of Gloucester's reason for marrying Anne Neville and the besmirching of the memory of my proud fearless father. Any who dared break that rule found themselves penniless, homeless and unemployed in a very short time. I only wish that my family had been so determined to protect me, but perhaps I do them an injustice, perhaps they have fought harder than I realise for my life.

What matter anyway; the hours pass by, the flames drop low and the chill in the room is preparing me for the chill of the tomb which I will share with Isobel.

What do I say of the endless arguments, the final division of land, the agreements we signed and in between all that, my first child being born, my daughter

Margaret? She was a joy to me, such a pretty child and so quick to recognise me when I visited her. Isobel was overjoyed and looked unbelievably pretty as a mother, flushed with pride and motherhood.

What do I say of the time when the printer William Caxton, now in London with the new printing press wonder which transformed books, worked on his second book, 'The Game and Playe of Chesse' and dedicated it to me? What do I say of my pride in this, what it said about my standing in England? I so loved books and he knew it.

What do I say of the time Durian died? What do I say of his wasting away, his fighting for breath, the smell of the burning herbs infiltrating every part of my home and I not allowed to enter the room to say goodbye to the one person I loved beyond all other, for fear of my contracting the disease myself? If my household thought I paced endlessly before, they knew nothing until the days after Durian was lowered into the ground and I had a hole in my life big enough to fit Ludlow Castle into and leave room for Fotheringhay, too. I never thought I could ache for someone so much. I never believed I could miss someone so much. God knows in truth I would have joined him in the grave to take the pain from my life.

And at times to take the pain from my head. Of a surety it grew worse. I consulted my physician many times, asking for a draught to ease the pain. He spoke to me of the times I had fallen from my horse, asked if I had hit my head when falling, asking if I had caused damage that was coming back to trouble me. I said I recalled once having a very large lump on the side of my head, but my falls were trivial to me, nothing broken, just damaged muscles and aches and pains for a time, not to mention the serious damage to my pride. Had I damaged myself? I knew not the truth of this and doubted whether he did, either. But he strove to help and at times he actually relieved the pain for a while. Then it would go and I would be blessed with peace.

What do I say about the rumours which my trusted staff brought to me that I was in collusion with this one and that to overthrow my brother the king? I could declare it to be nonsense but right now none would understand a word I said. Of a surety I spoke with this one and that, of a surety I was still ready to battle my brother of Gloucester for there were many unresolved matters between us regarding the inheritance and when the Countess went to live with the Gloucesters, my inheritance seemed to be undermined and this worried me. But through all this I held my hand; I was loyal, I was obedient to my king, brother or not. What my brother of Gloucester thought at this time is not something I am truly privy to, for he kept a closed household and without Durian's skills at piecing together small snippets of information or gossip, I was unable to put anything together and make sense of it. I had some ideas but nothing I could say was the real truth. I knew he considered me an enemy and was preparing for 'battle' in case I began another series of disputes, but that is the way we were. Ever at each other's throats. It makes his unexpected and unbelievably welcome visit to me here, in my bleak lonely prison, all the more surprising and sad, it showed me what we could have had and didn't have through our own temperament. I have asked myself many times, did he fight me for the Warwick lands for Anne's sake or his own? Did he fight me because I am who I am; someone who turned traitor for a while but who was showered with estates and titles when they returned? Did that cause resentment in my younger brother? Only he can answer these questions and I doubt he would, if anyone were to ask him, for he was a closed man when it came to what he really felt. I doubt anyone ever saw him weep, I doubt if many saw him smile. If anyone knows him at all, it is that little mouse of a wife whom he chose above all others and who has the key to his heart where no other has ever done.

It occurs to me, as I sit here with my memories and nothing else that I might be doing Anne a disservice. Underneath the submissive exterior she might be a woman of steel, someone who is a perfect helpmeet for my brother, maybe she has wisdom beyond her years, maybe –

These are mere speculations and cannot be proved by anyone other than my brother of Gloucester and he is a closed man.

What is not speculation is the fact that my brother the king drew up a bill of resumption which deprived me of my estates and I was forced to submit to his will if I wished to continue to live in some comfort. I knew I angered him with my persistence in fighting for every hectare of land but he knew nothing of my deep inner longing for security, for land and wealth to buffer me against the hostile world in which I lived. He knew nothing of my ever-present feeling of being second best and needing the comfort in my own heart of being a man of stature to give me stature. Instead he took from me much that was close to my heart, starting with Tutbury. Punishment? Very likely. Granting me an equitable settlement a sign of his affection, as was stated by some? I doubt it. Trust me? He did not. In return I did not trust my brother the king again, for he knew what Tutbury meant to me and he took it away and gave it to another. He could have taken any other estate I held title of and he knew it. I did not argue, not then. I kept my thoughts close to my heart and considered them well during the long dark nights when sleep evaded me.

Sleep evades me now, has done since I was interred here in this cold cell of a room. Ever do I refer to it that way, as it is my prison, regardless of how anyone else might view it. Sleep has evaded me and the hours are long and tiresome in their passing, what else is there to do but consider my years already lived?

My brother the king did me one disservice after another. He deprived me of this role and of that, took from me the Lord-Lieutenantship of Ireland and gave it to another, no doubt fearful that if he let me go there, I would foment an uprising. I had no intention of doing so but he did not know that and, had I expressed the thought to him, he would have dismissed it as mere talk on my part. Of a surety he would. Under pressure from the leeches who had attached themselves to him, he took from me that which gave me my stature and in doing so, pushed me further from him. I took great exception to his treatment of me and withdrew from court. I still had estates left to manage and live in, gardens to supervise, my second child, my son Edward, to be proud of and delight in and my daughter Margaret, growing fast and becoming as beautiful as her mother. Two children and possibly more to come, I thought then. I had enough and more to do without the intrigues and unpleasantness of court. It was as if I no longer had time for the façade of politeness that obscured the reality of court, it was as if I could no longer expend the energy to cope with the deviousness of those who were around my brother the king and, of a surety, I could no longer cope with my brother the king whose feelings toward me were more than evident.

There were rewards in being away from court. I could spend more time riding, hunting, hawking, being entertained by my minstrels and singers. I had a new Fool, not one I entrusted with anything but a man of wry humour and great insight and he was good to have by me when my spirits needed lifting. I had my ever-faithful secretary and chancellor; I had my physician and my squires. I had my wife, my two children and a household of servants, ladies, squires, pages, all manner of people doing all manner of tasks to ensure that my wife and I were kept in the luxurious way we took as our right.

It is of one of these ladies I have to speak at some point; my thoughts are already travelling in her direction. Ankarette Twynho, will you ever know what you did to me? Her part in my life is yet to come, there are events prior to that but she is there, ever there, in the back of my mind, ever waiting to come forward and flash those covetous eyes at me again. Did I not say this at the beginning of this walk into my past, her covetous eyes? Believe me, you shades of darkness and death, covetous indeed were her eyes. I was a pure man; I walked not outside my marriage vows. I believed in the words I spoke to bond myself to Isobel and kept to them. But Ankarette Twynho would have turned the head of many a man, with her buxom figure, her gold/red hair and eyes which melted a man when she looked at him.

If I had bedded her and not killed her, for I killed her as surely as if I had stabbed her through the heart myself, would my fate have been different?

Chapter 29

Everything was hustle and bustle, messengers rode frantically between Court and homes, arranging this, commanding that. Edward was taking a campaign to France. The soldier king had at last remembered he was a soldier and not only a king. He was about to put on a show of strength to impress the French. George immediately agreed to bring a hundred and twenty men at arms and a thousand archers to the army, having heard that Richard of Gloucester had agreed that same number. When the armies met, it was shown that Richard had brought an additional three hundred men, whether to deliberately show George in a bad light, to impress his brother the king or both, was not clear. George was quietly furious and the king openly delighted, showering yet more honours on his devoted and loyal younger brother. Swallowing his anger for the sake of family unity at such an important time, George, Richard and the king set sail for France.

The great expedition had required a massive amount of planning but Edward had the men and the resources to do it. All George had to do was equip his men at arms and archers and transport them to the loading point. This he did with his usual efficiency and with a sense of excitement that life was likely to become a little more interesting. It had to be said there was a certain pleasure in heading into possible combat once more. George was in his prime, full of energy, apart from the insistent pain in his head, ready to do battle, to prove himself as a knight and a duke. Tending gardens and managing vast estates had become almost too easy. As he never rode in a tournament, he sometimes sighed after the thrill of riding against someone in reality, not mock combat. If he was to be unhorsed, let it be on the battlefield, not in some joust where the spectators would see his shame and humiliation. His pride, as ever, dictated his thoughts and his actions.

There was no battle. Duke Charles arrived at Calais with a bodyguard and high-blown phrases which were supposed to flatter the King of England and divert him from his chosen goal, victory for England. Everything conspired to ensure that the duke of Burgundy did not join forces with them to confront the king of France.

There was feasting, ceremonial, discussions and more discussions. Voices were raised in council, mostly for suing for peace. George was taken aback when Richard denounced the whole thing, demanding that war was not abandoned. It was the first time in many a long year, if ever, that he had spoken out and disagreed with his brother the king.

It made no difference, except that when the treaty was signed, Richard was not there.

But, the army returned to England without having tasted battle. Men were unhappy at not being in combat, not having the chance to bring home plunder. George was unhappy for he had left his wife and children for nothing more than an encampment on the battlefield of Agincourt and a showy signing ceremony. He was unhappy also because Isobel was pregnant again and was not in the best of health. He wanted to return to her covered in glory, to reinforce himself in her eyes as a man of stature, of wealth, of respect and of dignity. Instead he had to return, admitting that the whole campaign had been, for him, a waste of time. No matter that the fault lie with Edward and the duke of Burgundy, no matter that he was able to be present at the ceremonial signing of the treaty and guaranteeing his name in history for the being there, it had been a dismal failure.

Isobel was wan, tired, not able to hold her food well and spent a good deal of time in her chambers, resting and being cosseted by her ladies. Her physician was permanently in attendance. If he had worries about the child to come and Isobel's health, he was not saying anything to anyone. George visited her daily but found the presence of so many fluttering hands and fans rather overwhelming and escaped when he could to the company of squires and staff he trusted, men he could talk with, joke and laugh with and never ever say a word about the gnawing worry at the back of his mind, for her health and his.

He soon realised that everywhere he went, he was seeing the young girl, Ankarette. She was servant to his wife and apparently did her work well, according to those he spoke to about her. George was disconcerted for her eyes glowed and her smile was coy and seductive. He worked at ignoring her and the blatant invitation he saw in those glowing eyes and in the smile. He chose to overlook the fact that he saw her mostly standing in the doorway of the bedrooms, where it would have taken but a moment to walk in, kick the door shut behind him and take what she was offering. It had been some time since he had bedded Isobel and the need was there, but not with someone so blatant and so untrustworthy. He was convinced that if he so much as touched her arm, she would run and tell everyone about it. Her infatuation for him was obvious; he hoped his indifference was as obvious as it was real. He did not care for her at all and had no intention of taking up the invitation.

Just before the whole situation became ridiculous in the extreme, when he was beginning to feel he could not walk freely in his own home without being constantly on the lookout for a sly girl with covetous eyes who might entrap him and cause problems, Isobel went into labour.

It was a horribly long drawn out affair, quite unlike her earlier pregnancies when the babies seemed to come within a few hours. After a day and a night of unremitting pain, despite all the attentions and skills of her physician, the midwife and nurse hired for their specialist knowledge, Isobel birthed the child which would end her life. No one seemed able to stem the flow of blood gushing from her body. George heard the screams and shouts and something snapped in his mind. He ran like a man demented to the birthing chamber, thrusting aside all who would stand in his way, breaking all precedent and shocking those who were around her. He gathered her up in his arms, kissing her face, calling her name, rubbing her hands. He slowly became aware of the faces around him, shocked faces, felt the hand on his shoulder as Peke struggled to pull him away from his wife. Slowly he got up and looked at everyone.

"My apologies," he said in a voice on the edge of breaking. "I thought-"

He turned and walked out, making his way to his own chambers where he barred the door so none could enter. It was in her screams and in his instinctive reaction to them that he discovered a truth, he had a very deep emotion for his wife which he had denied, smothered beneath his own demands and interests. His occasional 'I love you' had been said to keep her happy, not said with conviction. Now he needed the chance, the opportunity, please God, just once! to say it and mean it.

Anyone who passed by the door as they went about the task of attending to Isobel and the new-born baby heard just the click of his boot heels as he paced endlessly, attempting to walk the pain from his mind. Everyone knew, from the volume of blood that had poured from Isobel, that she would find it hard to survive. Everyone knew it and none would say it to his face but George knew only too well that his wife's days were numbered. All he could do was ensure her final days on earth were as comfortable as his wealth could make it, the finest physicians, the most caring of nurses, the most devoted of attendants for his new son, christened Richard. The child was weak, sickly, for the pregnancy had been beset with problems throughout and it showed in the health of the child.

From October to December Isobel rested but was weak and showed no real signs of improvement but he took the opportunity God had given him and in the quiet moments when the nurse was busy elsewhere and the servants were despatched on many errands, he told her of his deep love for her and how much she had meant to him as helpmeet and wife. He knew, by the glow in her eyes, he had done the right thing. He prayed for her, for strength for his son as well as giving thanks for the gift of time with Isobel to tell her of his true feelings and give her that happiness. He prayed for her recovery whilst knowing full well it would not happen.

He decided, after lengthy discussions with Isobel, they would go to Warwick Castle for the Christmas festivities and invite many local nobles and other high ranking officials to the feasts each day, the better to show solidarity with the people who mattered, those who still revered him and would support him. On a bright December day the procession set out, Isobel in a horse litter, smiling happily at going home, as she referred to it. The words struck George as being odd. Everywhere they had lived had been home, for he had arranged it to be so. Isobel had the best of everything everywhere they lived. But Warwick had been her childhood home and she was inordinately pleased they were holding Christmas there. For her sake he was glad they had decided to go there, even though the journey would be fraught with danger for she was far from well and it was not the best of times to travel.

They made a good show for the local people, the armed men, the pennants, the pack horses laden with supplies, clothes and gifts. Many turned out to see them and shout greetings as they passed, pleasing George for he knew then he still had some standing with those on his lands and estates. But the journey was still long and worrisome for them all.

The cooks had been working hard to prepare for the great feasts, everywhere had been cleaned and prepared, the castle looked wonderful when they arrived. Immediately Isobel went to her chambers to rest, leaving George to prowl the corridors and rooms, searching for – he knew not what, only that he sought something.

If it was peace of mind he sought, it was not to come. The journey had after all proved too much for the invalid. She did not leave her chambers again and on the 22nd December Isobel went into a decline, just as the household was in the throes of preparation for the Christmas festivities, she quietly slipped away in her sleep.

The festivities were cancelled. It was considered unseemly to enjoy life when the duchess had just died and her baby son was so weak. The child Richard died without a fuss on the 1st January, marking the start of a New Year in the most terrible way imaginable. George took it as a sign that the year ahead would be bad and welcomed it, as if it was a penance for his sins, the sin of drinking too much and not being as attentive as he should have been to the needs of his pregnant wife, the sin of being in a condition of disunity with his liege lord, the sin of being tempted – although he had not succumbed - by the flirting Ankarette and his sudden burning desire for another wife, even though Isobel was not yet buried. His thoughts went around and around, turning in on themselves, becoming embroiled in their own passionate tangle so that he found hard to separate them. Confession didn't help, he needed a penance that was harsh enough to discipline him for the many sins he saw in himself and which his confessor refused to recognise, blaming it on grief and sorrow instead. Throughout it all he drank heavily, obtaining hogsheads of the sweet malmsey wine for his cellar and denying anyone else the chance to taste it, stating it was reserved for his own consumption and no other.

A courtier was overheard to say, "Of a surety he will drown in it!" This was reported back to George who snorted with laughter and said: "I can think of no finer way to go!" It was a grim laugh, an unnatural one. The messenger who brought the snippet of information to him was afraid enough to take several steps back. George laughed again at the thought his visage was frightening enough that a man would back away from him. He walked away, still laughing but it was then verging on hysteria and he knew he had to stop before it got out of hand. His reputation was already in shreds, it did not need hysteria to be added to it. What would his brother the king make of that if it was!

Chapter 30

My wife was just twenty-five years old when she died. We had been married for only seven years. If it had not been the most glorious of marriages, it had been rewarding in a number of ways. I look back at it now and know that I married for power and position but a degree of affection and love came with it. I know too that she married for power and protection and that she knew a degree of love and affection came with it. If it was not the love-bond my brother of Gloucester had with my sister-in-law, it was enough for me at the time. I can say in all honesty that I was faithful, which is more than can be said for many of my acquaintances.

The child Richard, my last son, clung to life so feebly I thought him dead many a time before he actually died. I knew him not, I held him not; I had nothing to do with him for he, in my eyes, took my wife from me. I mourned him not, poor helpless soul. God grant my chance to ask for his forgiveness when I finally walk through the door marked Death, the door he so easily slipped through without so much as a sigh, it would seem.

It was after Isobel's body was removed from Warwick that I began to – hallucinate? Lose contact with reality? Find the pain in my head too much to cope with? What excuse shall I offer myself for my behaviour?

I was more aware than ever of the ubiquitous Ankarette, ever just disappearing around a corner after casting a flirtatious smile my way, or flicking a skirt in my direction or casting one of her lingering glances at me as I walked past. I would have dismissed her but had no reason to, she did her work well enough and I had other thoughts to occupy me. Would that I had! Would that I had given way to my instinct, to pass her on to another family where perhaps she could bed the son of the house and give him the experience he needed to take into marriage. I did not. I allowed her to stay. I watched my own thinking spiral out of control and knew I had lost the ability to concentrate. I needed the funeral over and done to settle everything, to close that part of my life but it seemed to take forever. So many plans, so many people to be summoned, so many priests to say the masses, three of them, the vigil to be kept. I discussed and I talked and I decided and I kept an open mind on what my future might hold. Of a surety I needed another wife, I needed more heirs. I could see no one worthy of my standing.

Until the duke of Burgundy was killed, that was, and his daughter Mary was free and in need of a protector. I was still deep in grief but even I could see that she would be a fitting partner for me. The plans went ahead for Isobel's funeral, the formal lying in state and then internment in Tewkesbury Abbey - and my sister Margaret proposed my marriage to Mary.

My brother the king vetoed it, as he had tried to do with my marriage to Isobel. It was history repeating itself. There was no logical reason he should stop me, there was no reason apart from his own personal feelings and they were made very clear. Dislike and distrust were obvious in his words, in his manner, in his actions towards me. I was not a welcome person in his life. My brother of Gloucester was the favoured one, the chosen one, the recipient of estates, titles, gifts and affection. Clarence had nothing offered him at all. A possible marriage to the sister of the king of Scotland was likewise vetoed with my state of mourning quoted as a reason. It mattered not to my brother the king that a helpmeet and new wife would assist me in recovering from the shock of losing my wife and newborn child, that my life seemed empty and useless without her there as a pivotal point around which I would live my life. I was advised not to mention any of this to the king as he was of no mind to listen.

My feelings festered. Oh shades of death and darkness, I can confess this to you for you have no tongue with which to speak the treason I am confessing to you at this time. My feelings festered. I grew a plant of hatred in my stomach which threatened to burst through my heart and out through my chest and attack anyone who came near me. I was fierce of voice and manner; I was unapproachable on any topic that concerned my wife, my brothers or my state of health. I would speak on matters concerning the estates or the division of labour or adjudicate on some point of law or dispute between tenants and do it calmly and quietly. All else aroused an anger in me that was disproportionate to the matters in hand. I knew it for what it was, a manifestation of my grief and loss and a rage against my brother the king who once again appeared to want to stop me doing the things I wanted, to find a new partner and to settle my life. The pain in my head grew steadily worse in direct proportion to the anger that swelled within me and the amount of wine I consumed. Days, whole days went by without my having a moment free of the pain's intense biting presence. Nights were blissful only through quantities of wine which rendered the mornings a nightmare of blurred vision, rebellious stomach and a constant need to vomit the wine and the hatred and leave me empty and cleansed. I could lose the wine – and did – but the hatred remained.

What do I truthfully say about a life lived as second best, to my mother, to my liege lord, even to Warwick who chose to marry his younger daughter to the Prince of Wales and put me to one side? How can anyone who has not lived such a life begin to understand the hurt that it causes, to see someone else venerated, adored, admired and promoted above you when you are, in your own eyes, worthy of such attention? It is impossible. It is a pain like no other, an aching of the heart and mind that refuses to let go.

They talked of me, I knew that. They, members of the court, those who would try to impress with their 'knowledge'. I knew it without my spies bringing me back confidential information as well as those messengers who delighted in bringing me the words of the king and taking mine in return. An open dispute flared between us, all that had gone before was as kindling to the great fire of family disunity that erupted and would not be put out. Have I said not before, was it because we were three that we divided two against one in every permutation of that division that there could be? If I have, then shades, forgive me for my time is fast running out, even as time moves on and the fire burns low, my life is fast running out and it is impossible for me now to go back over my thoughts, my memories, my acceptances and say yes, I said it here or I said it there. I also realise how foolish it is of me to think like this, no one but the shades of death are able to hear and understand my thoughts anyway. What difference does it make? So I repeat it, was it because we were three we divided two against one?

It was in this time, this terrible time, that I began my alliance with the one who carries my child, or is it born already and walks this earth, a small part of me? Whilst the covetous Ankarette sought to distract me from my grief, I held another in my arms. She was one of Isobel's ladies, a quiet, demure person who did not flash her eyes and ankles at me, did not seek me in every corner of our home. But she was there, she was comfort, she was softness and gentleness and undemanding. She said 'sire, I love you' and I believed her but I could not tell her in truth I loved her for I did not truly understand the meaning of the word. I had told Isobel I loved her and in truth I believe I did, in a way. I cannot say I have ever felt the way I know my brother of Gloucester is with his wife. He has loved her, I do believe, from the moment he set eyes on her at Middleham all those long years ago. But this one, this one who will remain nameless, whose identity and that of the child will go with me into that elaborate tomb at Tewkesbury, this one gave me comfort and easement when I needed it so much, when the loneliness and sorrow threatened to overwhelm me, when I ached with emptiness, was as close to a love match as I ever had. She was there, willingly there; she filled the emptiness and gave me back my life, for a while. I gave no thought to the prospect of a child of our union; I sought only the consolation of a willing body which came with discretion and with love. But when she told me of the coming child, with eyes that glowed with happiness, I knew I had to send her out of my life, for fear of censure. I could not allow scandal to touch my name. I was hopeful of another marriage, one suited to my rank, even as I knew, deep inside where the truth lives and all lies are forbidden, that time was fast running out for me, in many ways. I knew I was walking a dangerous pathway with my brother the king, knew of his feelings toward me and yet I still committed acts which were guaranteed to destroy the last remnants of family loyalty he might have held for me. Why did I do such things? What possessed me? Was it still that sense of being second best, of having to try and be better than the others so he would notice me and give me that which I craved, his approbation of me as a duke, as someone of equal standing with the duke of Gloucester?

How quickly I divert from these thoughts into another path and how often do they return, endlessly, to my brothers again!

I had to let my new love go, for fear of censure. Let me state it clear and straight now to those shades around me. I know I loved her, as far as I am capable of loving anyone, and I know of a surety she loved me and

243

I know too that her consolation and comfort helped me beyond reason and belief during that sad troublesome time. Would that I could have raised her up, made her my consort, let the household know that this was my chosen one, but she was not high born enough. It would have given me yet more problems with my brother the king. After all, he had already stopped two potential marriages out forward for me and they did not come more highly ranked than those. This one he would have laughed out of the kingdom and I did not want that for her or the coming child. It would have denigrated and degraded that which we had. I held enough grievances against my brother; I did not need to create more. I heard no more of her when she had gone. It left yet another hole in my heart and my life.

I have to ask the shades now, why did I so believe that the covetous flirtatious minx Ankarette Twynho killed my wife? I say to you my mind was befuddled with grief and loneliness, with vexation against my brother the king, with resentment against my brother of Gloucester, with impatience with those around me who could not, seemingly, always understand my needs, despite their having been in my employ for some time, without my ordering them to do this and to do that to make life comfortable for me. I longed for Durian who somehow managed to correctly assume and presume my needs and arrange them for me without my having to so order it and if he did not do so, Isobel did. Now I found myself doing it all and that added to my bad temper and mood.

I recalled being told that Ankarette was supposedly sprinkling herbs on my wife's food. I recalled the drinks that were brought to her, mixtures of this and that and I did not question at the time they were nothing but good for her. Now I saw them as poison. I know not why it changed, I only know that it did.

My word was law. She and her 'associates', as I saw them, were brought to the Warwick Assizes, tried, convicted and hanged in the shortest possible time.

When they brought the news to me, in a moment of utter lucidity, I knew I had committed a terrible crime but there was no going back. There was no way to restore life to the body of a young girl whose only sin had been to desire me. In that moment I knew she had not poisoned my wife or that her associate had poisoned my son. I knew the pregnancy had been long, hard and difficult and my wife had not really survived the actual birth, despite her lingering for two months. In my eyes and in my mind, she actually died the night she gave birth and, as far as I was concerned, my son Richard had died that night, too, for all that he clung to life until after the Christmastide. I recalled only the pathetic white faced shrinking figure of my wife in her bed, asleep she looked dead to me. It turned my mind, of a surety it did.

I became convinced that my brothers were scheming against me. If they were not, they were creating that impression. Did I become insane through worry about it? I know not. I do know that I suffered mightily and prayed constantly for relief of body and mind and that relief did not come.

Where would this distrust, this dispute, this family disunity had gone had I not had my friend Thomas Burdet taken from me? Would we have healed the breach?

I know, of a surety I know, I have not mentioned many names to you, shades of darkness, for you have no need of names. You know my staff, my family, my retainers, my servants, my squires, my friends as well as I do. Why should I bother with names when you know them better than I at times, for at times my head was so dislocated from my body and the brain within it that I knew not who was standing before me. Drunken foolish Clarence. I have heard it said. I know it to be false, I know I had the mind and the sharpness of wit and clarity of vision to be a good ruler, to be a good duke, to be a trusted and loyal subject of His Grace King Edward IV of England and everywhere. I even feel I could have been cleverer than he, could have ruled better than he, could have conducted campaigns better than he but never got the chance to prove it to anyone, let alone myself.

Why then do I state my friend's name so clearly? Because it was the beginning of the end. My end. His beginning, my end. His move in the game and playe of chesse, to bring about my downfall. It is not something I will know but it is how I perceive it.

Did I know my friend dabbled in alchemy? I did but I also knew my brother the king had more than a passing interest in alchemy, too. He had books, he had alchemists he consulted, he had knowledge and I do not doubt he used it to suit himself. My sorrow when my friend was hanged for an act of necromancy is beyond belief. It came at a time when my heart was heavy with sadness for my wife, for my son, for the wasted lives I took – for what reason? - for the loss of friendship with my brother the king, when my own health was seriously undermined by –

If I were not seeing it with my own eyes, I would not believe it. Before me is a shadow, a moving shadow. It resembles a man and the sense coming from it is one of great compassion. I know not who it is or what it is and yet I am not afeared of it. I now know that the shades of death are indeed in the room with me, I now know to whom I speak, mind to mind, heart to heart and I feel the great depth of understanding. This is one who has lived my kind of life and who knows my innermost heart. Whoever you are, I give you thanks for comforting me in these final hours.

I wanted to protest Thomas's innocence. I wanted it protested in the highest place, the council. I did not want – I lie. I did want but my voice was betraying me at that time, it stuttered, it halted, it refused to enunciate the words properly. I could not stand up in the council and read a declaration of innocence for a man I trusted and liked without sounding like a fool. I chose a friend, a friar, to do it for me. I chose a day when my brother the king was not there. This was deliberate; I did not wish to provoke a public row with the King but wished it set on record that I believed in the innocence of those wrongfully hanged. What better way was there to do this than to have it announced in council and so recorded for the future? Or so I thought. It was also my way of saying 'I am still here, do not dismiss me!'

It was thrown back at me that I had arranged for others to be unlawfully hanged. They were right. I had. And where were those who would stand up and speak of their innocence? None ever did. I make that statement now to the shadows around me: they were innocent. Their deaths are on my conscience. Their lives were terminated by my insanity. It is another part of the confession I will need to make when the time comes. Oh God, in thy great mercy, make it soon! I cannot stand this waiting, this agonising, this pain any longer! If it be thy will, allow me to walk through the door marked Death and end this miserable existence which is no life for a duke used to luxury, used to commanding men, used to everything that being a prince of the royal blood entitles him to.

I now ask the question that has haunted me since I arrived here. Did my brother summon me to appear before him that fateful June, knowing he would commit me for trial for treason, or did he commit me for trial to teach me a lesson so that I would bow to his wishes in future? If it was the latter, what made him change his mind and bring a charge of treason against me?

Chapter 31

The mayor of London and the aldermen who sat in council the day George was summoned to attend looked at him with eyes that expressed curiosity, mild amusement and contempt that a royal prince should be brought before the King in such a manner. Edward's demeanour was entirely different. He literally seethed with anger; it spilled from him in his jerky movements, his reddened face and his heightened sense of regal behaviour. He wore his crown, rather than a circlet, he gestured with hands laden with expensive glittering rings. It took all of George's courage and determination to stand tall whilst his brother lashed out with vicious words, accusing him of disrupting the judicial system, of attempting to thwart the actions of legally appointed courts and of defying commands issued by the king himself. George stared at the figure before him, now growing large due to his love of fine foods and wine and seeming lack of exercise. He stared and told himself that this was not the brother who had once loved him and sent instructions that he and Dickon should be rescued from the imprisonment of the duchess of Buckingham and given succour and tuition at the Archbishop's home, the brother who visited him every day and lit up his life with his presence. The golden brother was being smothered under the weight of the heavy featured angry king who shouted, gesticulated, lectured, did everything to goad him into responding but he refused to do so.

It came as no real surprise to George when the men at arms were ordered to arrest him and convey him to the Tower but it was still unpleasant. He watched as a ripple of genuine surprise and shock ran through the gathered council at the words but no one raised a hand or uttered a word in his defence. All he could do was walk away with the men, proud, head held high, not looking back, not giving his king the satisfaction of knowing that his heart was leaden inside his chest, a heart that ached with sadness and bitter loneliness that threatened to eat away at the last remaining part of his sanity.

The journey was one fraught with emotion, for George at least. The men acted as if it was an everyday thing to escort the King's brother to the Tower of London, there to be imprisoned, awaiting trial. George felt as if every bone in his body was screaming 'This Is Wrong!' but none could hear it and if they could, what would they have done? No more than those who heard the command in the first place. Every step the horse took was a step nearer confinement and a step away from freedom. The grey looming walls drew ever nearer, nearer, then they were through the gate, into the courtyard and handing over the horses to stable hands. The escort closed in, as if he would run anywhere, as if he had anywhere to run to, and he finally walked into the Tower itself and was escorted to the rooms seemingly already allocated for him. George wondered for a moment whether the whole farcical situation had been arranged in advance, whether Edward had known precisely what he would do and how he would do it. Why else would no one question which rooms to take him to, or express with even so much as a lifted eyebrow why the Duke of Clarence should be incarcerated in the Tower?

And, the ever present question, would he ever walk free again? Would he ever know the relief of living his own life, making his own decisions, walking in his own gardens, again? Did Edward really mean to finish him? The question hung in the air, unspoken, unacknowledged, as the door slammed shut and he was left to contemplate grey thick cold all enclosing walls.

Confinement was cruelty in itself. He had paper and quills, he had access to his staff to make arrangements for the care and custody of his two children, of the

249

running of the estates which would soon enough be taken back into Treasury hands, to be given out to Wydevilles or anyone else Edward wanted to honour at that time. He had no freedom. For someone used to riding, hawking, hunting, walking in his beautiful gardens, attending services throughout the day, of consulting with tailors and cooks, of choosing his meals and entertainment, to be shut up alone was unbelievably hard. It gave him much time to think and in the thinking came great sorrow, heartbreak and, at times, overwhelming grief.

Throughout the time he grew more and more certain that Edward planned to have him executed. There was no other reason for the imprisonment that was ongoing, endless, utterly enervating and totally disheartening. How could he allow his wayward brother to walk free once again, to take up the reins of his life and carry on? It was inconceivable. With that in mind he made arrangements for the distribution of his jewellery, his wardrobe, his books and other favoured possessions, asking only for a few items to be brought to him in the Tower. He also arranged to make his peace with Earl Rivers, to calm that part of his uneasy conscience. He knew that he was very possibly going to die. The only question left was when.

George asked, but no word was brought to him of his brother of Gloucester's reaction to his arrest and imprisonment. He could not gain knowledge of the king's intentions, either. It seemed his spy network had shut down with his incarceration and no one was prepared to risk the wrath of the king in attempting to convey messages to him. So much for loyalty, he told himself, so much for devotion. Damn it to hell, Durian, why did you have to die? Of a surety you would have found a way to get word to me of what was going on, so I would not be here in a state of wonderment! How am I to die? Is this really my end? Is Ned so angry with me that he will terminate my life, me, a prince of the royal blood? Where is my lady mother in all this? Why does she not get word to Ned that he should be merciful to me? Captive thoughts, spinning wildly round and round in his mind, never ending, never giving him a moment of peace. Over and over he thought of what he should have said, what he should have done, shouted aloud the words that he wanted so much to say to those gathered to witness the proceedings whilst knowing deep in his heart that nothing could have been said to change the outcome in any way. He knew, by the whole elaborate way it had been carried out, that Edward had thought about it for some time, had planned it and finally carried it out. Maybe it was giving him intense pleasure to know George was under lock and key, away from life so that he could not get involved in any more problems, or again repeat the bastardy claim that had so infuriated Edward. It did not matter that George did not believe a single word of it, what mattered was that it was another weapon to use against the king, another opportunity to fire darts into that smiling countenance and see it change. But it had not been smiling when George had been escorted into the council chamber. Then the countenance had been truly regal, if puffy with excess weight and good living, severe and determined. Remembering that look, George knew full well all his protestations and arguments would have been to no avail. Edward had decided and the family knew that when that happened, there was no turning back.

The days dragged into weeks and the weeks dragged into months. George could do nothing but visualise the espaliered fruit trees heavy with their burdens ripe for plucking and envy others the chance to eat the fine fruits, think of the Autumn flowers in their glory and resent others enjoying their beauty, imagine his favourite chestnut stallion being ridden by others whilst recalling his own breakneck rides through forests, risking life limb and sanity by setting the horse at ditches or fences without knowing what was on the other side. He visualised his favourite hawk soaring above the forest, quivering, waiting for prey and wished he had the strength of mind to send his own spirit soaring outside the unbreachable walls of the Tower into freedom. He wanted to weep for his loss of freedom, for the loss of all he held dear but would not allow himself the luxury of tears. Who knew when someone would walk into his chamber, see his frailty and weakness and report it back to the king? That would not do. Ned had to believe he was defiant and strong to the very end. God willing, he would do it.

Day by day the pain grew fractionally worse, day by day he fought to hold on to the ability to speak, to stand tall, to walk. He knew sooner or later there would be a trial and he wished to defend himself well, not allow the king to walk over him and direct him to eternity without a fight. It would not do to walk away from such an eventuality, to have it known that at the end the duke of Clarence gave way without so much as a raised word in his own defence.

It would have to be his own defence for he knew well, from careful questions posed to those who brought food, wine and comforts for him, that no one was prepared to stand for him or with him. It took all his willpower and strength to practice speaking clearly and concisely, endlessly wondering how long it would be before it all came to its inevitable end. There was no physician available now to hand him the draughts of painkilling liquids, no one knew of his agony and he was determined no one would. Weakness would not be revealed, no matter what it took.

Autumn moved inevitably into winter, without word of what was to happen to him. Christmas was a bleak, lonely festival, food and wine was brought to him and the servers hastily departed, having their own festivities to attend. His priest came to say Mass but that was the only relief in a long endless cold isolated season. He imagined the revelries in court, wondered who had been appointed Lord of Misrule, thought of colour, light, movement, music, food and knew without knowing that his days were truly numbered. Sadness verging on grief consumed him so that the hours were long and the days even longer.

The New Year arrived unheralded and unnoticed in his lonely prison in the Tower. There was no word from Ned as to his intentions; George had no way of knowing how much longer his imprisonment would last. He was putting on even more weight through enforced inactivity; he grew a beard for ease and convenience, less time spent on himself when there was no longer any reason to be proud of his appearance. It also took from him the fear that in his shaking, someone would cut him, for he was beginning to shake like a man with palsy. His prayers were personal and directed to God, no intermediaries, he was done with intermediaries. He would talk to the Lord God himself, not ask someone to convey the message for him for fear of it not being delivered. He asked over and over again for the agony to be ended.

Beneath all the prayers, the concerns for his estates and family, his loneliness and isolation, ran the current of fear, fear of what was on the other side when he was finally killed. He would not use the word executed, even to himself. That fear caused gut wrenching agony at times as it wracked his body as well as his mind: intense, all consuming fear. Faith, apart from prayers to God, was eroding under the confinement and the enforced isolation which left his mind free to roam places it would not otherwise have gone. Fear wrote a scenario that was driving him toward insanity, combined as it was with the excruciating pain in his head. Oh God, he prayed endlessly, let it all be over and let it all be over soon! I am so afeared of my body betraying me and that would be shameful, humiliating and unworthy of a duke. Just let it be done, in the name of Heaven, let it be done!

He was summoned before the king and parliament on the 16th January by writ from Parliament.

Two of his squires came early to his chamber and helped him to dress in gold and black, his favourite colours. His long fair hair was brushed until it shone, a black cap with gold trimmings was set firmly on his head. He clenched his teeth against the sudden pain and hoped neither of them realised he was in agony. His beard was brushed until that too gleamed. An ermine lined cloak was placed around his shoulders, shining black leather boots were slid onto his feet and he stood straight and tall, smiling at them. The doublet might be a little tighter than he would have wished or desired but it looked fair enough to him.

"This is my time," he told them. "Whatever happens today is in the hands of Almighty God, not my brother the king, for only God can direct the course of our lives."

He was pleased the words came out clear and unequivocal. During the latter part of the old year and the first few days of the New Year his voice had begun to break up when he spoke. He carried a new fear that he would be incapable of defending himself against what he knew were false charges. It was simply that he was now an encumbrance to the Wydevilles – if not an actual danger - and a thorn to his king. Edward, being Edward, desired the removal of the thorn: permanently. None of this had been spoken aloud or even written anywhere. It was George's knowledge of his brother's nature and his own fey abilities which told him that this really was the final act in a masque of such ridiculous performances that of a surety history would laugh at it, were they to read the records in full.

They walked down the many steps, out through the huge intimidating doors and into the first truly fresh air George had breathed since June of the year before. A bitter cold wind blew sharp ice laden rain into his face but it was welcome, it was the ice experienced by free men. He mounted the horse brought for him, noted the armed escort, blank faced and immovable, who surrounded him. He was not being given a chance to escape, even if he had that thought in mind. They rode through all but deserted London streets, the weather keeping most citizens at home until they had of necessity to venture forth. Those who were going about their business did not look twice at the procession. They were well used to nobles and knights riding with armed guards and did not recognise the duke of Clarence, bearded as he was, heavier than he had been. His appearance had changed but in truth, he asked himself as he rode, would any of them have recognised me had I still been in my prime? How many commoners could recognise the aristocracy when they rode among them? Caps were doffed should anyone look their way, but that was about the limit of their subservience and recognition.

The fresh air was wonderful, even if it was bitterly cold and caused a constriction in his lungs each time he took a deep breath but the opportunity was too good to miss. Hold on, he told himself as he rode, hold on to the thoughts, speak clearly, speak strong and speak well. You have to go down fighting.

Go down? He asked himself the question as familiar buildings were passed and the horses snorted steam into the winter air, hooves clip clopping on the frost baked road. Go down? Why am I so sure I will go down? What an odd expression for me to use! But a true one, another voice argued. Ned is king, so no matter what you say, no matter what defence you raise, George

Plantagenet, he will have the last word and the last word is to rid his life of that which bothers him. No doubt it bothers the Wydevilles too, no doubt they had a hand in all of this.

He wondered, briefly, why he should be diverting his thoughts in this manner when he had known full well for months that this was no more than the final act before the curtain came down, until he realised he was bolstering himself for the ordeal to come, the struggle to speak clearly and stand straight and tall so no one would suspect any physical illness. He did not want to give them the satisfaction of knowing he was ill. He had long since decided that he could, with a small note to the king, dispense with this trial, this mockery of a trial, not give his brother the burden of having ordered him killed. He had long since decided he would not do so, he wanted to leave the stain of his murder on the reign of Edward IV as a lasting memorial, if history did not remember him any other way. It was, he thought, a very sad, almost heartbreaking verdict on our relationship that it has come to this.

Now, the question: should I, dare I, suggest before Parliament this day that all is not well with the marriage to the Queen? Dare I say aloud before the gathered officials that my brother the king is not legally married to Elizabeth Wydeville, as there is a –

No! Be not a total fool, Clarence! Be sure of this one thing, the truth will come out, one way or another, in the fullness of time. Let it not be from your lips, foolish man, for that will seal your fate sooner than anything else. Let it be on your behaviour, your actions alone, not on the actions of your brother the king.

The wiser voice prevailed. He resolved to say nothing of Stillington and his knowledge but wondered if anyone else knew or suspected he knew of the pre-contract and whether it would come back on his name in the future. Anything was possible in this world of spy and counter-spy, of deceit and double talk, of treachery and self-interest. It was all he could do not to laugh aloud at the last thought which entered his mind. Treachery and self-interest. Doubtless they were at the very core of his brother's accusations against him but ones which would not be voiced. They would be couched in terms which would make it look as if he were the guilty one in every way.

His escort rode stony-faced, staring ahead all the time. They had not observed any of his expressions, had not bothered to concern themselves with his feelings. They were doing their duty, escorting the duke to answer the King's summons. Nothing else mattered. Suddenly he was intensely lonely, even lonelier than he had been in his chambers in the Tower during the Christmas festivities, when he had sat alone before the fire, drunk on malmsey wine, imagining the gaiety of the court, wondering if any had given him so much as a passing thought during the whole twelve days. This loneliness, this feeling of being totally and completely alone, cut through him like a lance thrust, almost toppling him from the horse. He gripped the reins hard and clamped his knees against the horse's sides, determined to hold on to his dignity. It would not do to fall now, not when he had been so carefully groomed for this final walk onto life's public stage.

All too soon they arrived at Westminster.

Chapter 32

In the days since my trial I have gone over it a thousand times but I cannot recall any faces who looked on and did not speak. I only recall the face of the man I once called Ned and now called king, for the man who glared at me was not my brother of March, not the golden presence who filled my life with joy when he came to visit us, not the one who rode out to battle with a smile and a word for us all, inspiring us as only he could to do our best for him and for England. This man was a stranger, even more so than the one who had glared at me in similar fashion in council so many months earlier.

I knew others were there, heard their shifting feet and bodies, heard the collective sighs and breaths, felt the collective intense interest in the proceedings but name them? I could not, were I now to face the rack or anything else in the Tower torture chambers. They were blank to me, as blank as I will doubtless be to them when the writ is executed and I am killed. Still I refuse to use the word executed when referring to my death. It does not sit right in my mind or in my mouth.

Oh the king was so calm at first, detailing the case against me, my relationship with our cousin of Warwick, fighting against him, taking him prisoner, taking the law into my own hands with the trial and execution of Ankarette Twynho and those who died with her by my actions, my seeking the hand of Mary of Burgundy in order to strengthen my case to take the English throne. At this point I laughed aloud and Edward's face grew dark as thunder.

"Our sister Margaret proposed the marriage, Your Grace," I said with great formality. "It seemed a marriage that would befit my status as a royal prince and duke of this kingdom. It had nothing whatsoever to do with claiming the throne. Your Grace has a son who will take the throne when Your Grace leaves this mortal life."

"It is immaterial!" Edward shouted, literally shouted and those around him drew back from the sheer force of his anger. "It could have been!"

"Could have been but was not. Does Your Grace not realise I know full well my standing in this court, in this country, when it comes to the succession? Does Your Grace not realise that my previous attempts to claim that which Your Grace accorded me before the marriage to Queen Elizabeth and the result thereof, your son Edward, came to naught and so I put away all thoughts of becoming king?"

"So full of smooth words, Clarence, as always! Have I not held out the hand of forgiveness time and again for your indiscretions and treacherous acts? But this time you have gone too far. Taking the law into your own hands, subverting the judiciary, executing innocent people-"

"They were as innocent as Thomas Burdet!"

"Without a shred of evidence and against all due process of law!" he continued as if I had not spoken. The gathered masses seemed to hold their collective breath for all become totally still.

I waited, waited several heartbeats and then said, quietly:

"Your Grace had no evidence against Thomas Burdet either. I understand he protested his innocence to the moment his life was taken from him."

Edward was not to be dissuaded. He continued his imprecations, my treachery, my disloyalty, my dishonour to the House of York. I said no more for no more could be said. His mind was set and my words only inflamed the situation. He said over and over that he would even now forgive me but I had gone too far. It was nonsense and we both knew it was so. He had made up his mind – or had it made up for him – and there was no turning back.

It was almost a relief to be found guilty. I could turn and walk from the council chamber, I could remount the horse and endure the lonely ride back to the Tower and my official residence, all communications to George Plantagenet, Duke of Clarence, to be delivered to the Constable of the Tower, please, where I would await the official sentence. At least then I no longer had to fight to speak clearly, to see clearly and stand straight. I could, at long last and with great relief, give way to that which was eating my life away day by day. Let them think I was in shock, let them think the ordeal of the trial had caused its own problems, let them think what they would. I alone knew the truth, I and the shades around me who are, of a surety, moving in closer and closer.

Buckingham pronounced the sentence, death as a traitor. Edward IV signed the writ himself, befitting my rank as a royal prince, or so I liked to believe, or was he just making sure I knew that it was by his hand I was to die? I still do not know the manner of my death, but I am sure that it is not by hanging, drawing and quartering, the standard horrific death for a traitor, for I believe he will be merciful in that way. Whether I am to be beheaded instead, as befits one of my rank, is something I do not know but do not fear so much, it will be quick and my agony will be ended, at long last. My fear, this ongoing endless stomach clenching fear, is still what will happen when I walk through that door marked Death, the one that ever grows larger and clearer in my mind whilst all else seems to fade. I keep saying that, it is true. It is a constant in my life and I cannot escape it. I find it hard to recall the faces of those I loved: Durian, Isobel, my lady mother, my lord father, they are misty, so indistinct. What was it about Thomas Burdet that made me care for him and how did he look, I do not recall. It is sliding away from me, I am afraid for my sanity before the end.

Does the king regret the trial now, I wonder? Does he have any compassion left in him for me? What of Dickon, gone from me to the North, what will he truly feel when he hears the news, for of a surety someone will ride north with a message or a letter or official document detailing the trial and its outcome. There is nothing more he can do, will he feel useless, helpless in the face of such implacable royal will?

What are my children thinking of me now? Are they safe, are they in good custody and will they be told of the way I died? What of my estates, my staff, my animals, my –

There is no need to go on, Clarence, foolish man. What good is any of this to your mind right now? It is out of your hands, out of your control in its entirety. Let it go.

And so I go back, back to those far off days at Ludlow when Ned would reach for me and swing me round with such a huge smile it was unbelievable and then he would, with great courtesy and dignity, solemnly hold out his hand to Dickon, that small dark-eyed boy I shared my early life with, the boy that once clung to me and sobbed in his loneliness and homesickness.

I recall one night he came to my room, ignored the page and got into bed with me. He put those thin arms around me and held me as I cried after yet another whipping. No matter what they did, I could not learn to behave as a royal prince should and was forever getting into trouble. It seemed that tendency has stayed with me throughout my life. He slid quietly out of bed and out of my room when I stopped crying, never looking back and never speaking of it afterwards. I remember the feeling of love that came to me. Dickon only did that once but I never forgot it.

I remember my beautiful brother Edmund, who lived so short a time and died so dreadfully at the hand of someone who could have spared his life. I remember

261

my proud father, his head ignominiously on a spike crowned with a paper crown. I will not forgive that act if I spend eternity in Purgatory. I think now of my sorrowful mother, losing her husband, her babies, her daughters to marriage and her sons, one by cold blooded murder and one by execution. This time I say the word. In the name of heaven, how much more will she have to endure before she walks through the door marked Death herself?

I remember the good times as well as the bad; I remember the Christmas festivities, the great religious ceremonies, the coronations where I officiated and the great regard in which I was held. I remember it all.

I have come to the end. I have come through the twenty-eight years of my troubled life and looked at it all. I am left with the question, why did it all go wrong?

Chapter 33

The angel hovered by the huge arras over the fireplace, unseen, unnoticed, as she had virtually been throughout his life. Her sigh sent the tapestry rippling and he looked up, maybe wondering where the air had come from to disturb such heavy cloth. But then he looked down again, staring into the depths of the mazer before him, the empty mazer. Once again it seemed the wine had disappeared into his body and once again it seemed to have done nothing to take away his pain, physical or mental.

Could I have done more, the angel asked herself, staring at the fair hair of the man she had loved, shadowed and protected for 28 years. Could I have persuaded him not to take the pathways he insisted on travelling, could I have directed him in other ways, better ways?

It is at the very end of someone's life the questions are asked, the answers unforgiving. No. He could not have walked any other pathway. It was his karma, his fate that he should do those things, endure the hardships, the losses and the grief for his soul's progression. He would not have understood this if she had told him, for his mind had been clouded by wine and devious thoughts, by elements of greed, ambition, need and, at the last, the all devouring tumour eating his brain cells. It was the karma, the fate of others, to live with the legacy he would donate to them, his death on their conscience, his life on their minds, his memory a haunting reminder of what might have been.

The angel stirred, moved, cast one last loving look at George Plantagenet and prepared to leave him. He had no further need of protection but she had work to do. She had to find Isobel, duchess of Clarence, and advise her that the time was close. She might wish to be there when the moment arrived. If not, well, the angel

263

would do her duty and greet her charge when he crossed the divide. At least it would give her the chance to say 'sorry, I did my best but only on one occasion did you know I was there. After that you ignored me. You really thought it was imagination, didn't you? No, I really was there in the chapel with you, longing to reach out to you and help.'

She sighed once more and again he looked up at the arras. This time he gave the radiant smile that had won so many hearts and minds, the smile no one would see on this side of life after this day. She reached out a wing and touched his forehead. He put a hand up and rubbed his face, looking puzzled.

Then she was gone.

Chapter 34

I dreamed:

Of being king.
Of being the owner of Fotheringhay.
Of having a wonderful marriage.
Of fathering many children.
Of having power.
Of being part of the York family.
Of living to an old age.

My dreams are dead.

Soon, of a surety, I will be dead, too. My brother the king signed the warrant on the 7th February. Today is the 18th, by my reckoning. He will not allow me to live much longer. I am an embarrassment, I am a burden; I am a blot on his conscience. I know my brother; he will not delay further. That which troubles him is dismissed, disposed of, removed from his life. He wishes a peaceful reign. As long as I live he cannot guarantee peace. Little does he know I wish for it to be done, that every day is a torment to my body and my soul. But I still cannot bring myself to give him the satisfaction of requesting that it be over, any more than I can bring myself to tell him I would die anyway. Even now I am not prepared to be magnanimous.

To Hell with it, it no longer matters. I can no longer see clearly, the words run together on the paper, so burn it, burn it and be done with it, as my life will be done with before too long.

Oh the words I will not give the priest, for all that I trust him with my soul. I say them now, I say them to the stark cold stone walls that absorb everything and give nothing back.

God, forgive me my sins.
Richard, forgive me for all I did.

Edward, forgive me for all I did.

Mother, forgive me for not being the son you wanted.

Father, forgive me for not honouring you in my memory as I should.

Isobel, forgive me for not being the husband you really wanted. I loved you dearly – for a time.

My dear children, forgive me for not being there as you grow up.

Warwick, forgive me for not saving you at Barnet. I tried but it was too late.

Ankarette, forgive me for taking your life. Now I wonder why I did it.

John, forgive me for taking your life. Now I wonder why I did it.

The wine is long gone. I hear footsteps on the stairs; they come at last, with what? The door creaks, it is not opened much these days. At last the priest is come; my squires carry more wine. Outside the guards stand firm, as if I can run anywhere, as if I would!

There is a sense of sadness about them all. There is a sense – of termination. My squires bow and leave. The guards step in. I understand suddenly. It is they who will take my life. Of a moment all my fear has gone, drained out of me into the flagstones, the uncaring unmoving unmoved flagstones that have felt my feet trample on them these long tedious days of waiting for this moment. Of a moment every nerve that has been tight woven and painful has released itself. The calm is amazing, I welcome it, as I am able to confront that which is to happen without the knowledge that my body will betray me, that one stupid fear that has haunted me these long tedious days of waiting for this moment. At last it has come and with it has come the calm to face whatever is ahead.

The priest moves towards me.

"Your Grace," and I swear his voice quavers as he speaks, "I am bid to hear your confession, to offer the last rites, to give you this wine and to ask you to take the bath now being prepared for you."

Ned was merciful at the last, or did my lady mother plead for clemency? It all shines clearly in my mind. I doubt not that the wine is drugged, I doubt not that I shall be quietly drowned in a warm bath. So be it. There are worse ways of leaving this troublesome, troubled life. I could, as he ordained, have been forced to suffer the traditional traitor's death of hanging, drawing and quartering. I could, had he ordered it, been taken to the scaffold and there waited for the sword to sever my head from my body. Somehow I knew it would not come to that; I was most sure my brother the king would want a quiet, dignified execution for someone of his own blood. I was also sure my lady mother would have pleaded with him and he, being a dutiful and loving son, would have listened to her words and acquiesced.

So it has proved to be. I am not able to send my thanks, but in any event they would be inappropriate. In truth, what would I say to him? Forgive me? If he had a mind to offer forgiveness, I would not be staring Death in the face in the form of a drugged mazer of wine, two strong guards and a priest shaking in his robes at what he was to witness. Thank you for a kind death? I think not. No death is kind, even if it will release me from this agony and this turmoil.

Forget the thanks, Clarence, consider that which is ahead of you, the next few minutes, the next half hour or hour, however long it takes to confess. It is time to leave this world.

It is of no importance that this man will not be able to understand a word of my confession; God will hear and He is the only one who matters.

With a silent prayer of thanks for mercy shown,
I sink to my knees on the cold, unforgiving floor.

Epilogue

On the 18th February 1478 the physical life of George, duke of Clarence, came to an abrupt end. Legend has it that he was drowned in a butt of malmsey wine, a tale promoted by Shakespeare and believed by many historians. Quite why anyone would believe that is a mystery to me: malmsey wine is very expensive, why waste a hogshead of it? It is said that the fumes from an open butt would cause men to pass out but we are expected to believe servants held a possibly heavy person head down in the wine until he drowned. I didn't think it made sense … and that was before I met the duke and got the real story.

The facts of the ending of his life came from the duke himself, as did the whole book. At no time did I have any input into the writing of this life; the entire story came from the spirit who came to me in 2005, saying he was George, duke of Clarence and asked if I would write his life story.

We began writing the book in 2006, in just six months the work was done. How much of it has been 'added to' for the sake of a good story by the spirit author is anyone's guess, but his intention was throughout to make a good read for anyone interested enough to buy the book. His comment is, if he has strayed from the truth here and there for the sake of the story, it is no more and no less than many academically qualified and experienced historians have done, those who do not bother to check their facts and go on what others, equally careless, have written over the years. But essentially he assures me it is his life, as he remembers it.

You may well decide not to believe that this is a channelled book direct from spirit, that I am a good author and wrote an interesting work of fiction, in which case I hope you enjoyed your read. If you choose to believe that I channelled the work, then you will have had an insight into a period of history usually only seen through the eyes of historians. There are more such insights to come from a great variety of people, who have approached me with the same request, to tell their story and put the truth in front of the world.

My next book is observations on the life of His Majesty King Henry VIII. The same criteria applies: you can enjoy it as a piece of fiction or you can accept that it is channelled from His Majesty himself. Either way, I hope you will look out for the book and when you buy it, you will enjoy the reading of it.

Thank you for buying this book and thank you for reading it to the end. If nothing else, you should have a different opinion on the 'false, fleeting, perjur'd Clarence' beloved of Shakespearean scholars and readers alike – which is what we set out to do.

Dorothy Davies,
Isle of Wight, 2008.

Books By Dorothy Davies

Brief and Bitter Hearts
Captain Of The Wight
Cast In Stone
Daniel A Life
Death Be Pardoner To Me
Fools and Kings And Fighting Men
Forever
Ghosts, Mediums, Spirits and 'Death'
I Bid You Welcome
I Diced With God
Living In The Shadow Of The Cross
Not The Shadow Of A Man
Then Came The Liars, Then Came The Fools
Thirty Pieces Of Silver

Available from
www.fiction4all.com
and other book stores

Lightning Source UK Ltd.
Milton Keynes UK
UKOW01f0347101017
310695UK00005B/293/P